MARS WILL DIVIDE US

The Collector's Universe

Paul A. Smith

© Paul Anthony Smith

In the near future, when a disgruntled employee is ready to leave Mars for good, her plans are upset by making first contact with unwanted consequences.

Writing a Sci-Fi novel had been on my bucket list for a long time. I would like to thank my amazing wife, Sarah, for her continuous support to help me cross this off. Without her, this book would not have come to life.

Secondly, I would also like to thank my friends Ali, Anna, Carolina, Itzik and Sven for reading early drafts and providing valuable feedback. Thank you very much.

I (ELISA)

Mars was a lie, the colony was going to fail and it cost her everything to leave. Elisa was lying on her back, strapped into a seat in the front row and ready to launch into orbit. She had to go.

Finally, I can leave this fucking place! she thought and closed her eyes.

I am leaving!

Grinding her teeth, she began counting down in her head. Slowly, at half the pace of her heartbeat drumming in her chest, trying to ease her inner tension. Staring at the inside of her eyelids, she first saw darkness, then her eyes adjusted to pick up the glow of the lights from the inside of the space shuttle around her. She wiggled her eyes, blinked a couple of times, then opened them again, focussing on the curved screen in front of her. In the middle of it was the countdown, just passing the two-minute mark. It hadn't decreased half as much as she hoped it would have while she had her eyes closed.

The screen was filled with applications, showing various angles of the spaceship she was in. A rocket with a matte, white paint on the back and a mesh of dark, black tiles covering its belly from the tip to the engines. Two forward fins covered half in white paint, half in black tiles, stood out at the top and two similar but bigger aft fins at the bottom. The entire ship was covered in a fine brown dust, shading the original colours underneath. The shuttle stood upright on a pale, round launch pad, with another three space ships of the same type visible in the distance.

Please, please, please, faster! she thought, staring at the screen, creasing her forehead, her feet restlessly rocking in her seat. Minutes before, she had to impatiently sit still while waiting for the seat to adjust its shape to her body in her space suit.

The number trickled slowly below one minute and forty seconds, each second feeling slower, as if stretching against Elisa's wish to get away from Mars.

She was done with this place. Living on Mars hadn't developed into anything close to what she had been promised. The limitations of being in the same cramped place for half a decade, the constant brown dust and daily routine were the reality. The same food, the same people, the same mentality and the constant pressure to expand the colony did not leave room for any actual improvements to life on Mars. The advertisements for working on Mars had promised glass domes with spiralling ramps, on which you could go on evening walks while watching the pale, grey sun set, walking above trees growing under the dome. Plans to build anything like it had never materialised, nor had any trees been planted.

I (ELISA)

The countdown read 1 minute and 30 seconds.

The beginning had been exciting and Elisa had nurtured the thought that Mars was going to be different to anything she had experienced so far. Mars was going to be something else. She had been honoured and amazed to be allowed to work on Mars. The gratification of realising she was qualified for work in space, on another planet. No job offer could have matched this opportunity. A new world to explore, to contribute to something much greater than anything she had done before. Elisa had spent countless hours imagining challenges and how she would overcome them, to be recognised for her hard work, building a new home.

But as with every job she had worked in before, she burnt through the initial phase of excitement. The motivational feedback she got in the beginning boosted her morale to work even harder and she even spent additional time after work to improve her skills. This initial phase only lasted for a couple of months and soon the routine at work increased and the motivational feedback diminished. Her colleagues made sure to let her know how they had been running things and there was no point in being overly motivated. Soon, she realised she wasn't going to have an impact on Mars.

With the periodic influx of new workers landing on Mars, Elisa eventually went under in the crowd. The people she worked with almost forgot she was on the planet, unless there was a chance to blame something on her.

Mars turned out to be worse than any of her previous jobs. She was stuck in an endless cycle of fixing things for someone else and any value she created beyond that never belonged to her, but to the Interplanetary Corporation who owned the entire colony. Anything that came close to a career had been already set out for those who had been there the longest and provided the least resistance for management.

Even if she had quit working on Mars, it didn't mean she could stop working. She had signed up to start working on the preparation of the interplanetary shuttles headed for Earth, docked in Mars' orbit on the gateway station called The Gateway To Earth. At least it was a first step away from Mars, as leaving was not as easy as putting her personal items in a box and leave the building, as she had done on Earth in the past.

The countdown had gone down to one minute and ten seconds. Unconsciously, Elisa increased the intensity of her rocking.

I'm gone, I'm leaving!

Her heart beat harder at the thought and her nervousness turned into excitement.

Earlier that day, she had stomped out of the almost windowless dome of the cafeteria with her hand up high in the air, presenting her raised middle finger like a final trophy for everyone to see. And now she felt glad she had done it.

During her last week, she had said to everyone who crossed her path what she had to say and she didn't hold back when she did. She told some of them to go fuck themselves. She made clear to everyone she was happy to leave, that she was done with Mars.

Fifty-eight seconds.

No private life, no worklife. No life. On Mars.

Fifty-six seconds.

She had returned her inventory back to recycling and left nothing behind. The only things she had with her were her two big red duffle bags filled with her clothes and favourite blankets.

She felt stressed, rocking with her feet so hard she instinctively looked to her left to the next passenger, expecting a complaint. Her eyes met those of an older lady, roughly twice her age, mid-sixties, with grey hair and dark green eyes. The woman raised an eyebrow, staring back at her, shook her head and turned away facing her own screen. It was empty besides the countdown on the left half and the view ahead into the sky above Mars on the right.

Elisa turned her eyes back to her own display and followed the countdown inside her head. She pushed her feet into the seat, trying to keep them still, squeezing her arms tight down onto her thighs through layers of spacesuit and clothing. She felt the smooth rubbery texture inside her gloves, moving her finger tips up and down, slightly pulling at the fabric.

Thirty-two, thirty-one.

Elisa inhaled and held her breath.

Twenty-nine, twenty-eight, twenty-seven.

She exhaled and watched the screen pause at the last number for a second.

"Twenty-six!" she said out loud, staring at the screen. "Twenty-six!" This time, she shouted. But instead of watching the numbers continue to count down, two words appeared on the screen: Launch cancelled.

She looked to her left to meet the annoyed stare of the older lady who pointed at her screen.

Elisa looked at her own, which now read: Prepare for egress.

At the same time her helmet closed, spinning the visor to the front, locking it in place.

"Are you fucking with me now?" She angrily shouted as she tapped against the screen, but the controls were already locked. Animations depicting how to proceed with crawling out of her seat, climb down the ladder and walk down the jet bridge cycled on the display.

"These fuckers fly every day, for a decade, and *now* is the day the fucker doesn't want to fly?" She exaggerated a bit with the number of flights, knowing once a week would have been more accurate.

She turned her wrist and unlocked the display of her terminal strapped to her left arm, navigated to the list of latest messages of her inbox. The newest read: Flight cancelled.

With rage, Elisa looked at the lady next to her, who was already turning over to her side to climb out of her seat. Elisa waved at her and gestured with two fingers pointing to her ear and tapped against the side of her own helmet to start an audio link between them. As soon as the lady repeated the gesture she could hear her responding with a calm, but distant "Yes?"

Elisa didn't hesitate. "Check your messages, is your flight cancelled?" Impatiently, she leaned on her left arm, to get out of her seat, but also to get a better view of the older lady's display. She observed how well her space suit fitted her slender figure, with not a crinkle too many anywhere in the fabric. It also appeared softer and stronger than her own, and immediately made Elisa guess how much more money this woman must have had compared to her.

Eagerly, she waited for her response. Instead, the devices in her ears responded with the ship's neutral voice:

"Please proceed with egress. This flight has been cancelled by orbital controls. More information will be available soon. Please proceed with egress."

The woman's answer followed right after.

"Yes, it says 'cancelled' on mine, too".

She followed the lady down the ladder and continued talking to her.

"But why cancel the flight? Why wasn't it delayed, or postponed?" Watching the woman from above, she didn't expect an answer, as the lady below her was focusing on the short metal bars in front of her hands and under her feet, working herself down to the level of the jet bridge.

Elisa did the same, until her own feet reached the floor, standing next to the older woman, who was more than half a head taller than her.

The woman lifted her arm to read from her terminal and nodded at Elisa.

"Here, listen to this: Latest Information: All flights to the station are cancelled until further notice. Upcoming flights to Earth: cancelled."

She watched how the woman grabbed the metal bars they had just climbed down to steady herself, her eyes staring into an unreachable distance, searching for something invisible.

Elisa heard herself repeat the words slowly in her head.

All flights to Earth cancelled.

Then, she too felt the weight of these words pull at her arms and legs, like a sudden increase in gravity.

They were both pulled back to reality by the automated message telling them to continue with exiting the space shuttle.

They grabbed their bags from a storage lift and stepped down the stairs of the jet bridge that extended out the middle of the back of the rocket at a forty-five degree angle down to the launch pad. They exited through a small airlock at the bottom to walk into the Martian atmosphere and immediately left the launch pad. At the border of the pad, they descended down a set of stairs leading into the ground. They entered a small underground station, filled with the passengers who had left the shuttle before them, waiting for the transport vehicles to pick them up and return them to the city. The apparent confusion was visible by the posture and gestures of their fellow travellers, waving around in their space suits.

Elisa couldn't believe what was happening, she had been so close.

Twenty-seven fucking seconds!

Elisa's eyes began to jump from left to right, bouncing as if rapidly shaking her head. Her vision got blurry and she felt the effort it took her to breathe in and out. She closed her eyes and stumbled, instinctively holding onto the older woman in front of her to stop herself from falling over. And then, panic hit her. She heard her own words inside her head. *You're not going to leave Mars!*

The technicians, two men in their mid-forties, arrived with the first pod out of the tunnel that connected the launch pads with the city. They shuffled their way through the waiting passengers, apologising on a broadcast channel for not being able to help with the current situation. The only news Elisa learnt from them was that it was their job to prepare the shuttles for a longer downtime.

The transport station was located at the end of a tunnel slowly going downhill. A platform, not higher than a step from the track leading into the ground, was filled with around forty astronauts, all in almost the same shade of white. You could easily distinguish the basic company suits from the expensive and individualised fitted suits. The latter were either not visible at all, or elegantly aligned to pronounce a more muscular appearance. Whoever had worked long enough, or started with enough money could afford these.

Soon, more empty pods arrived. Each pod was a dozen metres long, the bottom half resembling a cargo container cut in half, with two hip-high wheels in the front and back. The top half was a cabin with square and triangular windows all around and a double door in the middle on both of the sides.

Once they stopped, the doors slid open, wide enough to let two people enter at a time. The inside was mostly empty, but for six rows of two slim chairs mechanically folding out of the floor shaped like a lambda symbol. The seats were shaped like a bicycle seat, a wide backrest with two belts to go across the shoulders and hooks in the floor to hold onto your boots.

Elisa looked around. Everything was quiet from the outside, but under each helmet was someone talking, discussing, moderating or live commenting about the current situation. The unpressurised pods did not significantly change the scene as she entered the vehicle with the older lady.

Instinctively, Elisa aimed for the standing seat next to her. She put on her shoulder straps like a backpack and closed the clasp in the front, then hooked her feet under the handles in the floor. She looked at the other passengers doing the same, dropping their baggage next to each other.

"I'm Iris." The voice of the older woman came from her left, only sounding from Elisa's left earpiece, giving her some orientation. She turned her head towards her to reply.

"If it's really cancelled–" She paused. "–why?"

Elisa couldn't remember any cancellations since she had landed on Mars over five years ago. She went through her memories, her training, and refresh courses. She slowly answered her own question herself as best as she could, word by word.

"An earthbound flight is only cancelled if all redundancy options to leave Mars are exhausted, or in case of a missed launch window. It can't be the last, because the launch window is still ahead of us and it can't be the first, because the flight was never delayed, to prepare a backup ship and fly on that."

Elisa thought of the possibilities of what could go wrong in space and went on.

"A meteor shower on the flight route would have been observable and predictable, but still improbable. So what was it? Is there something wrong with the interplanetary shuttles?"

She looked at her new travel companion, who had a tear running down each cheek.

"I'm going to have to wait to see my first grandchild for an additional twenty-six months." Iris immediately explained.

She tried to wipe away the tear but was stopped by the thin glass of her helmet, producing a quiet thud that Elisa could hear through her ear pieces, centred, now that she was looking at her.

"It just makes me a bit emotional, that's all." She smiled at her.

Elisa hadn't thought about her distant family waiting for her on Earth, if at all, but she understood her. Still, she didn't know how to respond and just nodded. To occupy herself, she quickly checked her suit was charging while connected to the seat.

The pod accelerated down the tunnel, picked up speed, and eventually continued on a level straight towards the city. The dim, white glow of the pod's lights around them illuminated the greyish walls enough to see that they were racing past the walls like an express train, painting a glowing blur outside the windows.

Suddenly, Elisa burst out laughing, much to the confusion of her emotional opposite. She smirked and turned to Iris.

"I'm sorry, it's just that I realised that I have to see a lot of people again who I literally told that they could go fuck themselves. Big time. And I mean a lot of people. I guess this doesn't put me on the spectrum of nice people you could hang out with right now."

Elisa turned her head towards the front of the pod, shaking her head.

She listened to the awkward silence between them, considered disconnecting the audio link, but quickly decided against it. She turned to Iris, with something nicer in her head.

"You were looking forward to something beautiful, and I get that. It's just that I was looking forward to get away from this place, you know, forever." She felt a wave of sadness flush through her body. It stopped and lingered at the back of her throat, a feeling which quickly turned into helplessness. She had no one here, and needed a place to stay.

The pod travelled the thirty kilometres back to the city within minutes. On arrival, it gently decelerated and stopped in a slot of one of the group air locks. The passengers left the vehicle, and filed into the air lock, two sliding doors closing behind them. Vapour shot down from the ceiling and up from the floor engulfing them in a dense fog. Wetting everything and washing down dust and sand clinging to the passengers and their luggage.

Elisa stretched her arms and legs in every direction, trying to move every crease of her suit inside the fine spray. Her suit confirmed her movements for the required procedure with a short message popping up on the terminal on her arm. Next, she shook her duffle bags.

As quickly as the spray had appeared, it was sucked away again, warm air heating up the chamber round them, blowing from the top, rattling at their suits and gear.

They continued through the airlock straight into a lift. Once they were all inside, it ascended into the ceiling, accelerating gently. One by one they opened their helmets. Elisa confirmed the action on her terminal and her visor swivelled out of view. Faces were now poking out of oval collars that went from below the chin to the back of the head.

The elevator doors slid open and Elisa stepped into a long round tunnel. To her left and right more elevators arrived filling the limited space with more passengers. Some immediately walked away into either direction to the left or right of her, others remained chattering about the cancelled flight. A group was joking around. "Earth has finally nuked itself!" But, only a handful of those present laughed.

She glanced at the old woman, who was mustering her. Iris was travelling lighter than her, a single grey duffle bag, matching her spacesuit carrying it on her back versus Elisa carrying her own two, a red bag in each hand.

"When was the last time you had a coffee, Elisa?" Iris asked her, looking her up and down. "Let's get us a coffee, and see how this plays out, I'm paying."

Elisa shrugged. Coffee hadn't been part of her menu budget for two years by now. She released her helmet and secured it on top of one of her duffle bags.

"Okay, fair enough. Thanks!"

Iris led the way, following the arrows painted on the wall reading Cafeteria 1. Walking along the bare, grey tunnel, Elisa looked at the dark, smooth floor, polished for at least two decades by boots traveling between the transport station and the city, wishing deep inside her, for a way out.

II (ELISA)

They arrived inside the food court, a round dome, thirty metres high with white, bluish lights illuminating the pale ceiling. Big canvases hung on four sides from the curved walls with projections running short clips about the current expansion and future plans for Mars.

A quarter section of the dome had a thin row of windows at the bottom, facing outside. The reddish brown, dusty rocks of Mars lying behind the glass. Further away, Elisa could see the next dome, hidden under a hill of regolith, connected with other domes and tunnels reaching out from its sides. From the top the city looked like one big, flat molecule. In the centre was a cluster of big domes, connected with tunnels above ground. Towards the outside the tunnels continued underground to the remaining domes, which lay deeper under the surface revealing only small bumps of their true size.

The floor of the dome was filled with low, green walls, sparsely decorated with bushes and plants, providing nooks in which you could sit with a handful of people. The canteen was located opposite the windows. A group of people were waiting in a file, each with a tray in hand, to pick up their dinner.

They were dressed in functional wear, sweatpants or cargo pants in combination with hoodies, ready for work.

The two women aimed for one of the nooks in the middle and parked their luggage at the side of its entrance.

Iris unlocked her terminal and swiped around on the screen until she turned to Elisa.

"I ordered us two large coffees." She smiled, and they both sat down.

Their nook was almost in the centre of the dome, under the highest point of the round ceiling. Around them, about three hundred people were busying around either finishing, eating, or starting their dinner break.

"So, what's your job here?" Elisa curiously asked, taking off her gloves, folding them on top of each other and pushing them to the side of the table. Iris did the same with her gloves, and also took off her open helmet. Elisa hoped talking to someone would take her mind off her situation.

They were both in their space suits, as if still expecting to catch a flight, in contrast to all the others around them.

Iris looked at Elisa and lifted an eyebrow.

"You really don't look at the common channels here, right? You don't recognise me?"

But Elisa did not recognise her. She tapped on the table and drew a square.

"I stopped looking at online profiles here a while ago." She tapped at the invisible square. "I prefer to be surprised by someone, to avoid painting a picture from a profile in my head before I give them a chance to talk. Who are you again?"

Elisa felt she was lying, because she had already judged Iris by the quality of her space suit.

"My husband was the first to have a lethal accident on Mars." Iris crossed her arms, and Elisa remembered something vague.

There had been casualties, especially at the beginning of the colonisation twenty five years ago. Multiple companies were working together to create the first domes. Not everything went as planned and there were too many misunderstandings. The first person to die on Mars, due to a missing oxygen adapter, suffocated in his suit, while driving back in an unpressurised pod. Elisa wasn't sure if she remembered correctly, but there was something about the family being highly compensated and everything was promised in order to save the image of going to and working on Mars.

"And I'm still here, and this might sound stupid, so I can put a stone on his grave every week I get to walk outside. But now I have something else to look forward to, a reason to get back to Earth."

A knee-high box with small wheels arrived at the side of their table. It raised a tray with two coffee cups into the air and pushed the beverages gently across the table towards them. As quiet as it had arrived, it disappeared again.

They both picked up their cups, Elisa inhaled the hot aroma and mouthed a 'Thank you' towards Iris while nodding at the coffee, not to interrupt her.

"Even with the-" Iris drew quotation marks in the air. "-sacrifice for the project bullshit, they convinced me to join Mars. If they planned on sending thousands more to work on Mars, the least I could do was nose around enough to see that no one had to suffer such stupid accidents again."

Elisa was too focused on her coffee, to think of a response, and sipped from her cup. Eventually, she looked up. Iris was visibly grinding her teeth, then she went on.

"I have to admit that I don't like all the marketing that came with me going to Mars, but I did take all the extras they offered for it. You have to take what you can get here, you know?" She nodded at her suit then at Elisa's.

"Indeed, they didn't leave capitalism on Earth." Elisa added.

She waited for Iris to continue, just long enough to notice that the food court around them had grown silent.

Elisa creased her forehead in confusion, and listened to the sudden absence of the general rumble under the dome. She turned around, to see what was going on.

"What the fuck did I say now?" Elisa whispered to herself, as she saw how people were staring at their terminals or tablets, or whatever output device they had available, stopping whatever they were doing. Some were inaudibly whispering to each other in disbelief, eyes glued to their screens.

II (ELISA)

Iris pulled a device from her bag, as big as a lighter, and placed it upright between both of them. A screen appeared on the table, a projection that filled out the space between their cups. Iris opened the main news channel, swiping on the table's surface. Elisa observed how Iris split the screen in half and mirrored it, so they both could follow what she was looking at.

The latest headline read in bold letters: *Mars, 2086-05-28 13h27: More than 100 unknown objects landed on Mars.*

Elisa froze, re-reading the line over and over again, then looked up at Iris, her eyes wide open, staring at the table in shock. Elisa looked back down at the headline and summarised the situation with a single word.

"Fuck."

III (ELISA)

Elisa watched how the quiet dome transformed, the silence in the food court quickly replaced with agitation. People bouncing with long strides, ran or almost flew past their nook, with both feet in the air for longer than you would expect on Earth.

Some were cheering and laughing.

"It's happening! Aliens!"

Others were more cautious, quietly moving around the dome to stay away from the runners.

Elisa felt mocked. If a prank was the cause for why she couldn't leave Mars, she would explode. Everyone was getting excited because something was happening. And apparently something unknown. She was not impressed.

Still, she quietly manipulated her part of the screen to soak in all the information there was. She was curious.

She navigated a 3D realtime rendering of Mars, slowly spinning it across her side of the table. She studied the estimated landing points, repeatedly zooming in and out.

The screen updated with new information and notifications every second. She studied the map in front of her and the summary in the corner. Now, more than one hundred and fifty objects had been counted. They appeared out of nowhere in a low orbit and descended onto Mars, keeping an equal distance of about a thousand kilometres between each other in the shape of an icosphere. She zoomed in on the city, a small mesh in the basin of Simund Vallis. The closest reported landing site was about five-hundred km to the north in a flat area labelled Chryse Planitia. The next was marked six-hundred kilometres to the east in Arabia Terra, a region spotted with many craters, and another, at the same distance to the west in a higher region, with as many craters, but in addition streaked with deep canyons, labelled Xanthe Terra.

Elisa thought the first site, to the north, looked reachable within hours. She studied the projection, zooming in and out.

"The distribution of those points is not a coincidence, this is not random." she said, then sipped her coffee. "When zoomed out, the pattern is obvious."

Iris expanded the screen to only show the view Elisa had selected, studying it as well. She agreed.

Before Elisa could change the perspective again, they were interrupted by a broadcast message popping up on the screen that read: *Please proceed to your quarters and wait for updates.*

Iris stopped the projection and pushed the tiny device back into her bag.

Elisa switched her earpieces back on and was immediately greeted by an announcement.

"–proceed to your quarters and wait for updates."

said a calm voice.

"Shit, I don't have a –" Elisa began to say, but was interrupted by Iris. "Let's go to my place, you can figure out what you can do from there."

They finished their coffees and placed them at the edge of the table in reach for the waiter bot to pick them up. Elisa grabbed her bags and waited for Iris to lead the way. She followed her, half stumbling over the return service bot, that announced itself too late with a rattling beep. Elisa wasn't in a good mood, and banging her shin into a bot wasn't improving it. She contemplated kicking the device for a second, but already had to catch up with Iris, and decided against it.

They rushed through a long tunnel, sliding doors opened and closed around them along the way, each door with a number painted onto it with big red letters, marking the pressurised segments of the city. The walls of the tunnel had the same texture as the one connecting the city with the launch pads.

They passed through a large, windowless utility dome looking like a big market, with booths and workshops lining the perimeter and two concentric rings of booths and storage spaces stacking high up under the ceiling. Cargo bots were sliding up, down and sideways along rails to store or retrieve items as requested. In the middle of the dome was a round staircase leading them to a floor filled with hundreds of 3d printers quietly wiggling their printheads across the print surface, producing handles, cargo boxes, shoes, clothing, whatever had been placed in the queue to be manufactured. The printers which were stopped for maintenance were left unattended, as the technicians had already left.

They left the print farm behind and exited the dome through another long, grey tunnel, leading them slowly deeper into the ground. At the end of the tunnel they arrived at a hub connected to tunnels from multiple directions like a star. People appeared from one opening to disappear into another, accompanied by a constant clattering of footsteps.

Elisa instinctively aimed for the tunnel connected to the dome she used to live in, expecting the other woman to follow her. But instead, Iris pointed at the staircase.

"Up. I live at the top." She said and aimed for the staircase.

Elisa lifted an eyebrow in response.

"Right, you mentioned something about that earlier." she said dryly, and followed the grey duffle bag with legs up the stairs.

The higher they went up the stairs, the fewer people were left walking with them. Elisa had never been to the part of the city that was built into a rock formation overlooking the city. It housed the luxury tourist apartments, a half-abandoned project, where the flats that were finished were rented out to those who could afford a three-year or longer vacation to Mars.

She noticed the walls were painted white and everything looked more welcoming and brighter.

They arrived at the top floor and followed a corridor with doors only to their right side, one every one hundred metres.

Between the doors were islands of flower pots. Groups of orchids hung from the ceiling. A gardening bot was in the process of digging in a pot, replacing flowers with freshly flowering ones, from a stack of trays wheeling behind it.

Elise noticed it was the same base type of a machine as the waiter bot that she now wished she had kicked earlier. Her legs felt tired.

The city was big, counting just above twenty-two thousand inhabitants, increasing with every new wave of settlers every twenty-six months. She had arrived with the seventh wave, bringing up the number of inhabitants just above four and a half thousand. The last two waves added another six and another twelve thousand workers, more than doubling the number of inhabitants on Mars each time.

There were forty dormitory domes and twenty utility domes, each focused on either manufacturing, repairs or dining. The recreational domes had been scrapped for dormitory domes a year after Elisa had arrived on Mars. The tunnels connecting the utilities were growing things more for aesthetic reasons, to create a more comfortable atmosphere, a project run in the few hours of spare time by a group of individuals, always dreading the day the water supplies would be cut. The actual farms, the hydroponic systems, were deeper underground below the habitats, in a vast network of mines that were first dug for resource extraction and then converted into farms. In the first years the drilling was concentrated to a single strip mine below the city, but then the equipment was regrouped to drilling lanes of tunnels outwards into every direction to look for other feasible places to expand and build more settlements and cities. This expansion was one of the topics where Elisa had collided with her managers, about how the city was being managed. When she left Earth, there were roughly two thousand people working on Mars, building and expanding the city, around the clock, 25/7.

At the beginning, Elisa was hyped to do her part with enthusiasm: repairing drills, bots, and writing code for everything as requested. They managed to triple the resources and redundancies on Mars, there were fail-safes.

There was a constant stream of supplies coming in from Earth, almost every month hundreds of tons of equipment and material arrived, stored underground in the empty tunnels.

But when they announced the plans of tripling the size of the city, giving up living space for work space, half a year before the next wave arrived, it felt like a slap in the face. As expected, not everyone was happy with the management decision, but for Elisa it meant she lost her belief in building something greater. Giving up security for a head count, to accelerate the expansion, without even asking those who worked on the planet, did not make sense to her.

With every wave that doubled the population, the riches in resources, space and redundancies they had created were filled with thousands of more workers instead. The original plan of a constant increase of population with every wave, reducing the work load with each iteration, was thrown overboard to max out the capacity. Again and again. Once the transports were underway there was no stopping them from reaching Mars, and everything felt out of control to her. The colonisation had to be scaled up, the workloads were increased and the pressure on everyone was growing with each day. The initial excitement of a twenty-five-hour day only resulted in longer work days and less sleep. The result was that to this day they didn't have enough space for everyone to sleep in their own private room.

Even if Elisa didn't visibly see the exponential increase of humans on Mars during the day, living in tunnels and domes, designed for an equal distribution, she noticed it during her daily routine. Resources were prioritised for the newbies. Prices for commodities were suddenly calculated depending on how long you had been on Mars. For the newly arrived it all seemed perfect. Fish, coffee, everything was on the menu. But for Elisa it soon meant that coffee was only affordable once a week, then once a month, until she entirely gave up.

As a result of the scarcity, there was a plan to reward you an interest rate for being frugal, a limitation that Elisa did not agree with. She distanced herself from those who were proud to live on almost nothing, to abstain from all the luxuries. And as the majority of workers had never seen a Mars with backups and safety measures, the new status-quo had been accepted as the new normal. She increasingly distanced herself from her colleagues, just waiting for her time to leave.

In addition to the growing numbers, she wondered how many of the newbies ever passed the mental assessments to be allowed to work on Mars.

The straw that broke the camel's back for her was when Mars was announced to be equal with Earth. Everyone cheered. Everyone got their pat on the back for their work, for establishing a thriving colony and economy on Mars, a new world. But it also meant, that if someone had to pay to get from Earth to Mars, you now also had to pay to get from Mars to Earth. This meant that if you spent all your local money in the form of credits on Martian luxuries, you'd be stuck there forever.

With Mars running close to exhaustion and artificial rationing of resources the economy thrived in the eyes of the management. But for Elisa it meant that she had to borrow tools for work, work extra hours to repair her work tools to meet her quota and working through an ever growing list of to-do's and technical debt. It was chaos. She was exhausted and disappointed. And she did not agree with where things were heading. When she voiced her concerns about missing redundancies in the life support systems, she was tasked to read the manuals that would prove they were fail safe. Even after she was called out of bed for last minute repairs to stop an entire habitat from flooding with CO_2, no one had listened to her concerns. In the same situation her colleagues were proud to be the 'hero of the day', saving everyone and avoiding catastrophic failure at the last minute. And all of this happened over and over again. Soon she did the simple math, that she would just about manage to save up enough credits to book a seat back to Earth. And she did.

But instead of boarding one of the four interplanetary shuttles docked to *The Gateway To Earth*, the orbital station above Mars, she had arrived at one of the luxury flats after being denied her launch. A luxury flat designed for those who could afford guided tours through the canyons of Xanthe Terra. Elisa clenched her fists around the handles of her duffle bags.

The doors of the apartment opened, Iris stepped through and motioned Elisa to follow her inside. The door quietly closed behind her and she walked a few steps further inside. With a soft clunk her duffle bags hit the floor and her jaw dropped. She looked at a huge room, a hall with an unusually high ceiling for Mars habitats at almost 8 metres. In the middle of the room was a square of grey couches, with enough room for a dozen grownups to lie around. In its centre was a glass table, with a miniature landscape of the area surrounding the city, spanning hundreds of kilometres scaled down, printed from Mars sand into a square of two by two metres under the glass. A wall of ivy was growing up the high walls to her left. A small pond speckled with water lilies and a wobbly bubbling fountain was built into the tiled floor below the green. Elisa spotted a small group of goldfish swimming about. On each side of the pond was a door leading to the other rooms. On the other side was an open kitchen, and in between, on the opposite side of the entrance to this hall, she could see a conservatory overlooking the plains of Chryse Planitia, with the domes of the city like irregular bubble wrap spread out below. She was impressed. This was a beautiful place to stay on Mars. Even for Earth this would have been amazing.

"Feel free to look around." Iris said from the corner of the room. "I will take the master bedroom and get changed into something more comfortable. You can take the guest room." She pointed at the door to Elisa's left of the conservatory. When she was gone, Elisa looked around, walked past the couches, her fingers touching the soft fabric as she walked past. When she reached the conservatory, she noticed the coffee from earlier was demanding its service.

On the toilet, Elisa was resting on her elbows. She was angry, because she knew who had built this place, and who had worked hard for this in an invisible ant hill under the ground. She was angry because her flight had been cancelled and she didn't know if it was real or a prank. And she was angry because even if she took a shit on Mars, the company benefitted from her providing free fertiliser, crapping into a litter box, collected by a bot to be carted off to the farms to be reprocessed.

The next day, Elisa woke up and got dressed. She washed herself in the en-suite bathroom and looked at her own reflection. She liked her dark hair and grey eyes, but she'd stopped counting the grey hairs slowly taking over. At least they matched her eye colour. She was indifferent to everything else. Unplucked eyebrows, no makeup. Things you would run out of on Mars in any case. No piercings, no earrings and no modifications. She dried herself off with her pyjamas, laid it out to dry on the bed and got dressed.

When, she walked into the living room, Iris was already up, with a cup of coffee in her hand. A short ring sounded from the kitchen, from the other side of the hall.

"Good morning, that's your coffee." Iris said looking out of the window, standing in the sun, gazing outside.

Elisa navigated around the island of sofas, past a counter into the kitchen and found a fresh cup of coffee standing ready under a single purpose coffee machine. She glanced around and tried to inventorise, but everything was hidden behind arrays of neat panels she guessed were fake. A rack of herbs growing under long bright light strips, was showing off with every green colour and texture.

She picked up her coffee and joined Iris standing in the conservatory. Between exotic plants she recognised orchids, and could distinguish three types of carnivorous plants. Everything else was either tree, grass or flower to her.

"How did you know I was up?" She asked Iris, looking at her face, wondering what she would look like in thirty years herself. Iris was standing in the sun, now with her eyes closed.

"And is this thing radiation proof?" Elisa added to her question.

Iris looked at her.

"I didn't. The flat did. And they said something about semi conducting glass, so the second answer is a 'yes'." She tapped against the glass and turned her gaze outside again, to concentrate on something apparently elusive.

Elisa looked around, then out of the windows. She hadn't looked outside, especially from a viewpoint like this for a long time. She was still amazed by the luxury of the apartment, the space and much better tasting coffee, which she held under her nose. Any coffee would have improved her mornings in the last year, she thought, even the synthetic one.

In the distance Elisa spotted a trail of dust leading north. A caravan of vehicles was speeding away from the city. She immediately remembered the alien objects landing on Mars from the day before.

"Yes, right!" Elisa reminded herself, fumbled her earpieces from a pocket of her cargo pants, and inserted them. They turned on with a brief beep. She had fallen asleep without talking to Iris the night before, and had forgotten the events of the previous day for a brief moment, enjoying her coffee.

She listened to a voice reading the latest messages from her inbox.

"Recent events. One hundred and sixty objects have landed on Mars. Six hundred and forty on Earth. Latest analysis: The origins remain unknown. All relevant authorities and units are on alert and are monitoring the situation. No casualties have been reported. The objects appear to be made of solid metal. No energy based processes detectable. The current assumption is that these objects provide no threat. Report for duty, and remain calm. Investigations are ongoing. Further information will be published as soon as it becomes available."

The message woke her up quicker than any coffee could have. Her last days bubbled up inside her head. The unpleasant good byes. The cancelled launch. The cancelled flight. She took out a terminal from another pocket of her trousers and checked her flight status. The latest message read: Refunded.

"Fuck!" she cursed and turned to Iris, who looked pressed, as if unsure what to say.

Elisa checked her terminal for upcoming flights, to find the original flights reinstated, but the tickets resold from scratch. The booking system returned no available seats, so Elisa checked the local message boards. Those who had panicked had outbid each other for the rescheduled flights. The last bids had increased tenfold in price of what she could afford. She was stuck. There was no way she could come up with an insane amount of credits to book a flight back to Earth. She had just saved up enough for the standard ticket.

She looked at Iris, who had been watching her for the past minute and the older woman began to talk.

"I'm sorry, I have to leave you. I got lucky and got one of the last tickets. I had my system set to auto-buy. I'll be leaving in a few minutes already, I'm glad you woke up on time, so I could say good bye in person. If you need me to take something back to Earth let me know. You can stay at this place for the rest of the week, I left my reservation until then."

Elisa looked at Iris who was turning a cold expression into a forced smile, as if pretending to be happy to have helped Elisa with something.

Elisa was speechless. She felt empty and angry. She looked back at the trail of dust in the distance. Her heart was thumping in her chest with rage. She checked the prices again. They were unaffordable to her, out of reach. She thought about filing a complaint, but knew there was no one to complain to. Everything was automated by software and not a single person was ever responsible. She felt her arms beginning to tingle. Anger building up inside her.

Before she could react or decide on what to do or say, Iris was already leaving in her perfectly fitting space suit, waving goodbye, leaving through the door, a grey duffle bag with legs poking out at the bottom.

Elisa thought about threatening Iris, forcing her to give her her ticket, to leave her tied up and crying in her luxury flat. But focusing on a better version of herself, she pushed away her thoughts. She turned around, to watch the sliding doors of the apartment close and Iris was gone. She stood there, staring at the door. She felt disappointed, like so many times before.

This place turns people into shit.

She felt betrayed by everyone. Her grip tightened around her half empty cup of coffee. Her breathing got heavier, her teeth were grinding until she stopped keeping her emotions inside her. She screamed as loud and hard as she could at the plants around her, then threw her coffee cup across the spacious room towards the wall next to the entrance. A trail of dark liquid spilled out in midair, tracing the trajectory. The cup hit the wall and cracked neatly in half, into a short tube and a smaller cup, with half a handle each.

A small bot on two wheels appeared from the kitchen, picked up the pieces and began to wipe up the coffee droplets from the floor and the wall.

Elisa picked up the empty cup Iris had left behind on the edge of a flower pot and threw it at the bot. With a satisfying clang it knocked the device off course. It turned around, picked up the second mug, and disappeared quietly into the kitchen under Elisa's raging eyes.

She wanted to destroy something, she wanted to see things break like she was breaking at that moment.

She put her hand into the closest flower pot, fingernails digging into the soil, closing around the roots of a plant and clenching it into her fist, crushing it, feeling the thick roots separate from the stem, moisture filling the folds of her palm. She wanted retribution.

In the hazy distance, the caravan had become smaller, racing towards the horizon. She watched it shrink for a second.

IV (PHIL)

Phil was on his daily routine inspection of the experimental farm he managed at a depth of two hundred metres below the Martian city. He didn't care much about the amount of solid rock above his head that could theoretically come crushing down at any time depending on how much of an over-thinker he was. But that was not his concern this morning.

This morning was different. He rushed through the long, bright tunnels, dressed in a worn out, white lab coat, and newly printed shoes. Pearls of sweat ran down his forehead, into his bushy, grey eyebrows. His chin was covered in a curly, grey beard. He was one of the first settlers on Mars and had been running the farms for more than two decades.

With long strides he almost jogged through the first section. It was filled with glowing, green walls made out of dozens of semi-transparent trays, each the size of a bed, layered from the floor to the ceiling on each side of the tunnel. Upon closer inspection, he could make out the clumps and particles of algae slowly flowing from tray to tray. The stacks of algae panels lined the tunnel up to the doors leading into the next section. His eyes jumped from left to right, confirming the status reports he had read on his screens earlier. Even if they had all been positive, he still had to check in any case. Routine was routine. And the best way to teach routine was by living it, to make sure his new assistant understood exactly what she had to do in the next days or weeks, depending on how his expedition went.

"First, the algae okay? You need to check they all look healthy. Take a screenshot of the current colour, this is optimal, okay?" He said hastily, waving at the camera at the end of the tunnel, then drew an invisible rectangle in the air around the green panels and pointed at it.

Red, his new assistant, started this morning, after the previous one had spontaneously decided to ditch Mars, burn all his credits and head back to Earth. He called the new one 'Red', because she had two red stripes tattooed down her face, starting from her cheek bones, over her jawline and down her throat. He almost called her 'Pause', because to him her face looked like a huge pause button, but he wasn't sure if he wanted to be funny on her first day.

"Yes, Dr. Scruffy!" replied her voice through his earpieces.

I should have gone with 'Pause', he thought and moved on to the next section. In front of the heavy door, he stopped. The left side had a rectangular window with rounded corners, and the right had the door id UF27 written in big red letters on it.

"Red, remember: to get out from anywhere you have to keep the windows to your right. It will lead you right up, okay?" He said, briefly waited for a reply, then repeated himself.

"Window to the left means lower. Window to the right, right up, okay?"

He imagined her getting lost in these tunnels, and since he was responsible for her, it would make it his problem.

"Yes, wait–" She dragged her words. "–let me take a screenshot of the door to be extra sure where left and right is."

He heard the mocking undertone in her voice. It reassured him for a second, which then flipped into fear when he thought about the last part of her sentence, about where left and right were.

The door slid open as he walked through it and closed right behind him once he was in the next section of the tunnel. It had the same length as before, but this one was walled with waste high stainless steel tanks filled with water, swarming with goldfish.

"In case you get hungry down here, the red ones taste like salmon, the grey ones taste like tuna." He pointed at the genetically modified fish.

"Tuna was my contribution." he said, smiling to himself, wiping sweat from his forehead with the sleeve of his lab coat.

Immediately, he imagined Red putting her hands elbow-deep into the tanks trying to catch a fish.

"Keep your hands out of the water. At all times. If the bots fail to fish out the dead ones, please use one of the nets."

IV (PHIL)

He looked at a thin creature of a bot, standing at the end of the tunnel segment, overlooking all the tanks, one arm fitted with a net. He had to make sure she didn't mess this up.

"I know, they look like goldfish, but they bite like piranhas." Said her voice in his ears.

He stopped to stare at the next camera, not sure if she was serious, hoping she was at least watching.

"I know, fungi. I'm new here, but I'm not entirely stupid, okay? Only sometimes."

He had to trust her and moved on to the next section.

It was warmer in the farms than in the domes, a nice and steady twenty-three degrees Celsius and the humidity was higher, too. Usually, he would enjoy his routine, slowly walking through each section, proud of his work. At the current pace he was sweating under his overall, his hair clinging to his forehead.

He remembered to get a haircut anyday, for months now, but he never went, because eventually he would forget again.

The next section was a red-green blur as he hurried through. Walls of tomatoes growing out of both sides of meshed panels, alternating with bright panels illuminating the plants, assembling an almost infinite sandwich of light and tomatoes. He showed the different stages of growth the tomatoes went through, repeating from top to bottom, repeating on each panel. Each gradient started with rows of yellow flowers, fading into rows of small green fruit, to rows of bright red, ripe tomatoes. Each plant grew exactly one fruit on a tiny leafy arm, from a single cell of many, like peas in a pod, lined up in a row.

Phil navigated around a slim bot, that almost looked like a praying mantis, which was in the process of extending a long flat arm under a row of ripe tomatoes. Within seconds, the bot retracted its arm, cutting and collecting the fruit in a single swift motion.

"Make sure the bots don't drop anything. You can't imagine how many times I've had them retrained by IT. I think they still don't know how AI works. I'm sure it is getting worse every year now." He said, puffed.

In his head he saw the fruit falling on the floor, rolling under the panels, gathering dust and mould.

"And keep in mind, this is only the test lab, the actual farm is much, much bigger. Make note of everything that goes wrong. With the current growth of the colony we don't have room for errors anymore. So we need to find those here, fix them and see how we can upgrade the main farm." He hoped she was listening.

Even at the current pace, he enjoyed the aromatic profile of the section. The intense smell of tiny green tomato leaves, a characteristic once relevant for protection against insects, but totally useless in a sealed environment on Mars. But often he had thought that with how things were going, this protective feature would soon be required in the kilometres of tunnels

IV (PHIL)

that were growing food.

Next, he rushed past potatoes, growing in cylinders, harvested from the bottom, growing out the top, in an endless race from the bottom up, always being pushed down in a rotating plastic tube, refilled with soil from the top, and harvested from the roots.

He did his best to remind her of everything that he expected to go wrong with the latest changes, even after twenty years of optimising, rebuilding from scratch. He was especially concerned about the automation. From automation, to machines, to errors, his attention went back to aliens. The things that landed on Mars. His thoughts were racing about what he might find once he arrived at one of the alien landing sites, as they were now called.

He had many questions. Were they really alien? Were they alive? Was it an alien terraforming project? He imagined Mars suddenly becoming liveable on the surface, being able to plant the first seeds in an uncontrolled atmosphere on the red planet. Or maybe the colony was merely perceived as fruit flies and swatted away as soon as they arrived? He imagined being thrown into the air by a force field, falling down and breaking his neck while landing on his head. He snapped back to reality, feeling excited and scared at the same time. He continued with the remaining segments. Vegetables growing vertically stacked in rows and columns, adapted to their size and length. Cucumbers, zucchini and corn growing stacked like wine bottles in a wine rack, lining both sides of the tunnel. Then, strawberries, similarly grown like the tomatoes, but smelling a lot sweeter, followed by tunnel segments growing wheat, densely packed like light yellow carpets standing between thin glowing panels. Again, genetically modified for minimal vegetational growth and space requirements, but maximum yield.

He arrived at the last section, a bright tunnel filled with a jungle of cannabis plants, brushing through the leaves as he walked through, deeply inhaling the thick smell. The ceiling so bright it was almost blinding him. This was his favourite section. He had optimised his own strain from a variety of seeds he had brought from Earth. He had called it Nova Mars, because he had managed to improve it in such a way that it messed with your short-term memory in a way that experiencing something felt like you experienced it for the first time again. For example if he walked, or floated, depending how high he was in the domes and looked outside, it felt like the first time stepping on Mars again, bringing back the excitement of colonising a new planet. It lit that spark of excitement that seemed to fade over the years, reigniting a positive effect that was welcomed by the management, giving him extra room for resources and planning, even if it wasn't explicitly allowed.

"Never, ever go from the male section to the females, if you keep this rule in mind, you can consume as much as you want. We have to avoid pollination." He said into the plants, making his way to the exit at the end of the tunnel.

"Indica, nice! I think I got this one." Red answered.

He looked for a camera to smile back, but couldn't see one through the thicket of plants growing over his head.

Maybe she wasn't as bad as he had assumed from her CV.

◆ ◆ ◆

An hour later, Phil stood in one of the excursion airlocks, to the north of the city, twenty metres below the surface. It was a long double-wide tunnel, filled with three large vehicles in the progress of being loaded with his equipment. The vehicles had the same dimensions as the pods travelling between the city and the launchpads, but with a higher ground clearance, and bigger off-road wheels. Each vehicle had a set of folding stairs in the middle to let passengers climb into a slim airlock mounted onto each side.

The first artefact expedition, as they had been called, had already left half a day ago and had arrived about five hundred kilometres to the north of the city. The expedition had already set up a portable dome around the artefact, to provide the first team with room to analyse the spherical object resting on the Martian surface. The portable domes were initially designed to be used by research teams that wanted to spend more time in a certain spot on the planet to search for traces of ancient life. There weren't many left and now everyone and everything working on Mars was re-tasked to build as many as possible, to spread out the research, to gain more insights from the alien objects.

Phil read through his list of tasks again. It had been provided by the middle management. They were tasked to proceed the same way as the first mission, but almost three times further out to the north.

The search for ancient alien life was the reason he had come to Mars twenty years before. But unfortunately the rough start of the colonisation, followed by changes in the organisation of the entire undertaking by merging into a single enterprise, had changed his plans. The company had to resolve so called growth pains. But after that, the colony was soon run as an expanding business, which reprioritised everything into scaling up the colonisation, which did not leave any room for research and scientific exploration. New goals were set and requirements for the amount of food in order to feed now almost twenty-two thousand humans, with no room for error, did not leave any resources for the search for dead fossilised lifeforms or whatever he expected to find, except a few marketing stunts here and there in the first years. And even those few excursions did not turn up with definitive results. The samples that came back positive still left the possibility of stemming from a physical process, so until now, he called it Schrödinger's life on Mars. It was either there or not, but he hadn't been given the chance to thoroughly take a look yet and come to a final conclusion. He had spent every opportunity he got to venture around the city, outside, but eventually gave up. He didn't want to go outside alone. And in addition to that, they were nowhere close enough to the more potential sites, and every stone on top and around the city had been touched already.

Despite the circumstances, Phil was convinced that the era of science was yet to come. The artefacts could be the spark that might kickstart this time. His time. He saw himself helping out a skinny, big-headed alien crawl out of an alien shuttle, establishing first contact, a photo of him in his lab coat attached to the top headline.

He improvised as best as he could to make up a list of tools and equipment he required for his spontaneous ideas of what he could use to analyse the unknown object. PCR kits, DNA analysers, centrifuges, whatever the 3D print farm could manufacture in the last twelve hours. He hadn't slept all night, and he was too excited to feel tired.

"I'd prefer if we could take an excavator instead of trowels and buckets." he said, looking at the 3D scan the first team had provided. A round ball resting on the cold regolith.

"From the satellite images, all the artefacts look as if they have gently touched down, and I'm pretty sure the archaeology equipment will be useless, Pause." He said more to himself, but still addressing Pause.

He had upgraded her name from 'Red' to 'Pause'. As soon as he came out of the tunnel, half a day ago, she had tossed his hair for her amusement and called him Dr. Scruffy again, which was enough for him. He'd told her that even if space was sometimes sparse on Mars, he still had his personal space and begged her to stop arsing around. He wouldn't call her 'Pause', just because he liked it, trying to make an example. She just laughed at him with a surprising smile and said "'Pause' is fine with me, if it helps you get along with me." She definitely had surprised him. He was twice her age and had spent the bigger part of her age on Mars already. He had never considered himself to be any different to anyone half his age joining the colony on Mars, but she was raising his doubts about this view of himself.

As he watched her load his final crate of equipment into the long cabin of the second off-road vehicle, he still wasn't sure if he had to get along with her or she with him. He wasn't responsible for hiring her, and he was especially not in a position to choose from talent. The system chose from his requirements, which was void of any personal requirements to get along with someone. He also noticed that the focus of the new settlers coming to Mars definitely hadn't been on scientific profiles. They must have been focused on the willingness to be permanent settlers on a one-way trip. Otherwise he could not explain the situation. No matter what he thought of her, he thanked her for managing to pack his seemingly endless list of things he might need into crates and load them into the cargo vehicle on time. Seeing everything work out left him with a more optimistic feeling about her looking after his experiments.

He checked his terminal again, a worn out, matte screen, strapped onto his right arm, on the outside of his grey space suit. He wasn't sure if he was required to be wearing the suit while driving across the Martian surface at a speed of two hundred kilometres per hour, but his head produced too many ugly images showing him getting exposed to the Martian atmosphere, that he felt safer putting it on. Especially as they had to cover a distance of fourteen hundred kilometres in the next eight hours. According to the numbers on the display, that was the expected length of the journey. It was made clear that time was important, as they apparently now had been in a race with Earth, to find out what all these alien objects were about. Again, he thought, when things were rushed, that was when things went wrong, so he felt safer in a suit. At the same time he wasn't sure if he was over-thinking again.

He watched the group assemble. The driver of the caravan had a well-toned body, wearing a dark, long-sleeved shirt and grey sweatpants. Phil watched him parading around his bulge as he strutted into the hall, making him feel jealous. The driver's flip flops on his naked feet on the other hand presented to him a level of confidence he did not share. Looking at the driver's silhouette in front of the tall airlock doors separating them from the freezing, almost vacuum like atmosphere, made him feel comfortable about wearing a space suit instead. He pushed away the thought of the doors cracking open under pressure, the air escaping and leaving them maybe ten to thirty seconds to find an oxygen mask, or in his case his helmet to auto-close, but then leaving him to look after the others. He didn't even know how to help in that case, and made a mental note to visit a safety refresh course. For a second time, he tried to push his thoughts aside, looking around to distract himself.

Two more men appeared, also dressed in a similar leisure outfit. Phil checked his terminal and figured the three men made up the support team in charge of setting up the camp and unloading the equipment, once at the landing site. In addition to the driver, one was an electrician, mainly responsible for the power generator truck and the other was a manufacturing engineer to design and operate the 3D printers as well as to provide in-place manufacturing of tools they might require.

Phil looked at his terminal again, to review the crew list. With him being the fourth member, with a background in biology, the fifth member was like him focused on research, but from a different perspective: computer science. And to Phil it made sense. He had asked himself already, what if the alien object was not of biological origin, but entirely artificial instead.

He turned towards the last member as she appeared, a woman probably a bit older than Pause, carrying two red duffle bags across her back, also wearing a grey space suit.

Interesting! he thought.

At least I'm not the only one in a suit.

"Hi, I'm Phil." He said as he turned to her, extending his hand. "I run the farms. We haven't met yet, I suppose?"

She slowly turned to him, carefully shook his hand, and replied. "I think I used to belong to the IT department."

He looked into her grey eyes looking back at him as if he was about to do something suspicious.

"And what's your name? In case I need a skilled developer for the farm automation, you know, after all this blows over. I'd be happy to book you." He smiled at her, unsure if he accidentally insulted her.

She looked away, turned to the first pod and replied, dryly. "Elisa".

V (PHIL)

Phil checked his terminal on his arm to track the progress of their journey. They had been driving for five and a half hours, flying across the flat dusty landscape at an average speed of two-hundred and twenty kilometres per hour. The time to the destination was indicated to be just below an hour.

He was strapped onto one of the folding seats in the back of the first vehicle, the shoulder straps closed in front of his chest. He turned around to watch the other two vehicles, closely racing behind them, automatically following their course with a slight delay, but without any passengers. To his right was Elisa. She was also strapped into her seat, in the process of waking up from a long nap. He had been looking forward to exchanging ideas with her and about what was expecting them, to share his excitement. But as soon as the vehicles had set into motion, slowly crawling up the dusty ramp, out into the Martian atmosphere, she had fallen asleep.

He tried to converse with the three younger men, but apparently as he was the 'old geezer', as they called him, he didn't seem to fit in. Out of spite he had declined their offer to play cards with them. Also, he wanted to stay strapped into his seat, which made him stand out, literally. The three were sitting on cargo boxes around a bigger container between them, drinking shots and playing cards. Further to the front of the vehicle was the cockpit, with two empty seats and two steering wheels, automatically turning with the path the vehicle selected, surrounded by screens and arrays of buttons above and below.

The vehicle was autonomously ploughing ahead, throwing dust into the air from its wheels. Whenever he turned around to check if the following vehicles were still there, he saw them disappear from time to time behind a veil of dust. Watching the speeding caravan, stacked with equipment and technology, he thought the third was the most important one, the one with the fuel cells.

Considering the driver's and his new friends' drunkenness, he was relieved the vehicle was driving itself, no matter what training state the AI was in.

Phil had thought a dozen times if he could ask Elisa if she'd taken a sleeping pill or not, but decided against it. Maybe he had insulted her already once.

He looked at his terminal. There were still no new insights from the first team at the first landing site. The sphere was sitting motionless in the same spot, not moving, radioing or talking or anything, in contrast to the three men in front of him. So far, he had figured out their names. The driver was Ewald, which made Phil laugh inside every time he heard his name. The electrician was called Erik, which he found incredibly easy to remember, and the 3D-printing engineer was Ahmad. All three of them had arrived with the latest wave just over a year before, with the latter two travelling on the same squad of shuttles. Phil had watched them get along really well so far, which did not include him.

"So how much time did you guys actually spend learning on the trip here? Or what is your background?" asked the driver, throwing another card on the table. The card backs were black. Half of the set was filled with a picture of planet Earth, the other half with Mars.

"I applied during high school, had to wait to be old enough to sign the contract. Did nothing in between, and as I'm not a total dumb ass, had to learn everything on the trip here. And I did." said Erik, playing his card, carefully putting it on top of the other cards, then collecting them, moving them over to his side of the cargo box, repurposed as a table. "Found out I'm good with wires and remembering not to touch the wrong ones." The electrician looked at Ahmad.

The manufacturing engineer rearranged his cards and waited for Erik to lay out a new card to start the next round and presented his story with a thick accent.

"I had my own print farm in Syria. Hundreds of printers. Tried my luck and applied. During the interview I told them 3D printing on Mars is easy. Bridging and overhangs at a third of gravity: easy. Maybe I got extra points for saying I'm used to living with sand and dust. Saw no big difference, thought we didn't even need an AC."

The answers made things a lot clearer to Phil. He thought about what he had heard: Hire as young as possible, so they could work as long as possible on Mars. Crash course on the flight, no experience required. It explained many of the delays, because throwing more under-qualified people at a task did not speed things up if they needed to be taught first.

The three men looked as if they had forgotten about him and Elisa, so he turned his head towards her and tried his luck.

"Good morning?" He whispered.

She didn't react, so he continued to watch another round of cards being won by the driver, and listened to the electrician tell another one of his stories.

"One time, during the trip here, we had this bet going, if I could jizz into this girl's mouth in nearly zero g, you know, in the centre where the jet bridges connect. The centre bit, between the doors that only open when you approach them really slow. What is that, eight metres?"

Erik had put down his cards and gestured two tunnels meeting with his hands. The others burst out laughing, while Ewald poured another round of shots and they all drank.

"Yeah man! Did you do it?" The driver was eager to know.

"No Dude, my dick is bent like fuck, of course not." Eric sneered, slapping his hands into his lap.

Ahmad laughed. "I saw the stain on the wall the next day. Motherfucker didn't even clean it off."

"At least you tried the stunt!" said the driver, wiping away his tears from laughing, then turned around to look at the driverless cockpit, and complained.

"Damn bro, still an hour to go, this feels longer than the trip between Earth and Mars!"

"Like your mom's dick?" joked Ahmad, pretending to evade invisible punches.

Phil turned his head and looked at Elisa. She was awake, her lips tightly pressed against each other, with a mix of a smile, a frown and slowly nodding her head, watching the group in front of them. Phil turned over to her and whispered.

"Yeah, right–", but didn't finish his sentence on purpose. For him it was one of those moments where saying nothing at all said all that was to be said. She faced him and raised an eyebrow.

"And who are you?" she asked.

Happy to have someone to talk to he did his best to start a conversation.

"Well, I'm still Phil." He smiled and added a short laugh. "And I spend most of my time in the experimental farms, researching ways to make sure their kids have enough to eat." He said nodding his head slightly towards the three men in front of them, trying to hide his disappointment in his voice, but apparently they had heard him.

"Hey, fuck off man. Without us you would have no space or things to build your farms, okay?" The electrician barked across the makeshift table.

"Fuck you elitist cunt." Mumbled the driver, and got up.

The other two watched him climb over the boxes they had rearranged for their game, and quickly followed him to the front of the vehicle. Ahmad went for a piss in a portable toilet, a big plastic box standing in the front left part of the vehicle, with the door facing the cockpit, leaving it open.

"Feeding the kids? Interesting!" Elisa sounded interested. "Is this something you *planned* to do here or is it something you *ended up* doing here?"

Phil felt she had hit him in an area he rarely thought about himself. He was proud of his work, but not entirely happy.

"I enjoy what I'm doing. I'm a scientist, biology is my area. And engineering crops is what I've been doing most of the time. I'm good at it." He replied.

"That was not my question!"

"Well, I've been here for a long time, and things have changed a lot, and I'm sure they will change again, so I can eventually do what I came here to do."

"That is a really long way of saying 'no'." she said, while Ahmad walked out of the toilet and sat down on a box behind the other two.

"Well, does it matter, if you're happy with what you're doing?" He felt strange answering the question and turned his head towards her, shifting on his narrow seat. He thought for a second what else to say. "I mean, you are right. My answer should be 'no'. But I'm not a pessimist."

Elisa shrugged.

"It's okay. If it doesn't bother you, it's okay for you. I just think in the end the only person you have to answer anything to is–" She paused, looked him in the eyes and pointed at him. "–is you! No supervisor, no god. Just yourself, and you will think about these things and ask yourself, was this what I wanted to do? Was this what I planned?"

She shrugged inside her suit.

He scratched his cheek with a rubbery glove. This wasn't small talk at all, he thought. He asked the question back at her. "And? Have you been doing what you planned to do?"

"No. I came here to be part of something greater, to push the boundaries of exploration, not to be a meaningless hamster in yet another broken wheel. And it's everybody here. I thought it would be different from Earth. Like-minded explorers. But there is nothing of that left here. There is nothing close to it." She sounded disappointed. "And it's getting worse, it's all growing too quickly. Everything is done to push more people onto Mars, for the sake of fucking expansion."

He felt he was listening to a response that had been given a hundred times and wasn't sure what else he had to listen to.

At least time is going faster! he thought as he checked his terminal.

He turned his attention back to Elisa, who was looking straight ahead, focused on the cockpit. To keep up the conversation, he replied as best as he could.

"Well, I can agree on the growing part. Those expectations have been insane. We managed to meet them, but it really was a lot to do."

Waiting for her reaction, he noticed she was looking more and more concerned, stretching in her seat to get a better view of what was happening in the front.

He turned to the front as well and watched the driver and the electrician sitting in the front seats, fumbling with the control panels.

"As long as they leave it on autopilot, there's nothing that could happen." He said to Elisa but felt the opposite.

Phil studied her suit, it was the newer generation, so she couldn't have been that long on Mars, eight years at the most. Right-handed, he thought, looking at the panel on her left arm, showing the current speed. Two hundred and fifty kilometres per hour and slowly rising.

"What are you guys up to?" she shouted at the group in the front.

Without turning around, the driver shouted back.

"Nothing, just want to get there sooner. Really gunning it now. I'm not driving, just adjusting the parameters a little."

Elisa looked at her terminal, navigated around her screen, but Phil couldn't see what she was looking at.

He tried to inconspicuously stretch in his seat, to

get a better view. Right when he thought he could see the schematics of the vehicle on his display, he heard a dull bang. The straps around his shoulders tightened in an instant, pressing his back into the chair, forcing him to look at the ceiling. He felt the pressure of something clamping down on his feet, stretching his legs.

"Fuck!" Elisa's scream rang in his ears.

He felt his body shift to the left inside his suit. He tried to hold on to the shoulder straps, but was unable to push a gloved finger underneath. The vehicle leaned towards the front, turning to the right. He could hear the sound of metal scraping on rocks under him for a second. The light inside the vehicle flickered. He closed his eyes, tried to hold his arms up with his elbows in front of his face to shield his head. He felt the collar of his spacesuit briefly inflate against his neck and head, locking him in place and suddenly letting go again. A high pitched whining noise rang from behind his head, something pushed his hands away to one side like a guillotine, then he felt his own breath deflecting from the inside of his closed helmet. He opened his eyes and followed with terror the trajectory of the unsecured cargo boxes, first lifting, turning, and then smashing into the ceiling, cracking the glass. He watched the boxes crashing down, opening, spilling their contents. The ambient light of the vehicle switched off and he saw daylight spinning around him, the cabin filling with fine brown dust, scooped up from outside, shaking him in his suit.

The last thing Phil could see was the team in the front trying to hold on to the frame of the vehicle, gasping for air, heads crushing into the ceiling, turning over, crashing down, heads bent, coughing up red dust.

Then, his vision tunnelled, and everything faded to black.

VI (IRIS)

The orbital shuttle II was on its way to the space station called *The Gateway To Earth*, orbiting eight hundred kilometres above Mars. Iris watched the station getting closer on the screen in front of her while trying to ignore the man sitting to her right, who had been babbling on the entire time since they had launched an hour ago. She sat in the first row again and as the shuttle was full, could not avoid sitting next to someone. On the screen, she counted the sixteen segments of the ring that made up the station. The ring was six hundred and eighty metres across, rotating at exactly one round per minute, providing it with a gravity equal to that of Mars. Each segment had the length of approximately one-hundred and thirty metres and a diameter of thirty metres, giving it enough space to fit in three habitable floors, and an additional storage and maintenance floor, on the outermost level. The outward facing side of the ring was mostly covered with heat resistant tiles, except for the joints where each straight segment was joined to the next at an angle of nearly one-hundred and sixty degrees. The inside of the ring was painted with a dim white colour.

"Yes, the O-boat!" The man next to her chuckled,

VI (IRIS)

his finger pointing at her screen. His name was Hamza and he had just finished his ten-year contract on Mars and was excited to fly back home. "It's called the O-boat, because it feels like a U-boat inside, but is shaped like an O!" He chuckled a gain. "But it's ingenious if you think about it. Sending four extra ships with each of the first four waves to Mars, initially as cargo and backup, but it all went so well, none of them were eventually used as backup, and they had sixteen left, and joined them into a ring: *The Gateway to Earth*. This is such excellent planning!" His eyes were glowing with excitement.

I wish I could just mute him. she thought.

Iris felt a tapping on her shoulder, which made her instinctively turn to him.

Doesn't he get it? I'm not here to talk. she thought, as she contemplated shutting her visor, to block him out. But she didn't want to look like the crazy person leaving the helmet closed during the full flight and found it easier to breathe without the glass in front of her nose, so she had to endure him.

Hamza went on. "Hey, I've told you so much about me, how about you telling me something about you. It's not as if we have too many people here to hang around with and talk to, you know? I haven't seen you at all down there. What area did you work in? I'd be happy to know more about you." He smiled.

She hesitated, and gave in.

Not responding wouldn't be the right approach to blend in with the workers. she thought.

"Well, my name is Iris, and I work in public relations."

"Public relations, what exactly?"

"I don't do much work to be honest." She lowered her voice. "I'm the widow of the first casualty here on Mars. I stayed here for a while to be as close to him as possible, whenever I had the chance to go outside, you know." She paused on purpose. "To visit his grave." She forced herself not to blink, and waited until her eyes welled up from the dryness. A tear rolled down her cheek, and she kept looking at him, to make sure he saw.

It worked. He finally stopped talking.

She looked closer at him, still annoyed by all his constant jabbering. She despised him for it. And with that she put on a fake smile, and continued the conversation.

"Don't you worry, now that you know my secret, what is yours?"

If you want to talk. Talk!

She kept the fake smile on her face, waiting for his response.

He seemed to relax a little, but at first didn't reply. She enjoyed the brief silence between them which she knew made him uncomfortable.

He lowered his voice as if someone could be listening. "Do you want to know my *real* success story here?"

Iris smiled - this brightened her mood - and leaned a bit closer to him, ready to listen.

"I think the best part was that I made more money here by buying up the possessions of the arriving settlers. The stuff that they thought they wouldn't need. And then sold it back to them when they missed it. See, they all get a little shocked when they see that it's not filled with resources and luxuries for everyone out here. But they will give in at some point and want to give themselves a treat. Especially those not made for Mars will quickly begin selling their possessions for a few extras, to have some wonderful coffee in the morning, or a quality wine. But once they realise that those five or ten years are harder than they expected, they suddenly get homesick and want their stuff back. Easy. I store it for them, and sell it back for at least double the price. Of course there are those who want to buy other people's stuff, but they pay even more. All just to decorate their rooms, with things that remind them of Earth and who they once were, if they are able to pay. You don't need much room to sleep, so I just crammed everything into my room."

He grinned.

"Mars is looking for more economy, I found one. But let me tell you: These alien things are bad for business. Cost me way too much to get a ticket back. But I've still got two thirds left of my credits to trade with those from the next wave." His face beamed with a proud smile.

Iris raised an eyebrow and nodded. "Well, I gave away a few things, back to recycling, so if we'd met earlier I would still be able to get them. Memories do linger in the things we have!" She added another fake laugh and he joined in.

They were approaching the ring now sideways and it was close enough for them to see the docking ports, slowly rotating along the outside rim. She pointed at the screen. "Oh, we are already there. Need to make sure the seatbelts are fastened." Iris pretended to straighten up inside her seat and fake-laughed again.

"Yes, now comes the smooth bit." He shuffled in his seat as the seats in the shuttle leaned back. The approach slowed, the dock disappeared out of view on the screens, and with a brief acceleration the shuttle matched the spin of the station. A soft clunk, followed by a chime confirmed that the docking had completed. At the same time Iris felt how the gravity on the ship came back. The seats tilted forward and lowered the passenger's feet until they touched the ground. Iris was used to be suddenly standing on the wall she had climbed up earlier to get into her seat with the steps of the ladder disappearing into the floor and to climb up a ladder that emerged from the floor they had to walk on, into the shuttle earlier, rotating the direction of gravity experienced in the shuttle by ninety degrees.

She was the last to exit the ship.

As Iris appeared on the first floor of the station, she looked down the corridor to each side, up to the point where she could only see a part of the floor going up with the curvature of the ring.

It does seem like a U-boat. She thought that, being annoyed, because now he was talking inside her head.

VI (IRIS)

She started down the corridor, hoping that Hamza would depart in the opposite direction. But instead of getting a chance to say goodbye to him, he followed her and kept on talking.

"You know, isn't it amazing that we are actually not walking around the station, but the station is rotating under us? Relatively, we are always in the same place, infinitely walking uphill. But not only uphill. First you walk slightly downhill, and then uphill again, slowly waving up and down as you walk the station around you, under you."

When he didn't disappear down the next airlock towards a planetary shuttle, she stopped to look at her terminal, then made something up about waiting and catching up with a friend. She watched him disappear down the corridor, then walked back to her actual destination. She traced her path back to the previous staircase and went up to the third level, to walk down to the end of the corridor to her private apartment. It was located exactly in the middle of a segment, such that the pull of artificial gravity was mostly perpendicular, an important detail as Iris hated the imperfection of slightly leaning inside a room, practically standing on a ramp.

At her apartment, she shook herself as she heard Hamza babbling in her head again, as the biometric scanner above the door let her through without a delay and it closed behind her just as quickly. A thick, yellow glowing bar appeared across the door, right through its middle, across both frame and door, indicating it was now locked. She activated the terminal next to her door and signed in with her private keys. She looked up the passenger lists of the planetary shuttles and found out which planetary shuttle Hamza had just quartered.

The perks of having root rights in this segment. She grinned at the display.

The entrance to her flat was her office. The walls to both sides were lined with pictures from Earth on one side and pictures from Mars on the other. To her left, a door led into her bedroom and her ensuite bathroom, and another door, to her right, led into her private garden. These kinds of flats were called terra-suites, and the station had four of them. In the middle of the office was an L-shaped desk with a view through the curved windows down at Mars, eight-hundred kilometres below, filling the room with an orange-brown panorama circling behind the windows.

She turned left, and walked into her bedroom, placed her duffle bag on a counter on the side, and continued into the bathroom. Two robotic arms unfolded out of the wall next to the bathroom mirror and helped her unzip the suit. She stepped out, undressed from her leisure wear she wore underneath the suit and walked into the shower. At the same time the arms moved her space suit into a cabinet into the wall. A blue icon appeared on the cabinet indicating the suit was being cleaned. A steady rain of water gently fell on her, as wide as an umbrella. With her eyes closed, she stood under the shower, enjoying the warmth and humidity in contrast to the dry and cool city.

After unwinding under the shower, with her fingers soaked and wrinkled by the hot water, she stepped out and dried off, then walked through the bedroom, past the office into her garden. The garden was a room stretching across the entire width of the third floor, taking up the size of two tennis courts. The ceiling curved like a tunnel over the grass, lined with the same tall windows as her office, with a row of bushes in front. A bright blue light shining across the ceiling gave the impression of a blue sky, with the brown, glow of mars on one side and the darkness of space on the other. The floor was covered with perfectly trimmed grass, lined with flowerbeds all around, and a lofty seating area in the middle, two L-shaped deck chairs with a flat glass table in between.

Iris walked inside, lay on the grass, and listened to the buzzing bumble bees flying across the grass. She turned her head to watch them land and crawl around the flowers, scaring away small blue butterflies. She inhaled the air inside the garden and closed her eyes.

"Begin simulation." she said as she turned her head back to face the ceiling. From all around her, hidden speakers embedded into the walls and ceiling began to play sounds of wind and birds flying. She could hear them flitting about, flying past her, side to side. A mild heat radiated from the ceiling simulating sunlight.

VII (IRIS)

Later that day, Iris got dressed and ready for a company meeting in her role as marketing manager. She left early, to be inside the meeting room located in the neighbouring section, before her colleagues arrived. The meeting was a face to face review meeting, and the agenda the usual. Every division reported their status and next steps. It was her last meeting, before she flew back to earth, for retirement. Iris always preferred to be the first in the room. Not being the first meant to miss out on any unofficial discussions before the meeting started. Those usually were the most insightful to her, and she hated to be out of the loop. If one thing had brought her far in life, it was to always know more than others, always having the bigger picture.

She wore a white blouse, combined with a black suit and dark grey sneakers, sitting at the round meeting table, with her back to the dark space behind her, and the entrance on the opposite side. She was about to pour herself a glass of sparkling water when she caught a bumble bee crawling out of her collar onto her shoulder. Wondering how it had escaped her garden, she scooped it up with her glass, and poured the insect out on the table. She watched it rearrange its wings, wiggling its tiny legs across its head while she held her glass still in her hand, hovering above the insect. After a few seconds she slammed the glass down, crushing the life form with black and yellow stripes flat onto the table. Expressionless, she wiped away the stain from the glass surface with her napkin. Shortly afterwards, her colleagues came through the door one by one.

Here we go. She thought. *Why do meetings still exist?*

Around the table, there were four managers in total. In front of each participant the table curved up and displayed the company logo of the Interplanetary Corporation.

Mr. Moreno, an almost bald-headed, small figure, began the meeting. The first topic was to be an unusual topic for these kinds of meetings: the alien objects that had landed on Earth and Mars. He cast the latest message from the headquarter back on Earth to each screen. He read out the statement that the governments on Earth were not sharing any information about the spheres, but instructed the Interplanetary Corporation to stay away from them until being updated with further instructions. Anxiously, Iris listened to Mr. Moreno. She preferred to forget about the alien spheres as quickly as possible. They frightened her.

"We are continuing our efforts to send out as many teams as we can to the landing sites. Currently, they are either still travelling, or analysing them superficially. We are going to wait until tomorrow before we start either dissecting them or connecting them, whatever they are capable of doing, but not before we have more than one team onsite, to watch at least one other sphere as a reference. For everyone else we will be adjusting the shifts in a way that they won't have too much time thinking about these things. Better to keep everyone as busy as possible. The alien event has caused the number of seats being booked back to Earth to triple to the full capacity of six hundred passengers. We have all agreed that there is no way to extend this capacity out of security reasons, which means the capacity for flights back to Earth will remain at the current level. The workforce has shrunk by less than three percent because of this, but it hasn't impacted on the outcome of the simulations significantly. This is another reason to increase the shifts to make up for the loss of workforce in the city."

Iris felt uneasy, having to listen to them talking about the alien things that had swarmed in, landing on Earth and Mars. She kept quiet and waited for the meeting to continue with the first actual point of the agenda, the expansion review. A map of the city displayed on her screen, replacing the images of the round metallic objects.

Finally out of sight. she thought.

On the screen each inhabitant was shown as a tiny grey dot on a three-dimensional map. Larger point clouds inside the domes, working, eating or exercising. She saw strings of dots moving between domes, and in some places, two, three or four dots huddled in one area, a bedroom inside a dormitory dome.

"As we can see here, the growth of the perimeter has been as we expected." said Mr Moreno, manipulating his screen, looking down his narrow nose at the surface in front of him. The animation on the screens sped up to a time lapse, showing the tiny dots in repeating patterns, daily routines, buzzing around the city. Tiny clouds were running through newly dug tunnels expanding to all directions, then bursting into tiny fireworks, building new domes and habitats in a rapidly pulsing cycle of day and night.

"The data shows it's feasible to concentrate the expansion to the south. The density of ores has been higher there."

He drew an arc around the perimeter of the city with a short bony finger. New domes appeared inside the arc with a shimmering texture to indicate their theoretical place, and a small popup showed the estimated increase of workspaces and capacity of inhabitants it would add.

"They have more than enough space already. More than thirty-five square metres for an average of one point six inhabitants. If they print enough bunk beds we can double that density easily, and leave more rooms for the next wave. We might even do more than double the number of inhabitants we have now. The headquarter on Earth is still discussing this possibility. Either way we will guarantee the practicability of this."

Mr. Moreno looked around the room, looking for a reaction, then continued with his presentation.

"The next nuclear reactor should be ready with the following wave in under a year, and after that production capabilities will allow us to build our own. A single reactor will give us the capacity for forty-thousand people. Enough to produce food, warmth and electricity, and twice the amount of energy to run the automation, as well as the 3D print-"

The woman sitting opposite him, Mrs. Zhao, interrupted him.

"What if Earth does not deliver the reactor with the next wave in time? People will be ready to leave Earth and we can't let them wait until the next window opens up!"

Mrs. Zhao was visibly unhappy with this implied uncertainty. She was much younger than Iris, probably in her mid-thirties. Iris had never gotten her hands on the woman's private profile to look it up, which annoyed her and she was new to the board and still unknown to her. Mrs. Zhao went on with her complaint.

"You said *should* and not *will*. We were promised half of the seats on the next wave, to secure our joint position in space. We are not going to fund this if it's going to depend on a single element which is now uncertain."

Mrs. Zhao glared at the man opposite her. The nearly bald man shifted a smug smile across his face, crossed his arms and replied:

"In that case, we will remind the engineers that it's their job to analyse the unexpected situation and come up with a solution so this can be managed by us. Simple as that. They will have no other choice. Bao, we both have to see this from a business perspective and this is what we get paid to do here. If we get scared by the first challenge we see, like someone new to the stock market selling at the first dip, we are not going to build a new civilisation here on Mars. So please have some more trust in our strategy. Okay?"

Iris clenched her fist as she watched Mr. Moreno underline his superiority by addressing Mrs. Zhao's by her first name.

He leaned back, looking at the other faces in the room with a thin smile on his face.

"Any more objections?" He looked back and forth. "None? Thought so!"

A podgy, blonde guy opposite Iris, called Mr. Ginn, shuffled in his chair, fumbled with his controls and cast his screen to all the others.

"In that case we are well prepared, our social simulations show that the general happiness will go down a little, but we have enough ways to influence this. We can adjust the pay-out of frugal behaviour, not with immediate payments but with pensions. People are willing to come here to stay forever, covered by the contracts. And we can label this a retirement provision. There is no returning from this planet and this is only possible with a small sacrifice in luxury. Remember we don't have the capacity to bring everyone back, because we are not going to. We are here to stay. But we are more than prepared to influence and manage expectations."

Iris watched the others closely, resting her nose on the knuckle of her index finger, with her elbow supported by her chair's armrest.

The podgy Mr. Ginn always enjoys to bring up his socio-influential tactics to save the day, doesn't he?
She thought, looking him up and down.
We will see who has more to gain for and from the company really soon.

Mr. Moreno cleared his throat.

"We are here to constantly push the goals and make sure to remind everyone what they signed up for. Everyone should remember, the risks are stated in every contract. This is not a holiday resort. We don't have to make it comfortable for anyone here. They will be here to work. A missing reactor can and will not delay the expansion. We will have to find a way to build one here on our own. We have the plans and the workforce! We will ask them for an estimation, and expect it to be made manageable, to add the tasks to everyone's work schedule. It's just a matter of prioritisation."

Iris didn't care much about the expansion, or any possible conditions changing for the people working on Mars as long as she could follow her own goals: make sure to get her last bonus on Mars, then work as an advisor remotely from her island back home in the South Sea.

VII (IRIS)

When it was her turn to present the work of her marketing division on Mars, she opened her latest result and cast it to everyone in the room.

"I've been shooting excellent footage of the workspaces and the new cafeteria during the last weeks, but yesterday, as luck would have it, I had the chance to get to know one of the IT workers. She had a flight booked back to Earth, and she sat next to me. As we all know the events caused the system to cancel all flights, which were thankfully reinstated, otherwise I wouldn't be sitting here."

Iris smiled. On the one hand for being able to fly back to the station, and prepare for her trip back to Earth and on the other hand for circumscribing the alien artefacts with the word *events*. She went on.

"So I invited her to a coffee and listened to her, gave her my full attention. She was desperate to leave this place, full of disappointment. Why? Doesn't matter. She was tired, maybe. The usual complaints."

Iris looked at Mr. Ginn who was ignoring her, changing the controls of his simulations, dots moving around the map of the city changing their hues, resembling moods.

"But take a look at this."

Iris started a video with Elisa walking down the corridor to her apartment. She had edited herself out of the entire footage. Everyone in the room but Mr. Ginn watched her as she continued.

"Pay attention to her expressions, her face."

The narrator of the clip started to speak through speakers embedded into the round table.

"The trip to Mars is a long voyage, but in the end, you will see it's worth it: You will find what you have been longing for."

A time-lapse drone shot flying through the canyon of Shalbatana Vallis, then flying over the city ran across the screen. The shot crossed over into the camera rising out of the table inside Iris' apartment on Mars, the landscape of the drone shot blending into the matching 3D print under the glass tabletop, then turned towards the lush green of the conservatory overlooking the landscape outside.

The camera turned around and showed the bubbling fountain on the right side of the screen. The lights turned on in the apartment, lighting up the comfortable seats in the middle of the living room and the ivy growing up the wall. The door slid open to reveal Elisa. She looked frustrated and tired. The camera slowly zoomed in on her face as she took in the luxury of the room in front of her. Her expression changed, washing away her tiredness with a look of surprise. The next scene showed her dropping her luggage on the floor and walk around the flat, marvelling at the flowers and the sheer size of the place, her hand gliding along the back of the sofa. Then, a closeup shot of her fingers gliding over the soft fabric of the furniture. Accompanied by a melodic jingle, the camera faded to black. The crossover then faded into Elisa waking up in the guest room, undressing from her pyjamas, with the camera watching her half naked figure from the back as she walked into the bathroom.

The narrator went on.

"But wait until you arrive on Mars, you will enjoy your work and life here to the fullest."

The clip cut to her walking into the kitchen, pick up the cup of coffee waiting for her, followed by a closeup shot of the steam rising from the cup. The final scene showed her face, with the cup under her nose, gazing out of the conservatory, taking in the aroma and the view at the same time. Elisa looked relaxed and rested, smiling at the sun. Finally, the perspective changed, the video showed her silhouette among the plants, with the red dusty Martian landscape behind a wall of glass expanding into the distance. The narrator concluded the advertisement.

"What are you waiting for?"

Mr. Moreno smiled and Mrs. Zhao nodded at Iris. Mr. Ginn still wasn't paying attention, going through his simulations, ignoring her work as usual.

"Very natural. Nice."

Mr Moreno was the first to comment and Mrs. Zhao chimed in.

"Perfect, we will definitely miss your work here once you are heading back."

The last comment annoyed Iris.

And why is that exactly? Do you want me gone? she thought.

She closely watched Mr. Moreno scratch his bald

head, staring at the screen, straightened his suit and leaning forward to rewind the clip. Dryly, he turned to Iris.

"Can we replace her underpants in this shot with a thong and make her butt rounder? Also, her hair doesn't look fresh enough in the last part. We are aiming for a younger audience here."

Within seconds Iris added the finishing touches, which she had already prepared. The hair was died and the wakeup scene included the requested additional shape and skin. They rewatched it once more, and the two congratulated Iris on the natural reaction she had managed to capture. The video was labelled as *actual footage shot on Mars*. Iris was content, because she knew they would bring up the nudity as usual. Bread crumbs she had left out on purpose for them to find. Making sure to feed their need to feel important to have something to say and modify her work, without influencing her actual work. Mr. Ginn was still distracted, not even once looking at her work.

During the last part of their meeting they discussed the economic developments on Mars. One topic that Mrs. Zhao brought up, was the distribution and flow of credits, during which Iris navigated the map in front of her. She configured the brightness of the dots to visualise the amount of credits of each person. Those that had just moved from the city to the orbital station were on average a lot brighter than the thousands remaining on Mars.

Whoever travelled to the station with the last shuttles, had to be able to afford the bids on the last tickets to Earth. Iris cast her screen to the others showing the outflow of currency, and suggested her proposal as sincerely as she could.

"I'm sorry to interrupt you, Bao, and I know it's not my domain to be discussing the economic aspects of Mars, but maybe we should look into changing the terms and conditions to limit the amount of credits that can be taken back to Earth."

Iris pointed at the bright dots moving in realtime across the station, boarding the four big ships docked around it.

"Just a thought." she said and saw exactly which one was Hamza and smiled, imagining his face once he realised that he was going home with close to nothing. They unanimously agreed for measures to be put into place immediately.

The meeting ended with congratulations from Mr. Moreno and Mrs. Zhao wishing her a safe trip back to earth. She confirmed she also had a Terra-suite on her way back, so there would be no concerns about having enough privacy or room for herself to enjoy on her last trip between Mars and Earth.

VIII (IRIS)

Back in her Terra-suite, Iris sat on the chaise-longue, having changed into a leisure suit, with her naked feet in the grass. She waited for the latest news stream from her husband, awaiting a reply on how things were on Earth since the alien objects had landed.

To pass the time, she scrolled through the local channels to see how things were down on Mars. The glass table in front of her curled up to display the map from the meeting earlier.

Through the tall windows, above the bushes lining the room, the shadow of Olympus Mons grew around its base, slowly turning into the night crawling across the planet. The city below was already engulfed in darkness for a few hours now. Inside, her terra-suite was beginning to dim as well, simulating a red sunset on earth, a red orange gradient slowly illuminating to her right, and the opposite side tipping into a dark blue. The flight back would gradually shorten the daylight simulations to match the twenty-four hour cycle on Earth, to have her adjusted to the shorter days. As she was going to have her own terra-suite on the planetary shuttle, she could even adjust the daylight simulation to match her local time zone.

The bottom half of the door to her office opened and a small servant bot appeared, quietly rolled across the grass and stopped next to her. The lid opened and it lifted a tray with freshly cut fruit onto the chaise-longue next to her. Iris blindly picked up a strawberry from a bowl, used to the comforts that were at her disposal.

She scrolled through the reports from the away teams. One had reached the landing site more than half a day before. So far, all they could confirm was that they had found a metallic sphere, most likely similar to the ones from Earth. Initial scans revealed the sphere to be entirely made out of alternating layers of metal and further scanners were in the process of being assembled, keeping as many workers busy as possible. Two other teams had arrived an hour ago, also finding a sphere, but without any additional equipment for a deeper analysis. All teams were instructed to wait with literally scratching the surface until the next day or further details and recommendations had been provided by Earth. The third team was indicated as 'crashed' about fifty kilometres from their destination, roughly nine hundred kilometres from the first base and another five hundred from the city. Iris ignored the details of the message, and sent it to Mr Ginn with a request to handle the situation.

Finally, the notification of an incoming stream popped up on her screen which she hastily accepted. The stream opened, with a small map in the corner displaying the location of Mars in the solar system. Earth was a quarter orbit behind Mars, catching up. A line went from Mars almost perpendicular to the closest of Earth's Lagrange points, and from there to Earth indicating an active data link.

The video started. Her husband was walking along a beach, one arm holding his terminal in front of him. He waved at the camera and began to talk.

"Hi honey, I've finally found some time so I can tell you how things are going."

Iris smiled at the screen.

"The short version is: things are crazy. Most of the servants have left to look after their families. People are panicking. There is looting in the cities and there are curfews everywhere. It's not so bad on our island. We have plenty of supplies and there should be enough that we can buy from the locals from the neighbouring islands. With the servants gone, this leaves us with more for us in any case. So it's not that bad."

Her smile disappeared.

"Internationally, there is almost a blackout, ties have been cut, and everyone is blaming someone else for being behind those things. Those things have triggered all sorts of protocols and measures. I was so glad when I heard from you in person that those things landed on Mars as well. I forwarded that segment of your message to the administration, or what is left of it, as soon as possible. They publicised it immediately, which was good, because it halted the markets from crashing for a day. Enough time for us to sell before the rest did the next day. The markets are down, and I mean *down* down. People are on the streets."

Her eyes were glued to the screen as fear crept through her body, almost as if gripping her lungs.

"People are panicking everywhere. There has been so much chaos and confusion. People are on the streets demonstrating against those... things. Of course there are the hippie types that started to draw crop circles and praying and all this bullshit."

Her look didn't change.

"And yes, there is another thing, tomorrow I am going to – "

Suddenly, without warning, the feed was gone, a blank square left in the middle of the bent glass surface.

Iris tapped on the screen to pause and continue the feed, but it wouldn't resume. A message read that there was no more data coming in. She checked the tiny overview in the corner of the screen. The link between Mars and the relays was up. Both lines connecting the relay stations with Earth were gone. She scaled the connection overview across the screen, then selected one of the stations. A list of the available feeds appeared. Iris selected the cameras facing earth. There was nothing. Empty space. No Earth, no moon. She tried the same from the other relay station. Also nothing.

A half-eaten strawberry fell from her fingers into the grass. Her hands were trembling.

She called Mr. Moreno on a private channel and he

immediately picked up.

"Have you seen this?" She asked him and bent over the screen, clutching her elbows to stop her hands from uncontrollably shaking. He didn't respond and Iris started to freak out.

"Say something, have you seen this? Is this real?" She shrieked.

"Yes, we are seeing this as well. The Lagrange stations are drifting out of orbit. Earth is–"

The man hesitated. She could hear him swallow as they both watched the video of the Lagrange stations. The view on her table looked into nothing but then slowly turned towards the sun.

Iris felt her heart drop like a stone, a sudden loss clutching her chest, as she heard Mr. Moreno finish his sentence.

"Earth, is gone."

IX (PHIL)

The sun cast long shadows across the open space of Chryse Planitia, when Phil regained his consciousness. His head hurt, his stomach felt sick. He opened his eyes and looked at the dented ceiling of the vehicle. The blue sunset dimly illuminated the inside of the cabin, through the cracked or missing windows. His ears were ringing and he heard a constant beeping. He focused on the repeating sound and on his breathing. Fragments of the crash came up from his memory. He saw the result of the chaos strewn around him. Both his arms felt bruised and hurt. Fighting against the stinging pain in his elbow, he lifted his right arm to the side of his head. He forced himself to move it close enough to tap against the thin metal of his helmet, right above his ear. The beeping stopped. He tapped again and coughed a single word against his visor.

"Broadcast."

The radio turned on, but all he heard was a faint static hiss followed by a clicking sound confirming his channel selection.

"Hello?" he croaked. "Is there anyone?"

He bent his head down to inspect his suit. He was still breathing which meant it was intact. Cargo boxes were distributed around him, some were split open, their contents spilled out. He looked at his terminal to check his environmental controls, but the screen was cracked.

That explains why my arm hurts so bad!

He thought and moved his other arm which responded with even more pain. Without his terminal he couldn't say how long his suit would run on battery to provide him with breathable air and heat. His breathing got louder with each breath against his visor, fogging more with exhalation, his headache pulsing with his heartbeat. His suit being the only layer between him and the cold Martian atmosphere. He hadn't been outside for years.

How long was I out? How much time do I have left in the suit? he thought and began to panic, scrambling in his seat.

"Yes! I'm here!"

Elisa's voice crackled through his ear pieces. "Oh fuck, you alive?" She sounded surprised.

He turned to his right, her seat was empty.

"Yes! Where are you?" he replied with relief, he wasn't alone.

Luckily, the vehicle had stopped the right way up. He looked down his body and saw he was still strapped in his chair. He unlocked the belts, clumsily pushed them over his shoulders and lifted himself out of his seat. Stumbling over an overturned, open cargo box, while looking around. A square hole across the width of the vehicle opened up to the sky above in the front. A good part of the cargo was missing, the rest distributed through the vehicle as if everything had exploded at once. He stepped through trays, sample containers, a tangled mess of cables, displays and parts he didn't recognise. The portable toilet was dented, split open along one edge and the door broken from its hinges.

"If you can, don't look at the front!" Elisa's voice warned him, but she was too late. He was already looking ahead at what was left, at the mangled bodies of the crew who were still there, slowly freezing over, covered in blood and dust. Among the terrified, bloated faces and broken bones it took him a moment to figure out that one of them was missing.

"Fuck." he said and a chill went down his spine.

He climbed over the open boxes, on his way to the open airlock to his right. Stumbling through the mess he crawled outside.

He dragged his boots carefully across the grainy, dusty surface and looked around. Whichever direction he looked, he saw the same: The brown regolith with rocks and clumps varying in size and texture, slowly disappearing in the growing, dark shadows of craters and ridges of the setting sun, a pale white spot in a hazy grey-blueish, gloomy sunset. No feature in the landscape gave him any hints how big, deep, tall or far anything on the surface around him was.

He turned around to search for Elisa. He spotted her over a hundred metres out. She was tracing back the trail of their crash, walking through the debris that had been flung from the vehicle.

She waved. He heard her voice over the radio. "I have to get my stuff. It's literally the only things I have left. Can you get to the second vehicle?"

He spotted the body of the third team member lying face down in the dust, about halfway between him and Elisa. The trail of the crash had been carved into the regolith by the heavy vehicle, rolling and grinding to a halt. The other vehicles had stopped in parallel to the crashed, with their headlights already on.

He stumbled forward, towards the second one.

"Yes. My terminal is broken. How long was I out?"

"A bit over ten minutes."

He felt relieved, reassured by the energy his suit must still hold for him to get to safety.

After he had dragged himself to the second vehicle, he tapped on a small control panel and the doors cracked open with a hiss, the pressurised air escaping into the thin freezing atmosphere. He crawled inside, waited for the pressure to build up and the wet vapour wash the dust from his suit. The procedure took longer than he expected, until he painfully wiggled his arms to register the required movements to clean his suit within the airlock.

Before he managed to sit down into one of the driver seats, he heard the hum and hiss of the airlock, of Elisa returning. Once inside, she also sat down in the front of the off-roader. Together, they waited for it to warm up inside, after it had cooled down over the day since it had carried no passengers. Phil mustered a crack going across her visor as she opened her helmet and he opened his as well. Their visors lifted, rotated away behind their heads, almost in parallel. She unhinged the round glass from the back of her head and let it slide to the ground. Even with the low gravity of Mars it cracked neatly in half as it hit the floor, only held together by a thin plastic film around the edges.

Phil felt like shit. He sagged down into the chair, unlocked it to spin it around, looking aimlessly at the neatly stacked cargo boxes. He turned his eyes towards Elisa and met her blank stare.

"What the fuck happened?" he whispered.

She shook her head. "The wheels." She looked down. "They are not rated for speeds above two fifty, never, ever have been." She lifted her terminal on her wrist, it still showed the wiki page about the off-roaders. She let her arm drop into her lap. "I was about to look it up." She took a deep breath, looked around, opened her gloves and let them fall on the floor next to her broken visor. She kicked it away.

"I can't anymore. I'm done. I quit." She sounded frustrated.

Phil felt useless. Scenes of the crash kept replaying inside his head. And different versions of the crash where he didn't survive. Him being the one thrown out of the vehicle, breathing in the freezing, empty atmosphere. His lungs boiling. He felt horrible and began to talk, to address his own thoughts.

"You know, I've been always, always, *always* overthinking that the worst things could happen. *This* is why I was wearing a space suit in the first place. Not like those–" He paused, his eyes staring at nothing, out of focus, pointing at the crashed vehicle outside. "But does this mean I was right to think that way? I've been working on this for so long, just to find out, I was right?" Phil shook his head and looked at Elisa, trying to start a conversation. "Right now my head is bombarding me with images how you walk away from the crash site. Without me. And I die." He lost himself in his thoughts again.

She looked at him, shaking her head with disgust. Pointing with both hands at his head she screamed.

"LOOK. AT. YOUR. FACE!"

Snapping back to reality, he blinked with surprise, and his head finally stopped playing pictures of the crash. He spun his chair to the front to inspect his face for the first time since the crash. In the reflection of the front window, he saw his face. It looked like he had been beaten up with a barstool.

"I look like shit." He said to his reflection and remembered the safety cushion inflating, but then failing to retain pressure.

"You are lucky your head is still talking to your legs." she said dryly, calming down.

Phil's head had been bashed about inside his helmet. He had bitten his lip and blood had dried across his cheek and in his beard. He plucked the dry crust out of his facial hair. A vein had burst in his left eye, painting it half red. Phil took a deep breath, holding it for a few seconds. But instead of shouting, he allowed himself to cry. Tears running past his nose onto his lips. Even if he tried, he could not explain how he had survived. Phil turned back to Elisa, wiped the tears away with the back of his hand, leaving a brown, bloody smear on it. He half laughed, half cried, then pulled up his nose.

Her eyes welled up, but no tears ran down her cheeks.

"Ok, I'm sorry, I understand." Phil said, looking at her for help. He thought about the alien artefact. "What do we do now? Go back? I want to see it." He was sure of that.

Elisa leaned forward, unlocked the screens in the cockpit and opened a map to show their location and destination.

"It's just over an hour if we continue towards the alien artefact. We can think about what we do until then. I'm not going back either." she said.

Phil nodded in agreement. Immediately, she confirmed the suggested route and the two vehicles continued driving towards the alien landing site at half the previous speed.

His mind circled around the thought whether she would have left him there and if he would have left himself there. How much more time he would have had left. The controls of his suit were bust, so there was no way to check if he was still alive or how long his suit would have kept him alive. They had never paired their suits, so she couldn't have checked remotely if he was still breathing. He looked at his reflection, then focused his eyes on the surface of Mars rolling past them in the glow of the lights surrounding their vehicles. He realised how close to death they had been just moments before, that he had no idea where he was, where he was going and that he didn't care who the other woman next to him was. He continued to silently cry for a while, watching the lifeless landscape surrounding them roll past, into the night.

Eventually, he turned his seat towards Elisa, and laughed.

"I have no idea what is going to happen. I don't even know who you are, or why we are still going towards this thing. But if this is going to be a first contact, you'll have to do it. I'm for sure going to look like shit."

After reporting the accident, they followed the instructions to upload the logs and recordings of the crash for further analysis.

They continued their journey in silence, checking their suits and Elisa replacing the screen of Phil's terminal and the glass of her visor. When his terminal turned back on, the environmental controls indicated he still had forty minutes left. A long time to wait to die alone.

◆◆◆

The speed of the vehicles gradually decreased when they crept towards the metallic, unknown sphere waiting in the darkness, lying on the regolith, until they came to a stop.

Quietly, they watched the grey, round object in

IX (PHIL)

front of them. Both of them. Watching and waiting.

"So this is it."

Elisa was the first to break the silence inside the cabin.

"Yeah. Curious." he replied, eyes glued to the alien sphere.

Then instructions arrived from their expedition manager. Without the maintenance crew they had to set everything up themselves, but most of the steps were automated, if they required any manufacturing for tools, they would have to wait for further remote instructions. Through the dusty windows, they watched how the other vehicle drove in a circle around the sphere. Under the vehicle, a saw cut a seam into the regolith, ramming metal sheets deep into the cut, into the ground. After a full rotation, it continued to circle, placing row after row, stacking up a metallic igloo.

Their vehicle parked next to the small dome, aligning the airlock with a matching gap in the panels that connected them with the dome. This vehicle was now their habitable space, with access to the inside of the dome on one side and to the empty Martian landscape on the other side.

After an hour the dome was stacked and the last vehicle parked behind them. Elisa was quicker to understand the remaining instructions so she went outside to complete the process. Phil watched her connect the two vehicles to power the habitat from the fuel cells and confirm the process from inside. She released a tethered shoebox-sized bot that rolled up the seams of the dome with magnetic wheels to inspect the gaps and weld the remaining seams. A bot twice the size of the first drove around the dome and injected a grey slime into the seam that fused the panels with the regolith on the outside, sealing the dome.

Phil stood in front of the airlock, staring at the sphere, lost in his thoughts of what it could be and what could happen to him. The painkillers he had taken were finally working. At least he could move now without pain, walk around the cabin and re-organise the equipment. But every time he walked past the airlock, he couldn't keep his eyes off it. He had to distract himself. Spontaneously he closed his helmet and walked into the airlock leading outside. Once out of the vehicle, he walked over to Elisa, and asked her if she could use his help, hoping she would say yes.

"No, I'm alright. As long as the bots work, it should be airtight in half an hour."

After having repaired his terminal he insisted on pairing their space suits, to be on the safe side, to know if the other one was still alive, and allow them to open a direct, private channel.

They stood outside watching the work of the two bots, one dragging a bright white spark across the metal sheets as it rolled up and down the seams, the other quietly rolling along the edge of the dome, going back and forth checking its work and filling the transition between metal and stone.

Their dark shadows were cast across the sandy

rubble from the lights of their cabin. Everything else was surrounded in darkness, the sky lit up with the milky way and the universe. Phil watched Elisa as she looked up to the stars, turning her back to the lights and, followed her gaze. He heard her voice over the radio.

"Even if we are millions of kilometres away from Earth. The stars don't move a single bit. It makes me feel so small and insignificant, but at the same time this view makes me feel at home. Even so: Mars is not my home. I will go back to Earth. One way or another."

There was something in her voice that troubled him, but he couldn't put a finger on it. He pushed his feeling away, like the many images that liked to sneak inside his head.

His eyes wandered along the milky way. For a second he forgot they were standing next to one of hundreds of alien objects that had landed on Mars. As soon as this brief moment had passed, he replied.

"And even with all the emptiness and vast distances, somehow, something has found its way here."

The image of the sphere inside the dome appeared in his head and he shuddered.

They turned around and entered their vehicle through the airlock. Inside, they continued working through the instructions. The walls of the dome were to be sprayed with a thick, grey insulation foam, and the floor covered with tracks of light, padded fleece against the dust. As opposed to always being the one in charge of running the farms, Phil appreciated being told what to do and followed Elisa's instructions. It helped to keep him busy, focusing on his task to spray the walls with a regular pattern, up and down, working his way around the dome, with his back to the sphere. The painkillers were working, but he felt the weakness increase in his arms when only holding a spray gun connected to one of the three tall cylinders Elisa had placed around the dome for him.

After two hours, with breaks to recharge their suits, they were finally done with setting up the dome. Phil was tired. He felt as if more had happened in the past day compared to the last ten years.

"Time to take a closer look. I'll set up the lights and cameras." he said as he put the equipment in place, a tripod with bright LED panels and cameras looking at the sphere from four angles. Once his eyes had adjusted to the brightness, he slowly walked towards the alien object, until he was at arm's length. The surface was covered in endless, shimmering fractal patterns. As he moved around it he watched the pattern change and evolve. Impossible to find a starting point anywhere on its surface.

"They never told us how beautiful these things are." He said into his helmet, but Elisa didn't respond. He looked at her, standing motionless, staring at the sphere. After spending hours working next to it, he had got used to it. He felt brave walking around it. It hadn't lashed out as he had imagined numerous times by now, and he felt it must be unlikely that it would suddenly do so now. His headache began to return, pounding with every heartbeat, which troubled him more. As he completed his second round around the sphere, he noticed the notification on his terminal indicating the dome had been heated and pressurised by the two environment modules as big as two fridges, standing next to the airlock. Two devices Elisa had moved, with the help of a third of the gravity compared to Earth.

He opened his visor, breathing in the cool dry air. He heard the door open, from the other side of the sphere.

"I'm tired. I'll rearrange the cabin to find a place to sleep. Should I prepare yours, too?" he said, as he began to walk towards the airlock.

"Are the cameras on? Are they recording?" Her voice sounded demanding.

"Yes, they are."

He turned around to look for Elisa. He stepped aside to see her standing behind the sphere, holding a spray foam cylinder high above her head, reaching back.

"No!" he shouted, and sprinted towards her, but before he could even cover half the distance in his weakened state, she crashed the cylinder down, hard onto the alien object.

Phil's heart skipped a beat as he heard the metallic clang ring in his ears. He stumbled and crashed into her, tackling her to the ground. In the low gravity they flew further than he had expected, away from the sphere.

"Are you fucking crazy? What are you doing? Are you out of your fucking mind?" In his rage and panic he wanted to hit her, but his arms were too weak to even hold his own weight, and all he could do was roll off her, eyes wide open, looking at the sphere. Whatever strength he had left, was diminished by a rush of adrenaline. He was furious, angry and scared. His head was firing with images of the sphere unfolding arms that grabbed him and smashed him into the walls. Bolts of lightning shooting out, to fry him in his suit. But nothing happened. His body trembled and shook.

"Are you out of your fucking mind? Are you fucking dumber than those fucking newbies who killed themselves today?" he cried out at her, still lying next to him. She was grinning.

Again, he looked at the sphere, fear clutching his body. He looked for a scratch she might have left on the surface, but found nothing. The metallic clang of the cylinder repeated itself in his ears.

"We are all alone in this fucking universe, and the first thing you do when we have the first contact is to fucking hit it with a bloody gas bottle?" He was screaming now. His eyes jumped between looking at her face and the sphere. Elisa began to laugh.

His mental images continued. Over and over again. A force field blowing them up with the dome. Spikes shooting out of the sphere impaling him against the wall. He could almost feel the pain from his imagination running out of control. He cried and screamed.

He shook himself trying to push away his mental images and get back to observing reality, still waiting for a shockwave to blast him into the freezing desert outside, to join the driver with his face down in the regolith.

Phil lost control, he cried and screamed, kicking with his feet into the air.

"It's ok, Phil! It's ok. Look at me!" He heard her voice distantly, trying to calm him down. He felt her arms around him, hugging him tight, talking to him, holding his head.

"It's ok. Phil. Nothing has happened. It's ok!"

He looked at the sphere, the intricate patterns on its surface barely visible from his position lying on the ground, cradled in Elisa's arms.

"Breathe. In and out. In through your nose, and out through your mouth. Breathe, Phil."

He did as she said, his eyes fixed on the sphere, dragging hard on each breath in, holding it in, then trying to release his tension with every slow exhalation. Repeating his breathing while Elisa continued to reassure him nothing had happened.

Suddenly, but to his terror, the sphere changed. A faint, yellow glow crept into the fractal patterns, increasing in brightness with every second. He held his breath, and froze. Every muscle tensing in his body, watching the sphere awaken. Elisa's reassuring words fell silent, he felt her grip tighten around him.

The glowing increased, throwing shadows of the equipment against the dome.

A loud, deep hum shook them under the dome, the glowing sphere oscillating with the vibrations, the equipment rattled, a camera installation tipped over. The yellow light strobed, matching the sound.

Inaudibly under the noise, Phil squeaked in fear, closed his eyes, curled into a foetal position and peed himself.

After the humming had stopped, and the light had dimmed down, he looked up at the faintly illuminated sphere. Elisa had already gotten up, and walked towards the glowing object. She reached out and touched the surface with her fingers, admiring the detailed, infinite artwork, a trail of glowing traces following her where she had touched it with her fingertips.

◆◆◆

They sat inside the driver's seats, watching the glowing sphere on the screens, showing the angles of the cameras inside the dome. With a wide angle lens it looked as if the entire sphere was alight.

They had agreed that whatever they had witnessed hadn't stopped and it would have been too soon to report anything back, it being too early to come to any conclusions. Phil had accepted her suggestion not to report anything until the next day, as he shamefully changed his clothes, hiding his moist pants.

The original task from the expedition management was that they would be out here for at least a few days, and especially after the crash they were assumed to be asleep already, trying to recover. And indeed, Phil felt he had to recover more than ever. But given the unusual situation, for the first time he felt he had some limited freedom to decide what they could do next, inside their own mini city of a single dome, puzzling together how and why the sphere had reacted. Neither of them felt like stopping their observations to create a report. Even if he wasn't sure what to make of everything. He was the closest ever to find some sort of life on Mars he had ever been, and he knew that if he didn't have this motivation, he'd be on his way back to the city on the other off-roader. Both of them wanted to figure out what the sphere was about. It definitely was not from Earth nor Mars.

Phil's thoughts were racing. Breaking his stare from the sphere on the screen he turned to Elisa.

"Why did you hit it?" He was puzzled, her actions made no sense to him.

"I'm done here. I'm done with Mars." She played a recording of her crashing the cylinder into the sphere in a loop.

"I wanted proof I went against orders in the strongest way possible. That's why I wanted the recording. Fuck the terms and conditions. They will want to put me on trial on Earth for this."

He watched her stop the looping video.

"But now, I'm not so sure anymore if this is the smartest way to go ahead. This is your job. Even you have to admit it's not what you enjoy doing. And all the fucking expansion and colonisation bullshit.

They cancelled my flight back home, just to reinstate and resell the open slots again. This is so fucked up." She got up and walked around the small space inside the cabin. Phil spun his seat around to watch her.

"It's all a fucking lie! Look at us!" She went on. "We get up, we work, they make all the rules. Have you ever thought about how fucking difficult it has become to go back? There is no plan to let anyone go back. They have true monopoly here. They own us. Read the fucking terms and conditions. There are no laws, only their rules which they control. Of course your dreams and desires are blinded by their fucking marketing, and blinded by your own excitement to be an explorer, but what have we become? You've said it yourself. They let us drive out here with untrained morons who didn't deserve to be smashed to smithereens. The only reasons we survived are because you are paranoid as fuck and I had no reason or place to unpack. Those two bags are all I have, and I'm stuck here. Even if there is an alien race trying to contact us, it will never change a thing. I purposefully stumbled into this with an auto-matcher, with the only goal to do the worst damage I could do. So I can finally go fucking home. I just hope they haven't changed the rules in the meantime. Even if we are worth much less on Earth, at least you can get out. Literally."

He looked at her, slowly nodding his head, thinking over her words and logic. He felt the same, even if this was the start of an intergalactic exchange of some kind, it would all end up in the hands of some controlling entity, with power over others. He thought this had a different dimension than if he or someone else had found out if there had been traces of ancient life on Mars. It seemed to him that the alien objects landing was a change of reality compared to a small piece of information. And the latter was worthless to any company.

"It's sad." He agreed. "I believe you are right. Whatever comes from all this, all our actions are within the scope of the corporation, automatically giving them all the rights and benefits. It won't be much different on Earth I guess. All the inventions and experiments I've made are sold back to someone on Earth. We are technically biological robots to them."

Phil looked back at the screens and wondered.

"Do you think this is a robot of some kind?"

"Well, I'm pretty sure it's not a night lamp."

"I guess not."

"So, you screamed, it started to glow and it did this loud hum thing and the light strobed." She changed the topic and started walking around the cabin.

"You hit it first." He defended himself.

"Okay."

"Elisa, the first team said it seems to be entirely out of all sorts of metals, and they couldn't detect any organic matter on the surface. So whatever this is, it doesn't seem to be technically alive. Kind of reassuring, that you probably didn't try to crack open an alien lifeform's head."

"If I thought otherwise, I wouldn't have done it. I read their reports on the way here."

Elisa looked at the screens from a distance.

"This is amazing." She said with awe.

"And you still had to bang a cylinder into it?"

"You have a better idea to get back to Earth? I don't care how. Two more years here? I'll go nuts. Don't take this personally. Mars is a fucked up dusty shithole. If I could put a dent in this ball I would do it."

He watched her grind her teeth as she looked at the screens.

Phil fell into his own world of thoughts, analysing and overanalysing everything that had happened and every little detail he could remember.

"Bang, scream, glow, hum and strobe." He said to himself and turned away from the sphere. He got up, looking for something to eat. Between the stacked cargo boxes, he found a crate with shrink wrapped food. He continued talking to himself, scratching his beard at the same time.

"Whatever this is, wherever this came from, the distances in the universe are so vast I'd say it's impossible for any organic life form to travel anywhere. This thing must be ancient. Even if we could travel any practical distance to explore our galaxy it would take us more than a hundred thousand years to cross our own galaxy. Even at the speed of light, in a straight line, not checking anything, flying along a motorway. Physics is showing us our limits here, I'm pretty sure of that. I can't imagine any way this could work. Physics really is an asshole in this regard."

He grabbed a vacuum packed sausage from the box on the floor, ripped it out of its wrapping and bit into it, chewing on a mix of soy and insect proteins. He dropped the wrapper and watched it slowly glide back into the box it came from, landing on top of the remaining food. He grabbed another sausage from the box, tapping with it into the palm of his left hand, and went on to walk up and down the small space. Elisa returned back to the cockpit, slumping down into her seat.

"And even if you managed to build the technology to travel these distances, what a boring fucking time would it be? At the start you have a planet, and at the end you *might* have a planet, and in between, you'd have a hundred thousand years of nothing, flying through nothing. Who would want that?"

"Mars is enough for me already. Sitting on a space ship your entire life? Fuck, no!" Elisa interrupted his soliloquy.

Phil looked at her and used the time to take another bite. With his mouth full, he continued speaking out his thought.

"Ok, so basically there is no point for any intelligent life in the universe to go somewhere else, other than their own solar system. But let's assume, someone out there managed to do this, right? Because we have this, this, let us use your language for a second, 'fucking ball' here sitting in front of–"

"The glow is decreasing." She interrupted him

again and pointed at the screens in the cockpit. A chart showed the downgoing intensity over time. Phil walked to the airlock to see through the windows, to look with his own eyes if he could detect the change, even though it made him uneasy. Munching away on the soy sausage helped him relax.

"Bang, scream, glow, hum, strobe." He said again.

"Ok, listen Phil, I have a question for you. You came here, to Mars, to search for signs of ancient life, right?"

"Yes."

"You are not looking for life itself, because this place sucks, but you are looking for traces of previous life. Right?"

"Yes, why?"

"How would you do this?"

"Find a suitable spot to drill, dig, analyse, and find conclusive evidence of traces of life." He was curious about where she was going with her questions, but instead of asking her, he bit into another sausage.

"Let's play a different game. How would you go after looking for intelligent life, here, on Mars? The short version."

"Hmm, maybe dig a really deep hole and hope I burst into their game of Thursday poker?"

"Seriously?" Elisa looked disappointed.

He grinned, enjoying his brief moment of small talk and his mental image of interrupting four green little men smoking cigars and playing cards. Then, he remembered where the image of playing cards in his head recently came from, and his smile disappeared.

"Would you go looking for it in person?"

"Well, practically I would, but–"

"You wouldn't. It's inefficient!" She cut him off to finish his sentence.

"Yeah, I only have two hands. And considering the entire planet, it would take ages. Maybe I would use a bunch of robots–" He stopped in his track and turned towards the sphere. His mind was empty for a brief moment, then he turned his attention back to Elisa.

"Wait." He paused. In his head the sphere was unfolding legs and began walking around like a spider. Luckily, Elisa continued her thought experiment and caught his attention again.

"Phil? Let's go back a bit. Assume you would go from Mars to Earth to find life. What would change?"

"That would be pretty easy, you'd be happy to find a spot where there is no bacteria, once in a while."

"Exactly. If you assume there is life in the universe. What would you be really looking for? What would you be eager to find out?" Elisa got up and joined him at the airlock, picking up a new snack for him along the way.

"I'd try to find out if there is intelligent life on earth." He grinned. In his head he was already picturing primates bashing a research rover to pieces, sucking at the radiator fins standing out of the thermo electric generator, waiting to get zapped by wires torn from the instruments.

"But how would you do that?"

He was back to reality.

"Good question!"

He walked back to the cargo box filled with food and watched the next wrapper slowly glide back inside. Food was one of the few things that calmed him down, besides getting stoned.

"How would you detect something is intelligent? Like an intergalactic Turing test, but without humans."

"You mean what intelligence sensor would I build?"

"Yes!" Her eyes were bright with excitement. Without warning she jerked around, put her head into the airlock to face the sphere and screamed from the top of her lungs. Phil jumped out of his skin, almost choking on a piece of sausage, coughed and spat it on the floor. He was about to open his mouth to complain, when he was shut up by the deep, but quiet hum of the sphere. At first, he was annoyed to have lost a piece of his snack, but then was delighted not to have peed himself again.

He watched the sphere slightly increase its brightness, with his own eyes this time. It quickly fell back to its dim glow. He walked back to the airlock with his face as close to the window as possible without touching it with his nose.

"You're a genius." He whispered, his sausagy breath bouncing back at him from the glass.

"Phil! Phil! Let's think! Let's keep thinking!" Her words came rattling out of her mouth.

"Okay?" He agreed, quickly munching away on the last piece of his snack. He was also getting excited, forgetting how tired he was.

"Your scream was louder, and its response was louder. When I screamed, it reacted again, but less. Maybe, because we are insulated in here. But what's next?"

Phil remembered, how he had insisted to keep the airlock shut, although the inside was pressurised, quickly making up the open door would make it colder inside the cabin.

"Well, a minute ago, when you asked me about finding intelligent life on Earth, I had this image in my mind of monkeys hopping around a Mars rover, like the classical ones, ripping it apart and bashing it to pieces. Getting zapped by the battery, putting everything in their mouths like babies, and so on."

"Or bashing it with a spray cylinder?" She rubbed her forehead, hiding her eyes behind her hand, pretending to avoid his gaze, but still smiling with excitement.

"Yes, for example." He hoped she felt at least embarrassed about what she had tried to do. "But I don't know. I would wait for it to talk to me. But even then I wouldn't be able to tell if a dog barking or a cat meowing was trying to tell me something meaningful or if it was random noises. If it talked back I would be seriously surprised."

Elisa put her hand back down to look at him. Slowly, as if counting, she repeated his words.

"Scream. Glow. Hum. Strobe."

Phil watched her eyes wander through the vehicle, staring at nothing, her brain apparently working at full speed. After a short pause she shouted:

"Lights, we need the lights!"

Phil watched as Elisa franticly tapped on the screens in the cockpit. On one of them, a window opened up with a recording of her screaming in the cabin, next to it she placed a histogram of the audio track and on another she placed the recording of the sphere glowing. She also added the audio histogram, and matched against the chart that recorded the changing brightness.

"Look! Here!" She pointed at the screen. "The strobe has the same frequency as the hum!"

Elisa pulled out a keyboard from the console and started hacking away. Phil watched her actions on the screens, looking over her shoulder, but couldn't follow what she was doing.

Phil expected her to immediately produce a result, but he soon realised there was nothing he could do and nothing he understood, so he decided to go back to his box of snacks and fish another sausage from underneath a growing pile of empty wrappers. From a distance he watched her tapping on the keyboard, swiping the screen, flipping through one virtual page after another, looking for something, cursing missing documentation.

In the meantime the sphere's glow had almost diminished, now barely visible.

Time went by. He thought about interrupting her,

IX (PHIL)

to ask her what she was up to. The images of the crash earlier that day came up again. Phil gently touched the bruises on his head and his face. He probed the cut on his lip where he bit himself. His arms were sore and stiff. He searched for his personal luggage, a single duffle bag and found his weed stash, making sure it was still there. As he rolled a joint, Elisa interrupted him, calling from the front of the vehicle.

"Have you ever had any trouble with epilepsy or anything similar?"

He hesitated, and looked up.

"No, why?"

He heard her slam her hand onto the keyboard. She ran to the airlock, opened the doors and screamed. Phil flinched, pulling up his shoulders, to endure her shrill voice. Then, the lights in the cabin and in the dome went off. After a second, they came back on, strobing. Phil closed his eyes. The bright flashes made him dizzy, but he still tried to peak through his eyelids. He watched Elisa standing in the flashing lights as she looked into the dome. As quick as the flashing had started, it stopped, strobing for as long as her scream.

Phil blinked, then followed her into the airlock to look inside.

They watched the patterns on the sphere begin to pulse. For a brief moment it flashed brighter than the lights inside the dome and the cabin combined. Then, hundreds of glowing dots appeared circling around the surface all spinning in the same direction, slowly moving across the surface, all at the same speed. They watched in awe with their mouths open as the metallic surface appeared to become transparent, with a bright glowing dot at its centre. Then glowing dots squished into a plane, and without warning, the sphere turned entirely dark, leaving no light or metallic surface. Looking at the black object, Phil couldn't think of a darker colour that he had ever seen in his life.

X (ELISA)

The next morning, Elisa felt unreal. She woke up between the seats of the cockpit, lying on the floor, under her blanket. Her arms and legs felt stiff and her throat like sandpaper from breathing the dry, recycled air and smoking with Phil. She sat up, rubbed her face and watched him lying at the other end of the vehicle, curled up like a foetus under one of her spare blankets.

She had to pee and got up. They had placed two buckets inside the outside-facing airlock. One filled with coarse, wet regolith and a trowel, the other slowly filling with layers of regolith and whatever business they had left behind. She squatted down on the latter, looking at her sweatpants on the floor, then at the dark sphere inside the dome. Only the doors of the airlock separated them from each other. She tried to suppress her laugh. She felt too unreal to be pissing in a bucket while making eye contact with an enigmatic alien object.

They had stayed up late after the sphere had turned dark. They tried to repeat their experiment but without any success. She had even touched the dark surface, which felt icy cold in comparison to the first time she had touched it. Eventually, they gave up, being restless and spent the rest of the night talking about what had happened. Speculations about aliens and what they thought could happen or what any of it meant. They talked a bit about themselves, exchanged their views on the colony and what they planned to do and not to do.

They agreed that right now they were in the possession of something of value, the knowledge that these spheres were most likely alien, not a prank, although they thought that the surface had resembled art more than anything else. And they knew how they had changed it. What they didn't know was what they had changed, as well as what the 'final animation', as she called it, meant. They now had more questions than when they had started earlier that day. In the end they smoked weed to unwind, to finally fall asleep.

She finished her business and made sure to leave the bucket the way she had found it.

Through the window of the airlock she watched the dark sphere, while sucking on an orange juice paste from a shiny transparent pack as her breakfast. Phil was still snoring.

Poor guy. she thought and turned towards him. He looked terrible, as if someone had beaten him up and in addition to that she had the impression he had been going through hell mentally. And now he was one of the first human beings to make contact with something alien. The number of times she had caught him staring into the distance, distracted by his own imagination, in combination with his panic attack when she had hit the sphere, made her doubt he would mentally survive being alone with this unknown object.

She turned towards the screens in the front of the cabin, and as they had agreed the previous night, she wrote the first report, quietly sitting in the cockpit typing into one of the keyboards. She explained that they could confirm the findings of the other landing sites and weren't ready for any experiments, but were considering to return to the base due to lack of supplies and lack of mental capacity. She felt it easy to write because none of it was a lie. A good part of their supplies were strewn across the dry, dusty, freezing planes of Chryse Planitia and they were indeed recovering.

She sent the report and inspected her broken visor to pass the time, waiting for Phil to wake up. The visor wasn't supposed to break. She thought this was a taste of what Mars would become within the next few months and years. She didn't dare try to imagine if the next wave doubled the number of inhabitants again. It made her sad to know that the visions of going interplanetary, of the next big leaps of humankind, were slowly run down, into the ground. No one seemed to be willing to learn from the past.

She rewatched the videos more than a dozen times, trying to understand what it meant, the glowing lights followed by the sphere turning entirely dark, not responding to anything at all. She had no idea who could have sent or created these things that clearly responded to them, but then entirely stopped communicating after they had copied their behaviour. They had switched off all the lights, to mimic the dark colours of the sphere, but nothing happened. Watching the videos, it felt unreal to her, as if she had dreamt it.

She saw herself slamming the cylinder onto the sphere, how she had touched it, how it had responded to them copying the behaviour of syncing sound with light, until it basically switched off. The images of the glow increasing around the fractal lines, then intensifying as if dissolving the metallic surface around it. She remembered touching the sphere, how the glow followed her fingers, but the harder she tried to remember the details the fainter and more unbelievable it felt.

She rewatched the part where she touched the sphere, the glow tracing her fingers, and the part after her screaming followed by the strobing light. Elisa had instructed the computer to count the lights rotating around the sphere, to analyse the pattern if there was any information attached to it. But nothing that resolved to anything that resembled information. The only thing it reminded her of was that it looked like a star system, with too many planets to be physically possible, especially right before it turned dark.

Elisa knew she had changed. Even her attitude to getting away from Mars had changed. It was clear to her that she had to play her cards right, to get away. One part of it was, Phil had agreed to buying the tickets for both of them to get back at any price, using up his entire savings of over more than two decades on Mars.

Only once they were on Earth they would tell their stories and not give their information into the hands of a private company. Everyone had the right to know what had happened, and how, and where. They had agreed, that if something or someone managed to build an entity that could cross the vast distances of empty space, a few months delay wouldn't make any further difference. They had no trust in the company which was controlling Mars.

She turned around to Phil moving under the blanked, peeking at her, stretching his legs.

"Good Morning!" she said and threw a shiny pack of orange paste at him.

He coughed and grumbled back. Eventually, he sat upright, leaning against the frame of the cabin and stretched his arms.

"You think today can get any worse?" He sounded low.

"You look like it. But let's hope not. The sphere is still out, and even if I bonk any other things against it, I guess it will stay that way. I reported back as we agreed last night."

"They know nothing?"

"Nothing."

"Was there a response?"

She turned around, checked the screens in the front and read out loud.

"Immediately return to base!"

"Well, there we go." He sounded relieved.

After he had got up, they tidied up the cabin. Elisa made two copies of all the logs and recordings and encrypted them in the empty space of their terminals. She provided the first half of the password, and Phil the second, without exchanging it. This way both of them were required to be present to unlock the drives. They agreed not to say anything to anyone. At all. Even not to each other until they were on a squad back to earth. Elisa made sure to wipe all the drives from the off-road vehicle and factory reset the user space of the system. They looked at the black sphere one last time, dialled in a course back to the city, which avoided the crash site, and were headed on their long autonomous drive back. leaving behind the alien sphere.

They slept most of the time and only woke up to eat, drink, walk up and down the vehicle to stretch their legs or shovel regolith from one bucket to the next.

◆◆◆

The evening approached, and they could see the colourless domes of the city. If a perfectly round hill were something natural, the city would have gone unnoticed as such.

As their vehicle gently rolled down the ramp, into the open airlock, the heavy doors of the hangar slowly opened and closed around them. They were expecting a support crew to receive them and take over the vehicle for refills and maintenance, but there was noone waiting for them.

The airlock re-pressurised and arms reached down from the ceiling, spraying down the vehicles. They quietly sat in their seats, watching the empty hall in front of them, waiting for someone to appear during the process.

"Where is everyone gone?" asked Phil, sounding concerned, looking out of the windows around him, trying to see someone, as they rolled deeper into the hangar.

"No idea, but let me check the message channels."

She scrolled up the feed, and looked for nothing and everything at the same time.

"There is a compulsory meeting/broadcast in fifteen minutes, and we are supposed to assemble under the main domes." She summarised the latest message from her inbox, with relief. At least they knew why noone was receiving them.

"That explains the absence of any service I guess." Phil mumbled to her left.

She picked up her bags and they exited the vehicle, with opened helmets, breathing in the air from the city. Without any further talk they hurried through the tunnels and service domes, without meeting anyone along the way. Elisa tried to think of a topic to talk about, but her mind was revisiting the previous days before. The crash was already almost forgotten, but she had underestimated how much space and time the recent events were still taking up in her head.

They passed under a production dome, striding through rows of 3D printers stacked in rows or as single huge cubes behind glass walls, slowly doing their rounds, placing a thin layer upon layers. Others were burning objects out of sand, with a laser quickly firing an image at the neatly added surface of the next layer of material, hiding the objects to be built during the process.

When the last door between them and the nearest cafeteria dome opened, they were met with the grumble coming from the people inside. Elisa was unsure what to think of the situation, but was relieved to be among others again. Still, she was impressed by the sheer number of people in the dome at the same time. Usually, the inhabitants were more distributed across the city and during daytime. This was neatly planned out to provide everyone with as much space as possible. Now, it was crowded. People were moving around to find a place to sit or stand.

Nobody paid attention to them joining the assembly. They were one of many dressed in work clothes, suited to go outside. The four big canvases mounted under the roof of the dome slowly lit up as Elisa and Phil sat down behind a large group gathered around the entrance of the hall, looking at the canvas on the opposite side of the hall.

Elisa glanced around, scanning the faces illuminated by the massive screens above. Her sight jumped from face to face, trying to read the room, to guess what was about to be announced.

The company logo spun in the middle of the screen and renderings of the latest designs for the city's expansion scrolled past in the background.

Some people cheered, still impressed by the fake images. Elisa sighed.

They have no idea. She thought and shuddered, thinking about the colony doubling with the next expansion wave. Phil looked at her, his forehead creased, as if trying to push his bushy eyebrows closely enough together for them to meet in the middle. She could feel his concern, after having shared their thoughts the previous night: so many mouths to feed.

A small, bald man appeared on the screen, wearing a simple, black t-shirt and grey cargo pants. The subtitle labelled him as Robert Moreno, Lead Mars Expansion Architect. He stood behind a large desk, the surface being a screen filled with charts and animations of empty floor plans for new hubs, domes and new networks of new tunnels, charts and numbers indicating success and a steady growth. He began to talk.

"Fellow Martians!"

He left a pause to let people cheer and shout "Martians!" in return, while he kept his gaze at the camera, smiling.

"We all know that the last days and hours have been intense. We are facing new, unknown challenges. We are more than halfway towards the next wave of inhabitants and the progress we have made is incredible! The current situation will not stop us from succeeding to remain an interplanetary species."

Cheers went through the dome as the man on

the screen walked to the right towards another table, displaying images and videos of the spheres: three-dimensional renderings, with regular, repeating patterns on the surface.

"We have been studying these spheres for the past, almost two, days. They have appeared in regular distances across Mars and Earth."

He paused, staring into the camera.

"We ask you to remain calm, and carry on with your duties. Every day. We need to support each other and face the challenges. At this point, for transparency, we have to inform you, that last night we have lost radio contact with Earth."

An astonished grumble went through the dome, unnoticed by the speaker and he went on.

"But we have our best technicians working on re-establishing contact, here on the gateway to Earth."

The dome was listening intently.

"As of this morning we have confirmed that our old home–" The speaker paused for a second, swallowed, then continued, staring into the camera. "–that Earth has disappeared."

Elisa was shocked. She searched for Phil's eye contact. He was staring, frozen at the canvas above. She felt as if someone had kicked her into her guts. Her heart was trying to jump out of her chest. She talked to herself.

"Earth? Gone?" She couldn't believe it.

Cries of disbelief as well as cheers went through the crowds.

The speaker went on.

"We have verified this by analysing the available logs. With the absence of data streams and pilot tones from Earth and with the relay stations from Earth's Lagrange points losing their respective orbits, that in the place where Earth including the moon once have been, is nothing left but empty space."

Elisa watched a tall man faint, being caught by those around him. And like everyone around her, Elisa could not believe what she was hearing. Earth disappearing was not a possibility she could ever think of. Her chest stung with pain. She was re-evaluating everything in her mind at the same time. She saw the event from last night replay in her head, the lights, the touch and the sphere turning dark.

Was that us? Fuck! No!

She felt weak.

"The latest accepted theory is that the missing gravitational pull explains the decaying orbits from the Lagrange points. As Mars is outside of Earth's hill sphere there will be no effect on us. Without Earth's gravitation, the equilibrium of gravitational pull is gone, destabilising the relay points at L4 and L5."

The man pointed at an animation of Earth rotating around the sun.

"We can assure you, we are safe here on Mars. If there were any impact from Earth's disappearance on Mars, we would have felt it by now. Earth disappeared two nights ago."

People were mumbling, discussing and shouting questions at the screens. Elisa relaxed a bit, almost feeling relieved.

That was before we even went to the sphere!

An animation of the solar system ran in the corner of each canvas under the ceiling, with each planet sitting in a hole, bending down a mesh to depict its gravity well. With Earth disappearing the empty hole slowly filled and flattened and curved with the gravitational pull of the sun in the centre. The man on the screen continued.

"We have to reach out to everyone. In these times, we have to stand together. We will support each other and we have to be strong. Together we can do this. We are not alone. We have each other. Our undiminished drive to improve will guarantee us success, for years and decades to come. But in these times we have to be righteous. And we have to look after each other. And for those who don't, there will be consequences. We have had reports of assaults and thefts. This will stop. Now. This will not be tolerated. We have increased the number of personnel of the security wards, whose orders have to be respected. The terms and conditions of your contracts will be amended as we speak, expanding the authority of the wards as required. We are on our own now. And we need you to support each other to maintain peace and order."

He paused, staring at the camera, then he went on, his voice more serious than before.

"We need your help to support this city, and safeguard this colony. We need everyone to do their part. We have been forced to turn on monitoring measures for our safety. "

The viewers quietly watched and listened.

"As of now we are looking for two individuals involved in the death of three valued engineers. They are already back in the city."

The profile pictures of Elisa and Phil appeared next to each other on the screen, their names written below them.

"These two individuals are wanted for questioning. They are to proceed to the newly established ground stewards' office. This video will show you why this measure is necessary. These measures are for your safety."

A video filled the big screens, with the presenter now visible in small picture-in-picture embedded into the top left corner. The video began to play, showing the inside of the vehicle in which Phil and Elisa had begun their journey to the sphere, the camera looking over their own shoulders. They watched how Elisa lifted her arm to use her terminal, how Phil nodded at her, as if in confirmation. The diagram depicting the vehicle was visible on her terminal strapped to her space suit. She watched herself tap the wheel in the video. Just as she had lifted her finger from the screen, the crash followed. The video stopped with the last frame showing the cargo boxes in mid-air, hiding the three technicians in the front of the vehicle.

To her surprise the stream showing the presenter in the corner of the screens had stopped, too, and within seconds the broadcast broke off, a spinning animation depicting the reconnection attempts rotated a few times, and the screens turned dark.

When they turned back on, a message appeared on the screen: "We are The Mars Collective. We are freeing Mars from The Interplanetary Corporation."

XI (LUNA)

The Dolvar had been the first aliens to try and reach out to humans. A species shaped like a squid from a water planet three quarters the size of Earth, just about two weeks of space travel away, when travelling on one of their vessels.

Luna had joined the cultural exchange programme between Earth and *Dol* after she had finished her Masters in Technological History at The Rebuilt University. Everyone she knew had applied and she did as well, even if she was unsure if she was the right candidate. She understood why everyone wanted to be an ambassador for Earth, to represent humanity and experience something literally out of this world. She knew her chances were not zero, but with the applications being in the millions, she didn't expect to be drawn and it was a low risk versus being the odd one out.

When she was drawn, randomly selected by chance, she was stumped. She discussed stepping down from her ticket with her friends and family, but they had been unbearable with excitement and pushed her to accept, even if she tried to explain that she had doubts to be a suitable candidate. In the end, she had listened to everyone long enough to accept the opportunity of a lifetime, regardless of her convictions.

She remembered exactly when and how it happened. Everyone was glued to the living room screen watching the live feed, as the lucky ticket numbers appeared on the screen. And when it matched hers, the living room around her exploded with screams and congratulations, with her sitting frozen, staring at the confirmation message lighting up on a glowing display with her face and name.

About two months later, she sat inside the *The Second Blue Marble,* a space ship the length of two football fields, taking her time to adjust to travelling with her host, Erial. She had got used to the quietness inside, the absence of wind, birds, rain, and shrieking animals at night. Erial had setup a small number of rooms, just for her, all designed to fit her needs: A comfortable but simplistic living room with a desk for studying, a pile of cushions to rest, a bedroom with an attached bathroom as well as a fitness room, which she hardly ever used, and a sim-sphere.

The sim-sphere was the room that impressed her the most. Experiencing its dense technology alone had been worth accepting the result of the lottery to be participating in a cultural exchange with a Dolvar for months and years, away from Earth. Away from home. The room was a small spherical chamber attached to her living room through an oval hole in the wall, through which she had to step inside. Once inside, the door shrunk away, surrounding her entirely with the naked walls of the sphere. Standing inside this ball with a diameter twice her height, the walls could take on any shape, texture and colour, moving and rolling around her. Each and every movement of her was tracked and matched by the sphere reshaping its walls around her, redrawing its colours, creating the illusion of an infinite world.

The first time she had experienced the sphere in action, she chose a recreation of her university. The simulation began with her spawning inside in her dorm room. The level of detail and realism surprised her to the extent that she cursed for the first time in front of her alien host, who was listening to and instructing her remotely. Luckily, Erial had been knowledgeable enough about human language, that her expression of "Fuck me!" had not been literal.

When she walked up to a wall within the simulation she could touch, feel and smell it. The same worked for solid and coarse objects. With her bare feet, she could feel the texture of the carpet, and the cold hard surface of the tiles in the hallways. Whenever she sat down on a chair, the shape of the chair morphed out of the floor to create a solid surface to sit on. She had asked how it worked and listened to the detailed explanation, but eventually decided to call it magic micro mechanical matter. She had to accept she would never be able to explain it to anyone else other than by how she had experienced this level of technology.

With the sim-sphere to immerse herself into any of her recorded locations, provided her with the confidence to be travelling with the Dolvar on her own, away from friends and family for such a long time. Whenever she wanted to feel closer to home, she could enter the spherical room and accept the illusion of being in her bedroom, dorm room, or sitting in the forests behind her parents' house.

After the lottery, she had thought she'd have to go through space training, to be able to navigate a space ship, to know how to read star systems or calculate orbital manoeuvres. In short: to understand all the mathematical stuff she had always had a hard time learning. But none of it was required. She had a month to prepare, to visit her extended family and friends for a last time in at most half a decade and focus on her private matters. She found the time to give interviews and respond to fan mail, overwhelmed by the sudden attention. Like her, none of the other participants of the programme had any idea what was ahead of them. It was a first for everyone. All they knew was, that the Dolvar guaranteed their safety by any means necessary and that the mutual future depended on the outcome of the exchange.

Even if she knew she could return any time, she took the undertaking seriously enough to be willing to go through with it in its entirety.

Now, that she was travelling with Erial for just over a month, having spent not even two percent of their time and journey together, she still wasn't sure what was going to happen.

Luna took her time. Like on many days before, she

found herself in front of her desk inside her living room, staring at a blank page, after hours of discussions with her alien host, wondering what to write and what to make of it. She picked up her pen and began to draw a box for her entries date.

"What's the date today?" she asked, her voice directed at the paper in front of her.

"Earth or Dol?" Erial asked back, their voice resonating from the wall at the end of her desk.

"Here on Earth."

"It's the twenty-seventh of August, 2478. You have been travelling with me for thirty four days of your time. On Dol it's the 1204th rotation of the 4256th new orbit." The alien sounded nonchalant.

Over the last two decades, the Dolvar had been provided with every bit of information humanity still possessed or had recovered from archaeological findings. An offering to re-establish contact after almost four hundred years.

With the provided data, the Dolvar had a chance to paint a picture of what had happened in the past. Now, the cultural exchange was an exchange of information on a personal level, not to have their history retold, but to listen to all the random participants of the programme, to listen to what they thought and felt about what had happened on Earth during the last three-hundred and ninety-two years.

The Dolvar maintained that whatever had happened in the past of a species was one thing, but how that species looked at and felt about it said more about the species than their history itself.

Luna felt the empty paper with her finger tips, thinking of what to write, trying to summarise in her head before she wrote anything down. They had discussed the tragic events of the blackout and the Dolvar reaching out to Earth, trying to make first contact.

Luna had explained that the blackout marked humanity's technological climax. The three centuries that followed were called the second middle ages, a time where organised societies collapsed and the human population declined to less than two hundred million across the globe. The melting of the ice caps, the stopping of the gulf stream, the ice ages of Europe and natural disasters ravaging the planet had brought the once globalised civilisation to a downfall. It took the climate hundreds of years to settle, for the oceans to start moving and bring life back into the depths and transfer nutrients around the world, to feed ecosystems once held for granted. Too many generations paid the price for the economic boom of a few, all brought to a fall by a single event: the blackout.

It took humanity three centuries to finally find itself and rebuild a globalised society, to rebuild and rediscover the technologies that once existed, to re-establish contact with the Dolvar, to reach out and bring the two species closer together.

Luna wrote down her thoughts.

Maybe I'm wrong thinking that I'm not the right candidate for this exchange. Maybe my view that humans will inherently fuck things up, has to be said and it might be better to leave us alone for another four centuries, to see if we have understood what the future of intelligent life is about and how fragile intelligent life can be. There is nothing in this world that can explain the tragic events of our first contact with the Dolvar.

Luna put her pen down and thought of the first days aboard the space ship. Being the guest of an intelligent, aquatic species, that was superior if even only considering the technological aspects, had turned her stomach into a knot when she saw the alien floating behind a glass wall for the first time. She immediately explained to Erial the shame she felt about how humans had depleted the oceans, destroyed ecosystems and dumped their waste into the environment, especially the oceans. Compared to the status quo of the past, the current, strict controls on production as well as the use and spread of technology on Earth, seemed to her to be an environmentally better approach, even if she didn't agree with these restrictions, as they limited her in learning about existing technologies and build upon them.

These technological restrictions on Earth led to another discussion, where Luna described her fascination to Erial for the remnants of the technological antique on Earth, about what kind of technology had once been widely accessible. The magic of the old days, she had described it. The drastic changes of technology itself, spanning the decades before and after the turn of the second millennium, where technology itself was still in its infancy, where capacities and data rates had the potential of doubling every few years, then rapidly advancing into mankind establishing a colony on Mars during the following fifty years. She recounted how she had watched the specialists who taught themselves how to build liquid crystal displays from scratch for the first time, assembling them under the watchful eyes of an interested audience and auditors, bringing back a memory, a piece of history back to life, slowly puzzling together and reclaiming the lost technologies from the past, even only to archive and lock them away under the existing regulations.

Once, she had stumbled across a broken display on a bazaar, framed behind glass. She could still make out the shadows of the last page it had displayed, but not what the text actually read, its letters faded over centuries. She had searched the remains of the internet archives and found an advertisement for these paper-like displays, speaking of retaining the image on the display forever.

Remembering the faded, unreadable page of a book displayed on it, she learnt that the statement that it would last forever had not been truthful in any way.

Even if technological proficiency on Earth was slowly catching up, it wasn't pushing ahead as humanity had once seen it happen. The accessible technologies were restricted and regulated. From her own experience, switching from running a washing machine and a dishwasher meant you had to unplug the motor from the first and re-plug it into the other. A motor that was handed down from household to household. Instead of producing everything in the highest quantities to push down the price, the consensus was to manufacture as little as possible, to leave the remaining resources on Earth untouched. Any technology that was not a requirement for your health and safety was subject to the rationing of raw materials. The result was a global cleanup, that led to many people choosing a nomadic lifestyle of searching for recyclables, of which they were allowed to keep a stake of ten percent, to trade the obtained materials.

Luna put her pen down and watched it fasten into a slot on the desk. She closed the book, which also sank into a rectangular groove and the desk withdrew into the wall without leaving a visible seam or slot from which it had appeared.

She got up from the grey block that stood out of the floor, made from the same seamless material as the walls and walked through the living room, around the island of cushions that were stuck to the floor. Luna stopped at the window reaching from floor to ceiling, wall to wall, that looked into a dimly lit aquarium where Erial was swimming in a body of water twice the size of her rooms, all contained inside the space ship. The alien had the shape of a squid, but with two rings of tentacles instead of one. Where a squid had a body with two narrow fins along the side, the alien had four lobes, with a brain each, tightly intertwined around a smaller, brained core at its centre, all covered in a transparent shell when uncoloured. The inner tentacles were longer and stronger with arms that ended in thick paddles and the outer, smaller arms resembled a centipede more than a tentacle.

The alien pulsed with a low blue light, signalling it had seen her, then changed its colour to white to immediately dim to blue, then black. After a second the alien's body filled with curly, criss-crossing lines tracing around its body with an orange glow, almost resembling an ancient incandescent lightbulb, stretched across the almost five metre long body.

Luna smiled at Erial's presentation. She was still fascinated by the Dolvar's ability of being able to produce light and arbitrarily change colours. One day, she had asked if this ability gave the Dolvar an emotional advantage, as it provided a broader spectrum to communicate feelings without relying on the abstraction of words. Erial had answered 'no' and Luna had quietly disagreed.

Regardless of disagreeing in many points during their conversation, she was amazed how well they got along. They talked for hours, for example about whether the notion of a 'you' was necessary for a consciousness to evolve, or if visual patterns had the same expressivity as audio patterns, or if her brain was in a constant dialogue with its mental ancestor. Soon she had lost the feeling of talking to something or someone alien, but rather to someone she knew.

No matter how far they drifted during their discussions, eventually Erial brought them back to their assigned task of what they both called the biggest audit in human history.

XII (LUNA)

On the thirty-fifth day Luna decided she was ready to leave Earth. She woke up, undressed and walked barefoot across the warm rough surface into the bathroom. She stood in the middle of the small, round room, with the walls and floor made out of the same continuous, greyish material that made up her rooms on the spaceship. She looked at the ceiling, still wondering how the ship and everything worked the way it did, but still couldn't find any holes or a shower head.

"Warm." Luna commanded her preferences into the room and a comfortable curtain of warm water fell from the ceiling, landing on her and in a wide circle around her. Under the warm rain, she thought about the day she had joined Erial on their spaceship.

She had hugged her parents and friends as tight as she could. Tears were flowing, but all with bright smiles to catch them from running down their chins. She remembered, how she waved them goodbye from the car that picked her up.

Once in the harbour, she loaded her things into a water taxi, an old, rusty fishing boat, with two oars and a small electric motor attached at the back,

XII (LUNA)

pushing her and the driver across the gentle waves of the Baltic sea towards the announced time and location. Camera drones quietly circled them from above, broadcasting the signal back home to her parents and to anyone watching the stream.

She had never seen a rocket launch in person, let alone seeing one land and all she knew about it was from centuries-old recordings. The excitement was intense when she spotted the spaceship shaped like a cuttlebone, called *The Second Blue Marble*, falling silently, belly first, from the sky. With her head pressed into the nape of her neck, she watched it, falling straight down onto her. For seconds she feared it would crash down onto her, ending her journey on the first day, but then it gently drifted overhead and flipped to turn upright. Before it could hit the water, kilometres away from her, the lower end opened, producing eight tentacles spreading into a star, firing up arrays of rocket engines embedded into each arm. The spaceship gently stopped its free fall, lowered itself down to hover above the water for merely seconds and then gently breached the surface with one arm after the other, switching off its engines, slowly lowering itself below the water, until it disappeared. Before it vanished the cracking sound of the engines igniting made it across the sea, sending goose bumps across her skin and a chill down her spine. The driver had smiled and said how it impressed him every time, showing his own goose bumps on his hairy, suntanned arms, happy to be a witness to these events at his old age.

Within minutes the ship had resurfaced next to the water taxi, a massive, bulky shape slowly rising out of the water, like a gigantic whale, facing them with the tentacle end. One arm reached out and steadied the water taxi, another lifted itself on top of the edge of the boat forming a ramp for Luna to walk onto. She stepped across the railing onto the arm, which gently lifted her across the water towards the space ship. A hole opened on its top like a blowhole of a whale, revealing a ladder leading down. She turned around to wave goodbye to the drones and disappeared into *The Second Blue Marble*.

She had spent the first days with a mix of inside the ship and on deck, slowly cruising along the coast towards the North Atlantic. Erial was not in a hurry to leave, and had enough to see on Earth for themselves while cruising along. This gave Luna plenty of time to get used to her new surroundings. She had quickly forgotten she was on a space ship and it felt more like an ocean cruise on a mix of a submarine and yacht, but talking to an alien.

She had spent the majority of the past week inside as it was getting colder with every day they steered north.

As Luna stepped out of the stream of water, she knew she was ready to leave. She dried herself off, walked back into her bedroom, and made her bed as instructed, to avoid things from flying around during launch and got dressed.

Inside her living room, she turned to the wall of glass separating the two spaces, hers filled with air and the alien's with water.

"Erial? I'm ready." She said, searching for her extraterrestrial companion.

"We can see that." A pulsing, blue light at the end of the long room signalled amusement, swimming around in a figure of eight.

"No, I meant I'm ready. We can leave, now."

"Oh, we couldn't see that. You should think about adding some colours or lights to yourself, to make that clearer." Erial tried to sound amused.

Luna laughed. "I will. What do I need to do to launch this thing?"

She spun around and wiggled her arms as if they were her own excited tentacles.

"Nothing. The question is how much do you want to see, feel and experience?"

"The preview simulations looked so exciting, but I'm not sure how I will handle it and if I don't, I'm not going to be resentful. I'll switch it off if it gets too overwhelming." She crossed her arms, hugging herself, a sign of comfort for the Dolvar.

"Ok, We've prepared the sim-sphere for you. Once you are ready, we will swim out to sea, dive, build up speed and jump out of the water, then launch. Does that sound alright to you?"

"Yes." She agreed to the procedure and walked to the other side of the living room towards the oval opening in the wall. She turned around and waved at the now purple glowing alien on the other side of the glass.

"See you in space." She said and smiled, then

climbed through the hole into the sim-sphere.

Inside, the room had formed a mould into the curved, grey wall, shaped like a racing seat. She sat down and felt how the walls embraced her, carefully adjusting to the shape of her body, wrapping around her, holding her in place. She let her arms sink into the surface, gripping the handles that gently pushed into her palms from below. She moved her head from side to side to check the remaining sphere in front of her. Looking at the grey circular walls, she told Erial she was ready. Luna felt excited and unsure what to expect, her hands already sweating against the handles.

In an instant the oval hole looking into the living room disappeared, the walls changed from a light grey to a clear view of the world around them.

The first time the sim-sphere had turned on she had flinched at suddenly being somewhere else. By now she was used to it.

She watched how they cruised out of a fjord in Norway, picking up speed with every wave that rolled over the ship's body, inches below her feet. Luna pressed her head into the invisible wall embracing her, to swivel around and watch the ship's tail slowly waving up and down in big arched movements, propelling them out to sea.

The entire ship waved up and down increasing the acceleration with every of Luna's excited heartbeats. She turned her seat around again to face the front. At the same time the perspective changed: Instead of watching her own body sitting in an invisible seat with the ship under her feet, she now watched everything from the ship's and Erial's perspective.

Erial's voice came from the invisible walls.

"This is how we see it. How are you doing?"

"I'm great, let's do this!"

She turned her head towards the grey cloudy sky above and to the sides lined with the high, rocky walls of a fjord. In front of them lay the horizon. Below her, she could look deep down into the hidden depths of the water, the diffuse sunlight painting curtains of light around her invisible feet. Her body was now entirely hidden, submerged into the simsphere's walls, immersing her completely into the outside view.

She giggled at the splashing waves around her, as the rocks and slopes moved past her faster every second.

Just as they cleared the mouth of the fjord, she heard Erial's voice.

"Ready?"

"Ready!" She tightened her hands around the grips moulded into the walls, absorbing the sweat from her palms, feeling cool and dry.

"I'm ready!" Excitedly she repeated herself, looking forward to the launch.

A jolt of acceleration pressed her into the seat. She strained the muscles in her neck to steady her head against the sudden change of velocity. Immediately the seat shrunk around her, a soft pressure against the back of her head, holding her firmly in place. She relaxed and let the ship hold her tighter, giving in to the acceleration pushing through her body.

The waves foamed around her, as they continued to pick up speed. Without warning, the ship submerged, leaving the grey sky, shrieking seagulls, and waves above them. She watched the curtains of light of the breaking waves dance around her, as they sank into the blue darkness below, pushing her into the depths. She kicked out, to try to stop herself from falling and her stomach felt as if it wanted to sink faster than the rest of her body. She closed her eyes to hide from the masses of water building up above her head.

"We must say, we will miss the fish you have here. This has been a very unusual but pleasant taste in the past weeks." Erial's voice was now speaking almost inside her head, resonating from the embracing walls, reminding her she was still inside a spaceship.

Luna smiled and opened her eyes, staring into darkness, appreciating that Erial had picked up their own form of humour over the past weeks. A welcome distraction from the unknown surroundings. Watching a simulation had been one thing, but actually feeling it at the same time had been something else. She focused on Erial's voice.

"And we also accepted the offer to catch some supplies for both of us."

The angle of *The Second Blue Marble* decreased, travelling horizontally through the ocean, the acceleration diminishing. Testing her confinement, she tried to stretch herself.

"We promise you won't be eating a variation of flavoured bricks all the way and back." Erial continued. "We should pass one of the kelp blooms on *Dol*. The flowers taste great, and if you are interested you can get a taste of our avian varieties that nest on the kelp islands. Whatever we find first."

She felt the ship tilting upwards, picking up speed again, pressing her into the seat. She had her eyes fixed to the front, staring into the darkness.

"We are launching." confirmed Erial.

Luna blinked a couple of times, ready not to miss a thing. She looked around to orientate herself. The water ahead seemed brighter. Over the next seconds the brightness increased, and she saw the waves from below, like an inverted picture rippling ahead, a view she had never seen and felt before. In an instant, she crashed through the surface towards the clouds above. The sim-sphere's perspective changed onto the outside of the ship again, her body below her. She spun around to lock back down and instinctively tried to flail her arms and legs to stop her from rising and falling, to hold on to anything to stop her from flying through the air. The confinement of her body held her tight, the ship pulling her into the air, but her brain did its best to convince her she was not in fact inside the ship. She pushed her breath out of her lungs, forcing herself to take in the view. She screamed. First with fear, then with excitement. A thin water film raced down the ship, turning into a white trail of foamy rain falling back to the ocean, sinking rapidly away below her. Seagulls shrieked away, shrinking in size as the spaceship shot into the sky. Then their ascent slowed, almost stopped and Luna felt a brief weightlessness as she watched the tentacles at the back of the ship split open. The water falling and flowing past her evaporated into a plume of smoke and steam, ignited by the screaming engines below, drowning her own.

She turned back around to face the sky. To her right she could see a bright pillow of clouds crawling from the sea into the mountains, and on her left the endless ocean falling away as she hurtled towards space.

◆ ◆ ◆

Luna felt the wall around her release her from its grip. She took a deep breath and slowly pushed herself up. Her arms and legs felt weak, drained by the excitement. The lack of gravity sent her spinning up and around. She bumped her head into the invisible wall, then pushed herself away with her arms above her head and bumped with her feet into the opposite side. After a moment of adjusting to the absence of gravity, she stopped herself from rotating and gently manoeuvred herself into the centre of the sphere.

Only then did she register the visualisation of herself floating in space without a space suit. Luna's skin crawled with goosebumps and it took her breath away. She was exhilarated. She carefully spun herself around, to look at the original blue marble, Earth. The sight overwhelmed her and brought tears of happiness into her eyes.

"I have never seen such a beautiful sight." she said as she wiped away her tears with a smile.

Behind her was the huge body of the ship, shielding her from the sun. Above and below her was the vast emptiness of space awash with distant stars. Earth looked small from this far out, as if not bigger than the sphere that contained Luna. The atmosphere seemed so thin, as if she could blow it away as easily as the florets of a dandelion. She watched how they sped into space, her home planet shrinking in front of her eyes. A marble mixed with water, land and clouds, seemingly mixing and twisting forever on its own. The moon circling behind it, shining bright, Earth's lifeless companion facing the same side of the planet as if watching it, too.

"This is so beautiful. Thank you Erial, for showing it to me in this–" Luna found no words to describe what she wanted to say, and tried to form a sphere out of nothing in front of her eyes, tried to physically grasp it, caress it and hold it.

"You're welcome. It's the same for us." replied Erial.

Luna kept staring at the blue dot, now shrunk to the size of a tennis ball, accompanied by its tiny moon in the distance. She looked down the back of the space ship, its engines painting a burning glow around its tentacles, then turned her gaze down into the glowing emptiness painted with unmoving stars. Against her will, her mind tricked her into believing she was indeed floating in space and not watching it through a representation from inside the ship and she panicked. She felt a force pulling at her, building up inside her body, as if sinking down to the bottom of a pool. She reached out to grasp for the walls, her hands grabbing into empty air. She squeaked with fear.

"Close your eyes!" said Erial's calm voice from around her, and she followed the command in an instant, her arms and legs still flailing, crashing into the sim-sphere, while trying to control her quickening breathing. She shuddered. With her body tumbling in zero gravity, she had to fight the urge to reach out and hold onto something until she felt a flat surface on her back stopping her spin.

"I'm right here with you. You can open your eyes again." Erial's voice was welcome in her ears.

Right in front of her nose was a wall, covered with white-toned woodchip wallpaper, an easy surface for her eyes to focus on, an irregular pattern. It reminded her of her bedroom at her parents place in Woodside, Europe, from where she had left thirty five days before.

"You have a really fascinating history of decorating your walls." Erial was amused and Luna had to grin.

"Thanks, this helps." She was still floating in practically zero gravity. The wall of the sim-sphere opened to her left. She looked into the living room, upside down, her head pointing towards the floor. She was surprised by her total loss of orientation.

"We will start to spin now, if you could get upright, you can land on your feet."

Luna held onto the surface that caught her back and flipped herself around. She closed her eyes and waited for the gravity to increase. Her feet confirmed her touching down on the floor. She felt her blood sink back into her legs, as if standing up too quickly from crouching for too long, and she clenched her leg muscles to push the flow back up to her head. Still, she went tunnel visioned, sending her crawling out of the sim-sphere, to sit down on the floor inside the living room, leaning her back against the wall.

"Do you have carpets on *Dol*?" she asked the alien, resting her hands on the matte surface, textured with a mix of grey white and tiny green specks.

"We don't even have rooms, remember?" Erial sounded surprised by her question.

"Yes, I get the point."

Luna rested for a while, imagining what Erial's home world would be like. A planet covered completely with a single ocean, some areas covered with floating kelp islands, drifting in the vortices of an infinite stream of currents circulating around the hemispheres.

She stood up, walked towards the glass wall separating their breathable bubbles of water and air and looked inside. The alien was in the process of slowly retreating from a tangle of cables reaching out and around them. After disconnecting them one by one, Erial turned around, kicked out to propel themselves forward and stopped right in front of Luna. Their entire skin turned from their neutral pale grey to a black colour, sprinkled with tiny, glowing, yellowish, white dots, lined with a series of concentric circles with hundreds of bigger dots.

Luna agreed. "Yes, it is a beautiful system."

She rested her hands against the glass trying to touch the colourful alien skin on the other side. The colours changed and showed a blue wavy surface, with patches of green.

"I'm looking forward to *Dol*, too." she said, unsure if she had read it correctly.

"Try again!"

She took a step back, bent down to take a better look at the colours all around the alien. Inspecting the brighter, slightly glowing underside she remembered.

"Yes! I'm hungry, too!" Luna laughed. "I have totally forgotten about breakfast. In hindsight, maybe a good idea."

She walked towards the wall next to the opening that led to her bedroom.

"But don't you need to keep your eyes on the road?" She turned around to look at the alien's reaction, unable to hide her grin and laughed. The wall next to her bedroom opened and revealed a bowl with steaming rice mixed with cod, carrots and what looked like parsley. She grabbed the warm bowl and walked towards the pile of cushions in the centre of the room. At the same time, the creature kicked with is tentacles, darted around its room and sailed past the window.

"Let me explain this to you in your simple human terms. If you sit in a car, and it's going in a straight line, downhill, cruise control is making sure it's only slowly drifting away from its desired speed, and we assume your wheels are not wonky, so you won't drift aside. I think it's ok to let go of the steering, get a cup of tea and read a book."

As Erial finished their sentence, they bumped into the wall at the end of the window, sending dim rings of light circling around the length of its body.

"Ok, I'll do my best to be a good, watchful copilot then." She grinned and pointed with her chopsticks at the alien, as if lecturing it.

Luna often thought about what it was like for a Dolvar to be travelling with a human companion during this exchange. She had imagined travelling with a monkey or a dog or a cat, sitting with her in a camper van, talking about what cats and dogs and monkeys do, what they think and feel and what they want to do in the future. In her imagination it made her feel like a babysitter, looking after a lifeform and being responsible for keeping it alive, a strange duo, under the watchful eyes of society. In her mind she was trying to work out if cats were inherently evil, dogs only liked to play fetch because it made humans happy, and if monkeys enjoyed throwing their shit at the visitors in the zoos she had read about. She was sure, animals didn't care whether their food came out of a pan or a can when you fed them, similar to her now. But when she asked Erial how the kitchen worked on this ship, and they showed her the bouquet of tubes pooping out the elements of a meal into a bowl, she decided it was best to let this part be magic, and accepted whatever final presentation was randomly appearing in the hole on the wall. She just hoped that the hole the floor of the corner of the bathroom was not directly connected to the kitchen mechanism, and had enough things and devices between them. Either way, the kitchen had learned her tastes and she enjoyed her meals, even more than those of her parents.

During her first month Luna had learnt much about the Dolvar: how they didn't bond in pairs to mate, but in pods, spraying their eggs and sperm into the currents, and letting them flow with the currents. Millions of eggs, to be decimated by fish and sunlight. Those that sank to the bottom of the ocean, gently rolled across the ocean floor with the currents, just to be prayed on by the equivalent of stationary crustaceans. Those who went unharmed had a chance of hatching and produce schools of squid that grew in time and eventually took revenge on the fish that once fed on them. Then after years, they were herded by the grown Dolvar to undergo their final transformation. In the warm waters near underground vents of dormant volcanoes, they formed a cocoon, dissolving like a moth, their brain separating into the five lobes, increasing in size tenfold, and morphing into their grownup shape, to be born again, to be raised and taught to become a functioning, technologically advanced society. Erial was over four hundred human years old. In their years Erial had just turned eighty and was still considered to be young, but old enough to have auto-grown their own spaceship over the past century, ready to participate in the exchange between Earth and Dol.

When she had asked about their age, they drifted off into the discussion whether the effect of knowing to have a short life-expectancy had an impact on decision making. The question was if this could be a reason for the short -sightedness of humans during their history, their approach of abusing the planet, not caring who or what would be living on it for the next two hundred years, because the results of one's actions would often only be felt after one's lifetime. Luna thought there was a point to it. If she were stuck in the loop of getting up, going to work, getting back, finding the time to look after her kids, if that was her preference, just to fall into bed being exhausted, she could see herself not caring about her environment. Any convenience that she could apply to this lifestyle, hiding its true cost, would have been acceptable to her, as the life that was laid out to her by society was hostile in itself. She never understood how mankind never leveraged the use of automation for the general good for such a long time, especially in the twenty-first century.

As the end of the twenty-first century marked the beginning of the second middle ages, there had never been a chance for society to change the kind of life it dictated.

In comparison, she thought it was interesting that not all Dolvar kept the result of their second birth and chose to discard their outer brains. They then continued to live more or less like fish in the ocean, not burdened with the obligations and worries that came with an intelligent consciousness paired with a society. Instead they preferred to face the simple reality of eating and being eaten on a daily basis. Luna was sure, if she had a choice she would always chose life in a society over an animalistic daily routine.

She finished her bowl of rice and North Atlantic cod and placed it back into the hole from which it had appeared. As she returned to the glass wall between them, she watched the alien speed around, catching fish one after the other out of a shoal released into their living space. Luna studied them carefully and wondered about the alien's preferences.

"Erial, is there anything in particular that you would like to show me when we arrive on Dol?"

XIII (ELISA)

Still panting, Phil and Elisa arrived at the levels of the farms. They had scrambled down a seemingly endless flight of stairs, away from the chaos unfolding in the domes above. They jumped the stairs more than they ran, flying around corners, aided by the low gravity of Mars.

Phil led the way, running along a narrow corridor until they arrived at his room to monitor the farms.

"What the fuck was that?" she shouted, running behind him.

"What? The shit about us being murderers, or the stream being cut and this group taking over the city?" He looked at her, with his eyebrows almost touching again, visibly concerned as he fumbled with his terminal to unlock the door.

"The last part. What the fuck was that? Where did that come from?"

Once inside, they locked the door and removed the access rights, so nobody could open it from the outside.

When the stream was cut and *The Mars Collective* announced themselves, they had used the ensuing confusion to get out and run.

Elisa looked around, taking in the room. To her

right was a desk with an array of six screens screwed to the wall, a keyboard and a track pad. Two worn out swivel chairs were standing under the desk, the lining crumbling out of the armrests, the printed mesh of the back rests broken on every other layer. On the opposite side of the room was a couch converted into a bed with a pair of augmented reality glasses hanging on the wall above it. A small table stood in front of the couch with a chess set in grey and green colours and a stack of lunch trays piling up next to it. Leaning on the trays was a tower of plates and cutlery, dangerously close to falling over. The space along the wall between the bed and desk was a laboratory. The entire length was filled with two long tables set against a wall of shelves loaded with microscopes, tiny centrifuges, things that looked like miniature ovens and fridges. Everything was framed with beakers, flasks, cylinders and bottles filled with liquids ranging from transparent to brown, hiding their contents. Most of the labels were too washed-out or too small to read from her position. Another door led out this mess of a room from the opposite corner, a green glow shining through its window.

Phil ran around the room, his hands grabbing the curly hair on his head, words pouring out of his mouth.

"They could switch off the ventilation from the outside, but this is connected to the ventilation of the farms, so we still have air to breathe. They would have to switch off the electricity of the entire farm to cut us off, so we should have some time for negotiation first." He continued to look around the room, hiding his face between his elbows.

Elisa ignored him and walked over to the desk with the monitors to her right, pulled out a chair, then fell into it, making it creak under the sudden increase of her weight. She rubbed her forehead, then her eyes, and replied, to Phil's train of thought.

"They must have been watching us all the time."

"But how?"

Phil asked, the words shooting out of his mouth.

"Cameras. They must have a secondary system on the vehicles, that recorded or transmitted everything. Everything we did and said. Those videos were not part of our report."

"But why frame us?"

"I don't know! But, if they were watching us during the crash, they must have been watching us at the sphere as well." Elisa leaned forward, her left leg rocking up and down. "This is getting more and more fucked up with every day now!" she shouted and felt as if he was making her responsible for their situation. "Fuck, this. Fuck all of this. This place is so fucked!" Elisa looked at the overflowing trashcan and contemplated kicking it.

Phil was still walking aimlessly around the room, repeatedly looking at the door they had come in.

"Should we barricade the door?"

Elisa, looked at him, then at her terminal on her wrist.

"Well, at least we don't have a signal down here."

Then she looked around the room for holes in the wall, well knowing that the cameras would be too tiny to spot, especially among this mess. Immediately, she spun around to inspect the screens. He heart was racing, but not from running two hundred metres of stairs. She looked at the monitors overlooking the tunnel segments, filled with growing arrays of vegetables, panels with algae and tanks with fish. She pointed at the screen and tapped against it.

"Since when do we have strawberries?" she asked with surprise and shook her head.

"Those are still experimental, we send them up to the Gateway for evaluation. I think they are pretty nice."

"For evaluation?" She turned her head to look at Phil, who evaded her eyes.

"Yes." He shied away.

"I really don't have to repeat how sick I am of the mentality here and how this place is fucked, right?" Elisa paused, trying to make eye contact. "But I'm pretty sure whoever is on top of the food chain here is fucking mental. This entire company is run by psychopaths. Yes, you fucking motherfuckers, if you can hear this, I'm talking to you pricks!" she shouted at the monitors and checked each screen, then turned around to Phil and pointed at the keyboard.

"May I?"

He nodded.

Elisa opened up a console and her fingers drummed away, repeatedly hitting the enter key.

After half a minute of text scrolling up the screen, she turned back to Phil.

"This is nuts! The entire network is down, it's gone. No ping. They weren't joking. Nothing, it's entirely unplugged." She finally caught his gaze. "So this is how they are going to take over? Lucky we didn't use the elevators to get down here."

She checked the console again, columns of text now refreshing every second on the screen.

"Still nothing." She sounded confused.

By now she had caught her breath and got up again, and joined Phil, to start walking around the room, talking to herself.

"I don't get this place, they get special treatments, frame us for the crash, and then they get their asses kicked by a random group?"

Elisa combed the last days in her head. The cancelled flight, the spheres landing in a regular pattern on both Earth and Mars at the same time. Their first contact, of whatever it was that turned their sphere from grey to glowing and then black. Them driving back for hours, arriving on time for the presentation.

"If this is a *shit is going to hit the fan* thing, we are just an element of confusion, to occupy whoever needs this." She rubbed her face to get rid of the itchy sweat prickling on her forehead, she smelled her armpits revealing two days of physical effort and not showering.

Phil stood in her path, to catch her attention.

"What if we stopped Mars from disappearing?"

His idea made her feel uneasy, reminding her that Earth was apparently gone. She felt betrayed by the universe.

"Do you think this is possible? Just the part about Earth disappearing? Seriously?"

Phil, shrugged and sat down on his bed.

"If our interaction stopped us from disappearing like Earth, we might have saved this entire planet! And no one will know!"

She felt helplessness and sadness overwhelm her.

"Either way, this is too much. I don't care. The only thing I know for sure is I'm not getting away from this fucking planet any time soon." She shook her head, and sat back down into the worn out desk chair. Her mind was chaos and her stomach made its own. She felt her mouth water and build up saliva, swallowing it down instinctively. Without warning, she turned away from Phil, spun around and found the trashcan in time to decorate the overflowing trash with vomit.

◆ ◆ ◆

Half an hour later, her stomach seemed to be coming to its senses. Phil did his best to take care of her, handed her rough plastic towels to clean her face and some water to clear her throat. Tears had dried on her cheeks, and the acidic taste was still lingering in her mouth and nose. Elisa felt the mess of this room creeping onto her, like a symbol of what her life had become.

She looked around, pointed at the laboratory tables.

"I've noticed a bit how paranoid you are, but how do you live in this room, next to your experiments? Isn't this something that would never have been possible on Earth? Or is this why you like it down here so much?"

Phil looked hurt, his eyes jumping between her, his laboratory equipment and his makeshift bed.

"Might be true." He shrugged. "I can give you a guided tour if you want to get your mind away from things. Maybe it's the last thing we will see, I don't know. I haven't been here for more than a day, and I kind of want to check how things are going."

"Want to check or have to check?" She looked at him, and felt sorry for not having the capacity anymore to be nice.

He groaned and forced himself to smile.

"Maybe both?"

"Well, what the hell, let's go, might be better to not be here if someone comes looking through that window." She pointed at the door they had locked a short while ago.

Phil got up and opened the door to the experimental section of the farm and Elisa followed him inside.

Walking through the tunnel, she noticed how Phil was suddenly in his element, telling her everything about how he had set it up and where and how he still saw room for improvements. He told her about his findings and that without the limitations through laws on Earth he could finally progress with his work as he wanted, undisturbed for decades. She listened to his lecture, while inspecting the green glowing algae trays.

"Think about it. Mars is the perfect place to research GMO. If anything escapes, what should happen? It's not going to piss off any neighbouring farmers, is it? It's not going to escape from one of these tunnels anyways. And in addition to that, there are no regulations here, I have no limitations here. I can push into the necessary directions. I don't get to look for life on Mars, but this is special."

She watched him fumble with a set of valves.

"But are you doing this all on your own? Science is nothing that is done by anyone alone. Don't get me wrong, but all this output for a single person is insane!" She saw his eyes brighten at her question.

"Exactly! You are right. You are absolutely right. Most of the science is still done on Earth, the big brains, if you want to call it that way, are still there, back on Earth. I'm just their safe and secure test tube that can't be blocked by protesters, harassed on the way to work, and so on. They can theoretically write about their ideas in papers and I can pick and choose which ideas or DNA sequences I want to follow for my next experiment. It's not a problem to *think* about these things on Earth. You can propose an experiment, but you cannot do it. But we, or rather I, can see how it suits us on Mars, and select the most promising ideas. Although pursuing science is not a current goal on Mars, I realised this is the most scientific work I could find for myself here. And I've made some connections to management this way. Maybe they figured out to get some extra funding this way. I don't know. Either way, we had to push the farms to their limits to be able to sustain life, our life here on Mars. And it goes hand in hand with the limitations put on GMO on Earth. The only thing limiting my work is that the current output of semiconductors is still too low. I need more LED lights for example to let things grow."

In the meantime they had moved on to the next section of the farm and Phil pointed at one of the glowing panels walled in between rows of single tomatoes growing out of tiny boxes.

"It doesn't matter if the growth is a little bit slower, if we can scale up space and light utilisation this way." His hands waved up and down the gradient of plants growing into ripe fruit.

Elisa's thoughts trailed off. She thought about the beginning of colonisation on Mars. The private sector had advanced much quicker than anticipated to build and scale up the size and number of rockets that were required for going to Mars. First they built launch facilities on top of super tankers, avoiding the impact of rules and regulations, and to increase the number of launches per day. Then, they began moving the launch platforms across the world, offering travel times of half an hour to literally jump around the globe, between wherever they had stationed their floating space ports. The next step was the construction of *The Gateway to Mars*, a space station twice the size of *The Gateway to Earth*. Most of the station was dedicated to a seven star hotel called *The Beyond Earth*. Meeting rooms, private dining halls, massage parlours, saunas and everything the rich and elite could wish for while vacating in space. Selling the *Beyond Experience* to those who could afford it: lottery winners wasting their millions for a one-week stay, the ultra-rich and famous enjoying their repeated visits, industry bribing politicians or hosting the G24 meetings on a truly neutral ground as they had called it. A safe place, out of reach from protesters and any security concerns. Being launched into the sky sitting on two pressurised explosives, if mixed the right way, quickly had become the norm. Elisa thought that if she had the chance to tell anyone from the early days of human flight at the beginning of the twentieth century that humans would soon be flying four hundred people in an airplane weighing more than a quarter million kilograms from continent to continent, they would most likely answer it was impossible. The same way commercial passenger planes had been accepted as the new normal not even a hundred years later, commercial space flight did suddenly become accepted as the new normal, even less than half a century later.

After the initial waves of astronauts had successfully arrived on Mars, the following investments and resulting capacity that had been built to send more payloads to Mars out-scaled any national and international programmes that could come up with a plan to oversee this undertaking. The company in charge of the launch capabilities soon partnered with other private endeavours, providing drilling equipment, radiation proof shielding, transportation and finally a nuclear reactor to provide a source of energy. In the end they all merged into the Interplanetary Corporation, free from any national or international rules, technically operating from Mars.

Elisa fixed her attention back to Phil again, studying him in his own world, walking through his work, lecturing her about it.

"-you look at it, it's all necessary to make sure we don't starve here. The risks are higher, so we need to be ahead of the game. The rules are different in this case."

"Impressive work." She hadn't listened, and found something easy to say. At least it was not a lie, she thought, and it was free of her opinion. She looked him up and down.

They moved on to the next section, Phil let her enter first, to give her a better first impression. She looked at a small section of strawberries growing among peaches and plums. Not a single tree or plant was visible, just a tiny twig producing a single fruit, cradled within a couple of leaves reaching around it, in every little cell.

Phil went on with explaining his work.

"If you think of the benefits, of the progress we have made here on Mars and the possible applications back on Earth, the number of communities we can support by plants adapted to harsh environments–"

"When are we going to get the strawberries on our menu on Mars then?" Elisa interrupted him and pointed at the fruit, she could smell them from a few metres away.

"Well–" Phil was visibly searching for words. "–they haven't been cleared for production. The priority is on more nutritious foods at the moment."

"And what is happening with these once they are harvested?"

"I send them up to the Gateway."

"Isn't this a lot of strawberries for testing? I bet they are happily munching away, overlooking us how we work our asses off in this anthill, right?"

"More or less." He looked abashed.

"More or less? Do you even know who eats these? Just in case if something goes wrong?"

She laughed in his face, waiting for his reaction. When she saw there was none, she picked a strawberry and bit into it. The sweet taste caught her by surprise, she hadn't had anything like it in a long time.

"Usually the top management, the guy from the stream earlier. And the head of marketing." Phil was hesitant.

Elisa stopped for a second, stumped by his words. She had a suspicion, and continued digging with more questions. "Head of Marketing, you said. Who's that?"

She picked another strawberry.

"Prof. Iris Rens."

"She does take everything she can get here, doesn't she?"

Phil looked surprised, but she ignored him.

They finished their tour through the experiments and Elisa made sure to thank Phil for his generosity, to let him feel valued for his work. If Earth was truly gone, she had to play her cards right, even if she disagreed with him on his approach. But deep inside, she knew that without the experimental farms they were likely to starve on Mars. Elisa thought he could consider himself lucky if he was eventually working on something that mattered to him, even if he was yet another mind that had worked himself into a niche.

XIV (ELISA)

When they arrived back inside the lab, Elisa was surprised by a face with two red stripes that suddenly appeared behind the window of the entrance door.. Elisa jumped, watching the woman frantically wave at them to come closer.

"Pause?" Phil sounded surprised and briefly exchanged looks with Elisa.

Hesitantly they moved closer to the door, to hear what the woman was trying to say. Her muffled shouts came through the heavy metal door.

"- me in! - one here. The - video - bullshit!"

Elisa waited. She didn't know this woman, and had nothing to do with her.

"Let me - - see this!"

She watched Pause hold up her terminal to the tiny window. Through the thick, dirty glass, they both watched the screen. A short video was running in a loop. It was a screen grab showing a local streamer, dressed in a grey overall standing in front of the cafeteria glass windows talking to the camera. In the backdrop, behind the streamer, Elisa could make out the thin strips of light from the other domes. They watched the video loop over and over, but didn't get what the woman on the other side tried to say.

"– closer, – the sky!"

Phil made space to let Elisa move in front of him to get a closer look at the screen. She caught the video start from the beginning and spotted the milky way as well as the moon Phobos hanging above the black shadows of the Martian landscape. After a few seconds, the sky turned black, the outline of the domes against the stars vanishing in darkness. Everything behind the window disappeared but for the lights shining from the other domes. Elisa stepped back and shouted back through the door.

"What is this? What's happening?"

She watched the video once more, then moved aside to let Phil take a look as well.

"– sky, – stars, – sun. Every – gone!"

Elisa heard Phil whisper to himself, shaking his head.

"This is crazy!"

The terminal disappeared and was replaced with the face with the red tattoos again, this time visibly upset.

"– the door, you have – this!"

"What about the bullshit about us?" Elisa shouted back at her.

"No one – cares any – almost – freaking – now – Earth – now –"

The woman pulled up her terminal in front of the window again. This time with a different video: People were running around inside a dome, stewards in uniforms shouting and getting into fights, chairs flying, a food tray gliding through the air like an overpowered frisbee hitting someone in the head, sending them tumbling to the ground. More people were seen throwing fists and others running away.

Elisa decided she had enough of shouting through the door and waved at Phil to unlock the door. As soon as it slid open the other woman seemed visibly relieved.

"Finally! Thank you! I have waited here for ages. No one gives a crap about you."

Phil stepped aside to let her enter and immediately closed the door behind her.

"What happened to the stars in the first video?" Elisa looked at Pause, getting straight to the point. Phil nodded his head in agreement to her question. He looked worried.

Pause turned around to them, held up her terminal, looping the first video again.

"Here, look at the video! There isn't a star in the sky anymore. Nothing!" Her voice was shrill. "You've been silent all the way back, no message from you, really? And you've been hiding here inside. Has this got anything to do with you guys?" Her face screwed up with her question, looking from Elisa to Phil and back.

Elisa felt her stomach complain again. Luckily for her, Phil took over with asking questions.

"What's happening in the city? What about the Mars collective?"

"They cut the communication with the station.

XIV (ELISA)

Did you even see that? First thing they told us was to go back to our quarters and wait for further instructions. Then the local network was shut off and the stewards tried to control the situation. People panicked. This group is somehow organised and pulled up a new network. It's still peer to peer right now." Pause handed her terminal to Phil. "But this is for real. I saw the sky disappear with my own fucking eyes. I grabbed the video from the network while looking for you."

Elisa mustered the other woman. Only now did she take in that Pause towered almost a head taller than Elisa, even taller than Phil. Elisa caught herself staring back at the dark hair, bangs, dark eyebrows and the two red stripes tattooed from her cheekbones, past the corners of her mouth, down her throat, disappearing under her thick, black hoodie, the glowing terminal in her hand. She reckoned her to be at least ten years younger than her. Pause's pants were functional, she was wearing grey cargo pants, being dressed like almost everyone on Mars. Elisa had often thought that the only thing missing from everyone's clothing on Mars was the colour orange.

Pause stepped aside and pointed at the corridor behind her.

"No one is looking for you, trust me. When did you get back? Did you see the stream? What happened when you were out there? Are you okay?" Pause turned around, looking disgusted. "And what is that smell?"

Elisa had forgotten about the stench of her vomit which was drying in the overflowing trashcan standing next to them.

They moved into the middle of the room, with all of them standing around the stack of dirty lunch trays on the small table. Phil explained how they got back, after staring at the sphere for a night, but without any results. Elisa nodded along, keeping up her part of their made-up story regarding the sphere. He described how the crash had unfolded in reality and that they had nothing to do with it, other than being lucky enough to survive it, while presenting his bruised face and cracked lip.

Elisa looked at the room around her. A shiver went down her back and down her arms, as if she could feel darkness enclosing Mars and the city, reminding her how deep she was under ground. The walls, the stench and the chaos inside the room overwhelmed her. She looked at the other two, then turned away from them, shook herself and walked towards the exit.

"I'm sorry. I have to go. Upstairs. Out. I need to get out."

Elisa unlocked the door and stumbled into the corridor. Without looking back she walked off, leaving Phil and Reina behind. At the first stairs, she stopped and briefly looked back to see the other woman catch up with her. Without hesitating Elisa started her ascent.

"Here, let me help you get up. I'm Reina, sorry, I never introduced myself. Dr. Scruffy calls me Red or

Pause." Reina pointed at her tattoos, then smiled and stuck out her hand.

Elisa wedged her gloves under one arm and used the other to accept her handshake.

"Elisa."

"Nice to meet you!" Reina smiled.

They ascended the stairs without further talking. Elisa was tired, and the way up was tedious, even with the lower gravity of Mars.

Elisa wanted to be alone, but remembering how Phil had panicked next to the sphere, she appreciated not having to walk up the endless stairs and through the tunnels on her own.

◆◆◆

Once they reached the level of the domes, Reina broke the silence.

"Do I know you from somewhere?" Reina was out of breath, like Elisa who, surprised by her question, snapped back.

"Maybe from Mars' most wanted?"

"No. Not that bullshit. But I swear I've seen you before!" Reina shrugged, walking next to her, along the tunnel. "Never mind, my mistake. Don't worry."

Elisa shrugged and caught herself staring at her tattoos again, wondering where the lines stopped.

Walking towards the closest cafeteria, they passed through empty, grey tunnels. Occasionally, there were people rushing past them, packed with pillows, bags, alcohol, food or whatever they could grab, avoiding them as they passed. Everyone had only eyes for themselves or at most for Reina. As they walked through intersections, they triggered loud speakers announcing that everyone had to go to their accommodations and remain there for the night, unless required for essential maintenance.

The bar in the cafeteria was empty and raided, the lights had been left on and the big screens on the ceiling showed a single static message: *Remain in your dorms. The new network will be back up in the morning. Mars has been freed from the Interplanetary Corporation.*

"At least it's not running all the lies for a change!" Elisa nodded at the screens above.

"Well, I'm not sure how they are going to convince anyone, especially with this darkness going on outside." Reina looked sceptically at the canvas above her.

Elisa darted to the windows to look outside and found Reina's video was right: the stars, the universe were gone. Elisa was practically looking at nothing. The darkest night she had ever seen with her own eyes. Ever. She shielded her eyes against the glass with her hands, trying to cancel out any reflections from inside. She saw the slim glow of lights from the other domes a few hundred metres away from her. Like lights pointing at nothing, illuminating the fine dust and regolith. Everything else was pitch black. Nothing she could focus her eyes on.

Elisa shook her head, and looked again, blinking, trying to see anything. All she could see was that there was nothing to see but absolute darkness.

XIV (ELISA)

"Oh fuck, this is just like –" She began to say, then remembered her agreement with Phil, her breath fogging against the cold glass.

"This is like what?" She heard Reina behind her.

"Madness. This is madness." She lied. "I need to get my stuff, I left it in the cafeteria in the north."

They rushed through the tunnels, towards the dome where she had left her luggage earlier that evening and found it in the same place, untouched. Elisa grabbed her bags and turned to Reina.

"Thank you. I'll be going on my own now. I still have access to one of the luxury apartments for a few days. I'll stay there, just to see how this turns out. Also I can keep an eye on what's happening outside from there. They can't let us starve here, and whoever is trying to run this place right now can't let us starve either. So we will be in touch tomorrow at breakfast? Could you bring Phil his stuff?"

Elisa watched how Reina looked her up and down, then stepped back.

"What? What's wrong?" Elisa was confused.

"Oh, now I know where I've seen you before!" Reina's face lit up, visibly happy to finally remember.

"And that is?" Elisa grew impatient, she wanted to go and be on her own.

"The apartment, that's it!" Reina held her mouth, then continued to explain, "Okay, this will be a bit awkward."

"How can this be more awkward than the sky turning dark and someone trying to take over Mars?" She was impatient and felt the other woman was beginning to piss her off.

"I mean awkward for you. Let me explain: I've been in contact with my really fucking long distance girlfriend back on Earth until the day before yesterday, okay?" Reina grabbed her terminal from a knee pocket and scrolled around until she found what she was looking for. "She asked me if I had already had any of, let me quote her: this hot ass on Mars yet?" She held the terminal in front of Elisa's face.

It was a private message, the attachment was open, playing a loop of Elisa getting out of bed wearing nothing but a thong, entering the bathroom in the apartment she had just mentioned. She watched herself drinking coffee while looking out of the conservatory. Elisa raised her eyebrows in disgust and shook her head. She dropped her bags to the floor and grabbed the terminal to watch the clip again.

"No fucking way. What is this?" The clip was a slap in her face.

"I'm sorry. I'm really sorry. It's an advertisement they are running on Earth." Reina was apologising, trying to get her terminal back, but Elisa stepped away, staring at the video. She then turned away, evading Reina's attempts get back her device.

"That's not even my ass. They even died my hair! What the fuck?" Elisa fetched a lock of hair from the side of her head to the front, looked at her grey strands and compared them with the video on the screen.

"They modified my ass and coloured my hair. I don't even have a thong. Those fuckers." Elisa was speechless. She remembered the morning, how Iris had suddenly left her behind. The same anger she had felt that morning struck her again. She felt used. Used as an advertisement that was quietly sent back to earth, without her consent. She remembered in time she was not holding her own terminal and stopped herself from slamming it onto the floor. Instead she screamed at Reina.

"Well you think you're going to end up on a science magazine when you accept all the terms and conditions and write off the rights to your own picture to this fucking company. Instead, you get this shit!"

Elisa felt her arms tense, her legs painfully cramping up as if trying to run away and stay in place at the same time. She was aware of her breathing, her palms sweating. She remembered the satisfaction she had felt throwing the coffee cups. She handed the device back to Reina, grinding her teeth, looking for something to destroy. She grabbed the nearest tray and flung it away. Screaming, she watched it spin, rising up under the dome until it hit the wall and got stuck in the insulation.

Her eyes jumped from side to side, out of focus, ignoring the tall woman in front of her. She was still screaming.

"This place doesn't fucking stop! It doesn't stop!" Elisa slumped on the floor. Leaning against the green concrete wall, she cried.

Reina knelt down in front of her, first without saying a word. Eventually, she broke the silence.

"Hey, Elisa. You can stay at my place, until things calm down, okay?"

Elisa looked up at the face with the red stripes.

"Calm down? I'm going to stay calm. I'm going to stay real fucking calm right now. But that Iris bitch is done." She was furious. "Send me the file!"

XV (GÉRÔME)

Earth was a spinning under The Gateway to Mars, engulfed in darkness, four hundred kilometres below. The lights of populated areas lit up the land, tracing the outlines of the coast in a golden glow. On a usual day one would see the sun's glow in the atmosphere within minutes after passing through earth's shadow. Now, this beautiful event failed to appear, due to the blackout. For three days the planet below the station was drowned in what already felt like a depressing, eternal night.

Gérôme looked at the glow behind the glass pane separating him from the starless vacuum while sitting in a barber's chair. At the same time he could see his tired reflection, his body covered under a black chair cloth. His head was daubed with shaving cream in a semi-circle from ear to ear. Dark rings were under his eyes from sleepless nights. If he had ever had the impression the job as a hotel manager in space was exhausting, the previous days and nights had been worse by a magnitude.

The barber had just finished shaving the grey stubble from his face and moved on to shaving his receding hairline.

"How are you doing, Jonas?" he asked him, now

that he could move his face again. "Is there anything I can do for you?"

The barber, at most a third of his age, had been unusually quiet so far.

"I'm OK, I think." The young man paused, moving the blade across Gérôme's scalp, wiping it off on a towel. "I'm scared, to be honest. I'm scared."

Gérôme felt the sharp knife on the back of his head again, he wondered how the younger man could see anything in this dim light. He'd agreed with his technical staff that all energy and resources should be conserved as much as possible, to survive, as long as possible.

Gérôme continued the conversation.

"I think we all are. I'm scared, too. I'd be lying if I said otherwise."

He watched the glowing clouds hanging over cities, diffusing the light. Plumes of smoke from fires big enough to be seen from space. Not wild fires, but burning within cities. In the past hours, he had noticed that the lights started to go out in some parts of the cities and sometimes entire regions disappeared into darkness. Ground control had switched over to running on generators two days before, working with contractors to ensure a resupply of fuel. The last time they had heard from them was half a day ago. The global network of communication satellites had turned silent after two days, to ensure essential operation and remain operable in orbit. Everything orbiting Earth was designed to regularly pass around the bright side of the planet at least once a day to recharge the backup batteries, designed for operations during eclipses and to provide sufficient energy during peak loads. Nothing was designed to be running on batteries for more than a few days. Noone had ever thought of the sun going out.

Gérôme did his best to keep up the smalltalk.

"But as long as we keep going, we will get through this." He didn't like how his words came out and tried to sound more upbeat.

"I'm sure, if it was these alien orbs that put us in this dark place, they will get us out of it again. I'm sure." He still disliked his words.

With every day, he found it harder to be optimistic. People looked more desolate every hour. He made his rounds, determined to look after everyone. He wanted them to see that someone was at least trying to look out for them. He didn't care if he hadn't shaved in days, noone would have been aware of this. He wanted people to feel needed, to have a purpose and not sit in the dark, alone, staring at the void or civilisation crumbling below.

"How many more old geezers do you have to shave today?" he asked Jonas, trying to focus his mind on work.

"You are the only old geezer up here." Jonas laughed, much to Gérôme's delight.

He closed his eyes as he felt the finishing moves around his head, the moist towel cleaning away the remaining shaving cream. Once the barber was done, he focused on the reflection of the young man, waiting for him to remove the chair cloth.

Gérôme got up and straightened his tailor-made suit. He patted Jonas on the shoulder, thanked him and helped him clean up the barber shop. Eventually, he began his daily routine walk around the station, a five and a half kilometre walk along the outer ring. Most sections were empty. After the sun and stars had disappeared, it had taken less than an hour for the first guests on the station to request to be sent back down to Earth, and Gérôme was glad to let everyone depart who wanted to. The fewer people there were on the station, the easier it would be to manage and maintain it, give them more time to survive. Because now, they were stuck on the station. All the orbital shuttles had returned to the ground and with the communication satellites powered down for hibernation, it was impossible to contact any of the ground crews and ask them to pick them up. This meant about one hundred people remained on the station, half of them hotel staff, a quarter tourists, and the remaining quarter the operating crew preparing the departures to Mars.

Gérôme appreciated the joggers, who used the empty station for running in circles, breathing in a brief moment of life into the corridors while running past him. With his sixty-seven years, he wasn't going to pick up jogging, but he enjoyed his daily walk around the station, to stay active.

As he arrived inside the empty lobby of the hotel, he walked towards the counter, aiming for the old, brass call bell, the only thing resting on top of the three metre long marble surface. Gérôme imagined how the heavy counter top had been created on earth, riding into the sky on top of a heavy launcher, to be weightlessly transported through the station and installed, only to feel its real weight again, when the space station was spun up to one rotation per minute.

He slapped his hand on the call bell and listened to the ding fading in the empty foyer, then looked up at the sign behind the counter, which originally read *The Beyond Earth.* Someone had crossed out Earth and written *Darkness* in black paint underneath it. When this vandalism was presented to him, to decide what to do with it, he requested it to remain in place. He told his employees, that he agreed with whoever had altered the sign, because he also thought that beyond darkness there would be light, that they maybe just had to believe that this unknown, unchangeable darkness would be over soon. At the same time he thought it had to be very soon, as life on the station depended on Earth.

His walk lead him into the dining hall, a long, curved section which occupied the entire upper half of the ring, providing the full height of the radius to it. Glinting chandeliers hung from the ceiling, high above, now switched off to conserve energy. Only the glow from the emergency lights came from thin lines going across the ceiling, framing him in the darkness, inside a glowing cage. He looked across the hall. The best seats for dining were the ones directly in front of the long, tall windows, providing the opportunity to wine and dine with the planet directly rolling past the table, or if seated on the other side of the hall, to look at the stars and if the time was right, the moon. The windows would automatically dim as they passed in front of the sun, turning on their displays to simulate the stars hidden by the sun's glare.

The restaurant was divided in half. In the middle, on the side towards the stars outside, was a bar, and opposite it, on the earthbound side, was a narrow stage. The two were separated by a dance floor with parquet flooring.

As Gérôme walked past the tables, he remembered the events he had attended in the past. There had been weddings, business dinners and private parties. Tons of alcohol had to be launched with each supply vessel, destined for these events. He walked up to the bar, slid behind the counter and studied the selection of bottles. After squinting at the labels in the dim light, he chose an American bourbon whiskey from Kentucky and poured it into his glass. He drank it in a single sip. It tasted faintly sweet, and the after taste lingered in his mouth. He used the same cloth which he had used in the past two days to clean his glass and placed the bottle back onto the shelf.

He continued to walk along the tables to the windows on the side looking away from Earth. Even when he shielded his eyes with his hands pressed against the glass he couldn't see a single thing. Nothing. Not even a glimpse of light but the artefacts and noise from his own eyes. He was convinced it had something to do with the alien spheres landing on earth, spawning in an orbit above the station. The sheer number, their appearance out of nowhere, the symmetric distribution were proof enough for him. He took a step back from the glass, staring at his dim reflection, studying his suit. He looked upon the mirror image of the faintly glowing cities on Earth visible on the other side, rotating around him in the background. Gérôme felt tired and scared. He wasn't sure if anything he did still made sense. He didn't know if staying on the station had been the right choice, if they should have all cramped inside the last vessels, while hoping to avoid any injuries while landing. When he had asked his staff why they didn't request to return to Earth, they replied, that the thought had simply never occurred to them, that their job was to maintain the station. But now, he asked himself if that was because of their feeling of obligation to work or because of their loyalty to the hotel or station. As there was no choice left now to go back or not, he didn't see the point of asking to find out. He felt bad for all the young people stuck with him, working away from their families, unlike him, living with his wife at an altitude of four hundred kilometres. And as they had no kids, they were lucky not to have to worry about someone close, left behind on the Planet. They agreed, it was a blessing. But still, Gérôme felt responsible for so many on the station.

He continued his walk towards the next section,

leaving behind the bar and the second half of the dining hall. Like the dimmed lights, the heating had been regulated down to conserve energy almost everywhere on the station and he felt his fingers getting cold. He put his hands into his pockets to keep them warm, cursing the simplistic programming that only the entire station could be regulated at the same time.

It was the cold that made him turn around and walk back to the bar, grab two bottles of whiskey, and put them into the pockets of his suit, with an additional two bottles of gin for his wife.

◆ ◆ ◆

When he arrived back at his apartment, he was drunk. Stumbling through the door, he put the bottles down on a sideboard next to a group of small asteroids presented on glass trays, almost dropping them in the process.

His wife was already in bed, waiting for him, reading a book on a glowing screen. Gérôme changed into his pyjamas, dropped his suit in a chair and crawled into bed.

"I need to sleep. I love you." He mumbled his last words into the pillow before he fell asleep, snoring.

XVI (GÉRÔME)

The next day a fresh pair of socks, underpants and undershirt were neatly stacked on the chair where he had dropped his suit the night before. The suit itself was hanging inside the open closet behind the chair. He washed himself, got dressed, then left the bedroom to meet his wife in her studio. The bottles had disappeared from the counter in the hallway, and the small set of asteroids set back to their original presentation.

His wife was already up, painting the station above the dark Earth with acrylic paints on a canvas. A bright column of white paint shot diagonally across the picture, dividing it in half. She put down the paint brush and turned around to greet him.

"Good morning darling, could you get some sleep tonight?"

"Yes, the whiskey helped." he said as he thought about the bourbon, searching the room for his bottles, but couldn't see them. He turned back to his wife and caught her looking at him, up and down, and he returned her smile. She got up from her stool, embraced him, then shared her thoughts with him.

"Darling, before we go to meet the others for breakfast, here is what I think should happen today:

We will shut down most of the station and move everyone into the smallest number of segments possible. Make everyone clean out the bars, move everything into a single place. Those from the inner circle will move into the outer section, this way we can shut down the inner ring entirely. Maybe the living quarters next to the kitchens is the best choice. We will have infrastructure, and a place to sleep. We will have to check with IT that they find a way to rewrite the power management to allow us to run on single sections only. It will give people something to do. And if anyone wants to get drunk to get a good night of sleep, I don't want them wandering through an empty station for hours."

Gérôme felt the concern in her voice, especially during her last comment. Her words made an awful lot of sense to him and he slowly nodded in agreement, appreciating her support. He hugged her in return and thanked her.

They entered the staff's break room, Gérôme following his wife. Staff and guests were entering and leaving through further entrances on either side, with trays filled with omelette on toast, orange juice and coffee. People sat in small groups around two long rows of tables filling the lengthy room. Gérôme and his wife waited for their breakfast to appear from a chute in the wall, took their trays and sat down among a group of their staff.

The atmosphere in the room was quiet and depressing. Gérôme tried his best to initiate smalltalk with senior staff members among their group and listened to their thoughts. They voiced their concerns about how long they had to remain on the station and how long they could stay. There was still no radio contact with Earth and the darkness outside remained unchanged. When it came to the topic to organise the staff meeting Gérôme changed his routine. He got up from his chair and addressed the room.

"We will have the staff meeting now and here, and anyone who wants to listen can join."

He looked around at the young faces listening to him. Apart from his wife he was the oldest there, by far. He took a sip from his coffee and continued his speech.

"We don't know how long we will be up here. And we don't know what is happening down on Earth. But keep in mind: noone is alone here on this station, and noone has to go through this on their own."

People who had just left the break room, were coming back inside to listen.

Gérôme used his own words to repeat what his wife had said to him just minutes before. Then, he let his staff take over the discussion, falling back into his preferred role as an advisor. His principle was to provide the grounds for ideas and let his staff make the decisions and let them take over the planning. He sat back down, thanked his wife and rubbed his head not knowing if his headache came from the past night's booze or lack of sleep. He continued his breakfast in silence, watching his team unfold into action.

Within minutes, suggestions were piling up, ideas of what could be done. They defined the first steps that had to be made, which operations would have to move sections and what was required to allow them to move everyone into a single section. The break room would be the new control room, open to everyone and the living quarters re-distributed directly around it.

Watching them organise, Gérôme felt as if they were planning a sleepover, or setting up a camp, but in space instead of their neighbour's house. He liked the idea of keeping everyone busy with their own plans, and let everyone participate. The last thing he wanted to do was to command people around in these desolate times, when everything was engulfed with darkness.

After he had finished his breakfast, Gérôme stood up again, faced the people around him and raised his hand to speak.

"Please make sure not to leave any of the drinks and snacks in the restaurants and bars, especially not the minibars. We should think about rationing them, and how to do that, but let's get to that later. We should be fair and share it all. Everything is now on the house. And if this situation should be over in the next few days-" Gérôme paused to see he had everyone's attention to make his point: "-please make sure to blame it all on me. I will be retiring soon in any case." He was proud to see a few smiles appearing around him. "Oh, and if anyone is missing any whiskey or gin from the bar's inventory, I know where they are." He grinned as he sat back down and his wife gave him a playful smack across the back of his head.

◆ ◆ ◆

The plans of the morning kept everyone busy for the rest of the day. Gérôme's wife returned to their apartment to pack their clothes and move them into a smaller bedroom, above the break room. He himself joined his senior staff overseeing the operation.

He was amazed that many of his employees were still trying to stick to protocols, wanting to fill out the forms for security clearances to be able to access the rooms with the minibars. Especially the two from the IT department were reluctant in transferring the access rights to the entire station to so many others. He listened to their concerns about the existing rules and processes that had been established over the years and that security protocols were in place for a reason. But instead of letting his employees wait and discuss he already knew what kind of language he needed to convince them. When the two IT technicians arrived at the break room and finished setting up their new workplace, he addressed them directly in front of his staff, who were still waiting for their security clearance.

"I'm not sure if I want you to look up from your screens and take a look out the window or if I don't want you to look out the window. I don't want to frighten you, but whatever has been in place here to guarantee the rules and safety of this station does not apply anymore. As we speak, the world is burning, and entire cities are disappearing into darkness. If someone has to be blamed I will make sure it will be me. Until then we have to redefine who we are and how we work up here. If you tell me how to do it, I will do it myself, or I can let you watch me do it myself, searching with two fingers on your keyboard for the right keys to press. I'll make sure to manually click on the submit button with the mouse on every form instead of hitting 'enter'. I'd first start searching how to sign keys on the command line, or-"

Gérôme moved his fists with his index fingers sticking out, slowly typing on an invisible keyboard in front of his body, one finger after the other, to emphasise his point. At the same time he watched their faces. He wasn't sure if the reminder of what was going on outside or the mental torture they were already going through imagining him using their hardware in slow motion had scared them most. He knew noone wanted to be watching the oldest person in the room trying to use a computer. Of course he knew how to use a keyboard without looking and this wasn't the first time he played the card of repeating generational stereotypes of computer illiteracy to his advantage.

Quickly, they agreed and upgraded his employees' keys to root level, to be able to access all segments with no restrictions.

XVI (GÉRÔME)

In the afternoon he briefly looked after Jonas and helped him to move his barbershop. By now, more things than anyone had expected, had to fit into the section they had chosen, and things started to pile up. As a result, they agreed to use the neighbouring sections as a literal cold storage to move tools and equipment to be accessible as close-by as possible.

Until the end of the day the staff room had turned into the busiest place on the station. One wall had been covered in screens showing diagrams and stats of *The Gateway To Mars*. The two guys from IT had set themselves up next to it in the corner. When Gérôme entered the room, they were chatting with the engineers from the Mars support crew, trying to find the easiest way to rewrite the power management system, in order to adjust it to the current situation. Power saving had only been implemented on a global level, and did not allow a single section to switch off all others, again for security reasons. Behind the group, the chute in the wall was busy going up and down delivering biscuits and tea.

There was still a lot to do. So far they had only cleared a third of the station, twenty out of sixty segments. The inner ring was the same size as *The Gateway To Earth*, consisting of sixteen and the outer ring adding another forty-four sections, all originally launched into space like the interplanetary shuttles, sharing their dimension and framework.

Gérôme left the new makeshift control centre and walked past rows of trolleys parked along the hallway, ready to be carted away, to be filled up and returned the next day with more supplies and equipment. He watched as a small group of employees and guests who were still working, pushed away with their trolleys, down both directions of the corridor.

He walked to the section's staircase and descended down to the waiting area, usually an empty space around the hole in the ground leading into the airlock. The walls had been taken out to create an even bigger space and it had been redecorated with cushions and sofas from the private quarters, turning it into something resembling a lounge.

The remaining guests looked excited to consider themselves as part of the staff now, to be able to peak into every room and cabinet they were allowed to, learning about the workings of the station.

Gérôme took the stairs back up, leading up to the kitchens. The waiting area on the next level had been filled with trolleys stacked with hundreds of small glass bottles taken from the minibars, filled with water, soft drinks, beers, wines and liquor. He grabbed a water bottle, drank it and slid the empty bottle inside his jacket.

As he walked into the part of the section that was reorganised for general accommodation, he found his wife in the hallway, talking to a couple, maybe ten years younger than them.

His wife showed him their new room, much smaller than their private suite, no chair to put down clothes, just wide enough to walk around the bed. Additionally, it had no window facing outside.

XVI (GÉRÔME)

A blessing, he thought, not to be reminded of the depressing darkness lingering outside, like an invisible force watching them. The room had a tiny bathroom made from a single piece of plastic embedded in the wall. Their clothes were in a pile on the bed.

He turned to his wife. They hugged and he kissed her on her forehead, embracing her tightly. He thought how she had supported him all these years, had helped him for decades to follow his dream career of owning a hotel some day. That he ended up managing one in space had been more than he had ever imagined and more than he had ever asked for. Even if he knew he would retire within one or two years without having actually owned a hotel until now, they had saved up enough to be able to buy one. At least this had been their plan until a few days ago, before the alien objects landed and the universe disappeared just the day after. His wife had been an engineer, but retired early, to let her creativity flow into her art instead, but he knew she enjoyed consulting him on his job, more than she liked to admit. He couldn't imagine doing his job as a hotel manager in space without her being at his side, and practically they did it together.

Holding her and reflecting on the last days, weeks and years, he knew he had one more thing to do that day. He kissed her again, and excused himself.

"I'll have a few things on my mind that I want to check with my senior staff once more, one last thing I need to do for the day."

Instead of looking for his senior staff, he went

looking for Jonas. He found him, organising his utensils inside a small storage closet at the end of the section. Gérôme waited until Jonas noticed him and asked him for his help.

"Jonas, I could use your help with one last thing today. Would you mind helping me pack up Esra's studio and find a place to put it? I think one trolley won't be enough to pack everything, and I'm not really allowed to wonder off alone in the station anymore."

XVII (GÉRÔME)

Over the course of the next days the mood improved on *The Gateway to Mars*. They were wrapped in darkness for four days. With the changes and reorganisation they were able to maintain a night and day cycle with the days under the fully bright, artificial light of the station. Gérôme had given in to the group pressure to change from wearing a formal suit to sweatpants and a grey hoodie lined with teddy fleece. They had lowered the temperature to conserve energy, and he appreciated to swap his suit for something warmer. To provide every one of the remaining one hundred on the station with sufficient clothing, they had decided to gather the remaining personal items that were left behind under the rule that things of material or technological value were locked away on the inside ring, in the old control centre. Everyone was surprised about the amount of valuables that had been left behind, by those who had left in the first days. Piles of laptops, tablets, terminals, phones and boxes filled with jewellery were now awaiting an unknown fate at a third of Earth's gravity, with temperatures slowly dropping below zero.

On the night of the fourth day, he gathered

everyone around in the repurposed waiting area, to summarise the recent days and sketch out the next. People were sitting in the hallway, on the stairs on both sides of the room and inside islands made of couches and cushions. He stood in the middle of one of the staircases, on the lowest step, a glass of whiskey in one hand. His gaze wondered across the cozy place they had created. He lifted his glass to address those present.

"I'd like to thank all of you for your hard work in the recent days. And I'm looking forward to working with you in the days to come. We are one hundred and seven people here on board *The Beyond Darkness* which means we are using less than one tenth of its capacity. This includes food and power. Of course not all things will be as fresh as we are currently used to, starting presumably tomorrow."

Gérôme looked for his kitchen staff, to meet their eyes, waiting for them to nod in confirmation.

"The kitchen staff has done an incredible job in preserving as much as possible, and our estimate is that we will have enough for eight more weeks."

He looked around, took in the looks and expressions directed at him.

"Speaking of dishes, since four days ago we have adjusted our antennas to aim for the launch stations directly, requesting them to send up shuttles so we can all eventually leave the station and return to Earth. We assume this might already happen in the coming weeks. Unfortunately, we don't know why ground control is not responding, and I personally think it's not helpful to speculate. With an event of this scale it's impossible to tell what they have to deal with on the ground and we should hope for the best."

Gérôme drank from his whiskey.

"I'm impressed how quickly our former guests, now new staff, have picked up the craft of running a hotel. Really. And as soon as things go back to normal, I'd be happy to see your applications."

He returned the smiles he was seeing with his own.

"I'm not going to bullshit you with a 'we are going to be one big family' speech now, and if I have read some of your body language correctly in the recent days, it's better for you to not see yourselves as family members, to be honest. I hope I don't have to explain that starting a family right now might not be the best idea at the moment, but to be honest, that's none of my business."

Chuckles went across the room and some of those who had inched closer on the sofas tried to inconspicuously sit up, while others moved closer into each other's arms.

Gérôme took another sip and went on with his speech, while looking around to see everyone present.

"I'd like to thank you again for your support and respect in recent days, and I'm looking forward to working with you in the days to come."

He raised his glass, then finished his whiskey.

"Either way, Grandpa Joe is going to do the dishes

now. I'd be happy if there's someone who wants to help me."

◆ ◆ ◆

Later, in the kitchen, Gérôme was unloading the dishwasher, pulling the steaming tray of plates and glasses out, rolling it onto a trolley. A young man in his mid-twenties, who had been on a business trip, was babbling on about how he would redesign the station.

"You know the best way to expand the station? First we'd have to put a nuclear reactor running in the centre, like the one they have on Mars. We'd have nearly unlimited power and could add more rings to it. With every ring, we could decrease the angular velocity to have the outermost ring match Earth's gravity and downgrade the innermost rings to maintenance and storage facilities, which don't need full gravity. And then I would add a huge coral reef aquarium to the dining hall, the ultimate evolutionary achievement to bring aquatic life to space, the original source of life lifted into the skies. I'd love to see the expression of a fish looking into space for the first time."

Gérôme was in and out of listening to him. The reason *The Gateway to Mars* was not increased in size was because it was already making more than enough money for the Interplanetary Corporation, which was reinvested one hundred percent into the expansion of Mars. The outermost ring was used to refuel the interplanetary shuttles, and as a space port to let settlers arrive on orbital shuttles to board the interplanetary counterparts. Any changes to the station would have delayed the colony. But instead of speaking out his perspective he kept on nodding to show that he agreed and let him chatter on. He saw no point in telling someone that his ideas were wrong, especially if he saw no chance of them materializing.

He was about to finish stacking another set of warm plates, when one of his senior staff members burst into the kitchen, searching for him, visibly excited.

"Gérôme! Gérôme?"

He spun around, unsure about the reason for the excitement, but relieved to have an excuse to leave a rather one-sided conversation.

"They've sent a shuttle! The cameras picked up the launch."

Gérôme took off his apron and looked at his watch.

"When was the launch?"

"Fifteen minutes ago, about half past eight."

He excused himself and left the other man to finish the remaining dishes on his own.

The two walked out of the kitchen, aimed for the staircase and climbed the steps to the level of the new control centre.

Inside, the Mars engineers were already discussing which dock to prepare for berthing. Main engine cut-off had been confirmed, and the booster had successfully separated and was on its way back to return to the launch pad. The second stage, the shuttle itself, was heading towards the station.

After half an hour they managed to establish a link to the shuttle and the room went quiet, listening for a response over the radio.

"This is Low Earth Orbit Shuttle Romeo Hotel Seven, can you give us a dock number, thank you."

The captain's voice from inside the shuttle came through speakers embedded into the wall of screens. A chubby technician clipped on a headset and responded with instructions to proceed to dock ten, a section bordering the one where they had set up their camp. The technician waited for them to confirm the procedure, and responded with a question.

"Romeo Hotel Seven, how many beds would you like to reserve for the night? We are a hotel after all."

Nods and grins went through the room, a spark of hope lighting up in people's eyes.

"We had to launch with manual overrides. We are thirty-four. We'll explain more when we get there."

The smiles around Gérôme disappeared.

"Confirmed, have a good flight." The technician looked at Gérôme, uncertainty painted across his face, too.

"Thank you." The pilot of the shuttle ended the conversation.

The mood in the room had abruptly changed, everyone started to talk at the same time.

"Why is there so many on the shuttle?"

"Manual override?"

"Aren't two pilots enough to fly a shuttle?"

"Why are they sending up so many?"

Gérôme watched quietly, unsure what to make of the situation.

One and a half hours later the shuttle had successfully docked and the airlock opened.

Gérôme dug his hands into his pockets, trying to keep them warm in the cold segment where they were ready to receive whoever was on the ship. The number of passengers had been much higher than expected. He looked down the ladders going down the shaft, past the second airlock door into the ship. A man, who turned out to be the captain of the shuttle, looked up, waving at them from two metres below.

"Please tell us you have heating up here?" he asked, shivering in the cold air rushing down. His expression was tired and stressed. He helped the first group of ten climb up the ladder, all dressed in black track suits, with dark green backpacks. Gérôme watched them pull themselves up on the platform one by one. He greeted them, in the most friendly way he could, even if he found their outfits irritating.

"Welcome to the station. If you could follow Alex and Lee, they will show you to your rooms. Who are you?"

But instead of responding, they all quietly nodded at him and followed his staff down the corridor. The chubby engineer who had been the radio contact stood next to Gérôme and murmured under his breath.

"Who are these people, they look funny to me."

The next three who appeared at the bottom of the airlock took their time before they climbed up the ladder. For minutes they argued how to unload the luggage. One of them insisted on using the cargo elevator, but then they eventually agreed on two of them climbing up the ladder and passing the luggage along. In the meantime, two of the first arrivals returned to help with the unloading. After lifting the luggage into the waiting area, the three climbed up as well.

Impatiently, Gérôme took his hand from his warm pocket and pointed at the corridor.

"Please be so kind and follow my colleagues to your rooms. Thank you."

But instead of moving down the corridor the new guests drew guns and shouted at them.

"Don't move!"

Gérôme stared down the short barrel of a hand gun pointing at his face, his impatience turned into confusion and anger. His arms and legs tensed and immediately turned into an unusable, quivering mass, making him painfully aware of every cold breath he was taking, tingling in his lungs. He slowly raised his arms in defence.

"What are you doing? This is a hotel and not a war zone, please, put those down." He sounded confused, trying to hide his anger.

The new guests exchanged looks, but didn't respond to his request. They waited some more, gauging the situation, then waved at Gérôme and his team members to move away from the airlock to the side of the waiting area.

One of the new guests in the dark overalls shouted something into the shaft, in a language Gérôme didn't understand. He felt anger overwhelm him, triggered by the sudden hostility towards him and his crew.

"What is this? Who are you?" he began to shout back, just to be ignored by the men in track suits.

A minute later a woman appeared from the shaft, dressed in an orange suit, probably almost as old as Gérôme himself. She joined them on the platform and then walked towards him and his staff, who were still being held at gunpoint. The woman straightened her jacket and began to talk.

"Thank you for letting us board the station. We will be taking over from here. Please don't make this difficult and make sure you and your crew follow our instructions. No one has to get hurt, this all depends on you!"

"You can't do this! Who do you think you are?" Gérôme let his anger out.

"I'm her excellency Nila Chaudhary. And we have nothing to explain to you."

She crossed her arms, her hands holding onto her elbows, her face painted with impatience.

"Would you mind showing me our rooms? I'd like to warm up and have something to eat. Who is in charge of room service here? And as you might have noticed: *We* are in charge now."

The guy pointing a gun at his face moved closer, aiming it right at Gérôme's forehead.

The woman in orange feigned a smile and finished her introduction with a brief 'Thank you'.

Gérôme's stomach tied itself into a knot. Even his body agreed to the disgust he felt for the group standing in front of him. He shouted at the woman,

"I'm the manager here, and I'm responsible. And this is not going to happen!"

He refused to give up, but before he could go on to complain she interrupted him.

"If you refuse we will seal the airlock and undock the ship. If you have counted correctly, we are fourteen and there are still two dozen civilians on the shuttle. And we will make sure that without any pilots they will either starve, burn in the atmosphere or crash. Do you want to be responsible for their fate? It's your choice from now on."

The woman stepped closer and looked him up and down.

"What else do you need to show us to our rooms?"

She asked him without any emotion and scratched her nose without breaking eye contact.

Gérôme was filled with anger, grinding his teeth, clenching his hands into fists, contemplating to punch her in the face. But, before he could give in to his emotions, he was grabbed by one of the woman's entourage and felt a cold barrel pressed against the side of his head. Before he could make up his mind he was pushed forward, and dragged along the corridor.

As they moved through the only heated and inhabited section, more people woke up from the shouting, watching the apparent security guards force their way through the common room. Gérôme could see the surprise and shock among his colleagues. He pleaded them to remain calm and follow their orders, for the sake of their own safety. He was scared. At the same time he hoped his wife was sleeping through this and would not have to see him like this.

Gérôme was pushed into the first empty bedroom they found, soon followed by the captain and the co-pilot. He sat down on the side of the bed, looking at their reflections in the three tall windows that had nothing but darkness behind them, turning them into mirrors. He looked at the captain, then Gérôme rubbed his temple and felt the spot where the gun had been pressed against.

"And there was nothing you could have said to us? Nothing? You just let those idiots take over?" He shouted at the pilot.

Gérôme felt betrayed and disappointed. He waited for a response in silence, his gaze switching between the two reflections standing behind him on the other side of the bed.

His eyes met the glare of the captain looking straight down at him in the reflection. He turned his gaze ahead to stare at his own, avoiding eye contact with the other man.

The tall young man began to talk, with an unmistakable tension in his voice.

"Do you have any idea what we had to go through in the last four days? Do you? All this? It's the end! Those morons pointing guns at you is nothing compared to what is going on down there! Do you want to ask more stupid questions or do you want to pick a point and place where I should begin telling you what *is* actually going on? The point when suddenly day turned into night? Or when people started to panic and looted all the stores, leaving nothing behind."

The pilot made a pause, walked over to him, to stand right next to Gérôme, towering above him. He went on, his tension building into anger, shouting at Gérôme in return.

"Within a day! Within a day, all the stores and shops were empty! There was nothing! Zero! Nothing for families and children. Neighbours killing neighbours, fighting over food and water. Without the sun the power grids collapsed after a day. Nothing is running anymore. People left whatever they were doing. They were going crazy. And I'm not talking about the looting and killing. Have you heard nothing about the religious groups spawning everywhere, believing this is God's work, to punish us for our wrongdoing on *his* planet. Or the part where they go around destroying everything, to complete God's work of punishment? Or those that think there is going to be an alien invasion? Great! Have you seen anything from up here? Have you had to go through any of this? Do you know how cold it is on the surface? It's getting colder every hour, every day, every night. Or whatever this shit is. The temperature is dropping more than ten degrees every fucking day! The temperature has dropped almost thirty degrees already, and it will keep dropping without the sun. Maybe you can tell us from up here what is happening? No? From your comfortable seats in the first row? No? What else do I need to explain to you?"

Gérôme didn't respond.

"Without electricity people have no heating and are freezing in their homes, burning whatever they can find for warmth. Everyone's trying to survive.. It's chaos. It's crazy. So if you have any issues with a pissy president taking over this station, who thinks they can find out themselves what this is about, while you had it nice and warm and enough to fucking eat and drink every day, you might better keep in mind that I'm not going to fucking help you. Anything up here is better than everything on Earth right now. If they want to run the show, let them. Better than anything that happened in the past one hundred fucking hours. And even if we can survive an hour or a day or a week longer up here than down there, we are still going to eventually fucking freeze, starve or kill each other anyway. So what's the fucking point you are trying to make?"

Gérôme moved his head to the side to turn his ear away from the shouting directed at him, watching the captain in the reflection of the windows from the corner of his eye. The tall man dismissively walked away to the back of the room, leaned against the wall with his back and slid down, until he sat on the floor. He crossed his arms on his knees and fixed his eyes at the wall, shaking his head.

"Fucking asshole." were the captain's last words.

Gérôme thought about what the young man had said. His words filled in the blanks of watching the lights go out and smoke rise, and gave him the information of what was happening on Earth. It made him feel uneasy. The world had become an ugly place. He looked through the windows trying to see anything, a glimpse of hope, but saw nothing but the reflection of the tiny room bouncing off the glass.

Gérôme decided to remain quiet and watched as the co-pilot got up and sat down on his side of the bed at a distance.

He turned towards the woman, who looked like she was in her early thirties, with brown hair and brown eyes. She folded her hands into her lap and quietly began to talk.

"The last days have been really tough on everyone and I'm sure it will not get any easier. I'm sure you will understand. You *have* to understand. This is not easy for anyone."

She looked away and paused, her eyes searching the windows. She inhaled and sighed, quietly.

"I have to ask: Do you know what happened to Mars? Is there a way I could send a message?"

XVIII (LUNA)

The journey to *Dol* was a trip of thirteen days, without requiring a launch window. *The Second Blue Marble* was auto-piloting the gravitational slingshot manoeuvres, as Luna watched each planet they accelerated around fly by.

They had been travelling for a week and had found a new topic they both enjoyed to pass the time: Games. It had started with Luna learning and guessing the signals the Dolvar shared among each other in addition to the ones Erial had developed just between the two. At one point she had begun to pantomime and see if they could guess it. Soon their game turned to I spy, and riddles. At one point she was called a 'noob' for the lack of further extremities and chromatophores, to improve her miming. Soon, she suggested to play a game where physiology was not a deciding factor and told Erial about board games she had played before. At first, Luna was moving the pieces for Erial, their voice directing her from behind the glass. But soon Erial decided to put on a breather and join her inside the living room, to test if moving a hand above the board actually did help with thinking about which move to make next, as she suggested.

The day Luna saw Erial for the first time in the flesh was an unforgettable memory. Until then she had only seen the two metre body, with its double rings of tentacles, which added up to a length of 5 metres in total when stretched out, from a safe, comfortable personal distance behind a massive window as a barrier between them.

Erial had reassured her to always move as slowly as possible, and not to touch her at any time. She had agreed to behave with the same caution, but knew inside, that she was no threat to the alien. They both were aware that, no matter what mental relationship they had built so far, would be put to a test when they were confronted with each other in the same space, meeting face to face for the first time, in the same medium.

Luna had been sitting on the couch, not moving, waiting for the water level to sink behind the window, with the alien gently floating behind the glass, stretched out at full length, shimmering silvery purple, her favourite colour. When the water level was as low as the giant squid-like shape would allow to, the window separating them, slid down, joining their two living spaces. Erial had gently asked if they may enter her space, with Luna just nodding, her eyes admiring the process of it, and unable to speak. Slowly, one arm after the other, Erial lifted themselves over the glass wall, gliding into the living room. With a single flowing motion they arrived on the other side of the Chinese Checkers board set up on the table between them. She had watched the alien slowly lift themselves up to their full height, resting on the four big paddled tentacles spread out to the side and folded to the back, leaving two tentacles in the front with two rows of hundreds of tiny fingers waving in unison. All other unused tentacles were folded neatly away behind their body. Luna had just sat there with her mouth open, realising again, as if for the first time, that an extra-terrestrial being was sitting in front of her, allowing her to travel with them.

Now, two days later, Luna sat with Erial in the same place, still playing the same game. The glistening, towering body in front of her, with two black, shiny eyes in the shape of a kidney, twice the size of her fist, looking at her and the board at the same time with two pupils each. The alien's skin was constantly changing, slowly fading between colours and patterns. At first, Erial's eyes had blinked synchronously. But after a day they revealed that this was only for her comfort, and they soon started to blink independently, slowly, from the inside out, with a transparent skin moving across the dark surface and back. When she looked closely, she could see herself and the room reflected in them. Above the eyes were the towering lobes containing the four brains, folded around each other, with the fifth at the centre. Sometimes Erial's skin turned entirely transparent, giving her a glimpse at the brain tissue hidden underneath. This was a skill she could not imagine herself to possess, to be able to look at her own brain in the mirror.

Over the days, Luna was getting used to be dwarfed by Erial, in size and number of arms and legs, absorbed by the game between them. She was surprised the alien didn't have a smell, which Luna couldn't say about herself. She had imagined a fishy scent at least, but there was nothing that her nose could pick up. The first time the alien had sat down with her, Luna's hands and armpits were immediately sweaty with a mix of nervousness, excitement and an unconscious fear.

At the beginning, Erial had only used a single multi-fingered tentacle to manipulate the pieces on the board. Soon, the alien increased the number of tentacles until all eight, fingered arms were hovering above the board, changing places, planning their next move.

When Erial talked, their voice now came from the back of their body, from the breather, a transparent device slotted into and over the chamber that housed their brown, fern-like gills, slowly waving in the contained water, which Luna had inspected on their second day of playing board games, carefully walking around their body, making sure not to stumble over their tentacles.

Erial had been beating her nonstop when playing since they started working with all arms and Luna eventually protested.

"I think we should reduce the number of arms allowed to use to two while thinking. Seriously, I think you have an unfair advantage this way."

"Or maybe we are just better?" Erial responded,

arms still moving around above the pieces, patterns of purple blotches bursting and expanding, racing across their skin, matching the colours of the pieces on the board.

"Not funny!" Luna laughed, and she caught herself wanting to push the mess of tentacles away from the board.

She looked at Erial wondering what the tiny glistening fingers felt like. The alien moved a piece, pushing it across the board and it was her turn to concentrate on her next move again.

With Erial only thinking with two arms, she had a chance again. She won seven out of the next ten matches. It was her turn then and she was staring at the board. Erial, reorganised and stretched their large tentacles under their body and continued their conversation.

"It's interesting what we have in common, that our mental capacity is tied very much to our physiology. For example, if we think of a colour or emotion, we cannot do it without it appearing somewhere on our body. It is as if our emotions appear on our skin first before we even notice it ourselves."

"Hmm." Luna pulled on her lip, then moved a piece with a single hop and decided to join the conversation. "I have a different example. When I try to sing a note in my head, I cannot keep this note going on forever, even if my head does not have to actively breathe. I have to virtually breathe in my head which will interrupt me singing a note in my mind forever." She looked at the alien, satisfied with her example.

"But how do you play these instruments non-stop?"

"What instruments?"

"The long tree trunk things, didgeridoos?"

"That's because we can trap air in our cheeks, breathe in through the nose while pushing the air out with our cheek muscles, and then quickly breathe out through the mouth again, to rebuild pressure." She was lucky to have stumbled across this detail during her time at university.

The alien shook their arms, pointing with one at her head and the other waving around it.

"What if you imagined you were singing in your head making the noise with your lips instead?"

Luna thought about it, staring at the board. She made a vibrating noise with her lips in her head, as if playing a didgeridoo while looking down her nose to focus on the mental task. She imagined keeping her hum going while still breathing. Eventually it worked.

She watched Erial working on their next move, as she replaced the sound of her vibrating lips with her own voice in her head, singing a note. Luna kept the note going, while breathing in and out at the same time.

"Wow, it works." She said, excited and surprised.

Luna looked at the alien, wondering what else this intelligent creature could make up, to teach her something about herself. She watched Erial move the two arms across the board, then moving a piece, hopping over the other pieces to her side of the board.

"What if you used your chromatophores instead of your arms to plan your next move? As with your emotions, play the game on your skin first?" Initially she was proud of suggesting something in return, but quickly regretted her comment.

Within the next moves she saw the different lines and possible ways of jumping across the board flash across Erial's skin, a process too quick to give her a chance to remember what her opponent was planning. In addition it was difficult for her to see where the virtual playing board started and ended within the repeating patterns.

She found herself watching how Erial cleaned up the board, moving their game pieces into their side of the board, while giving her almost no chances to do the same. Instead of losing the game she decided to keep one of her pieces on its starting position, effectively blocking Erial from finishing the game. With another piece, she repeated the same useless move over and over again, pushing it left and right in the centre of the board, not even attempting to bring it closer to its intended destination.

"I see you don't want to lose, and I can't win."

Erial had analysed her repeating her move for the tenth time and changed their colour to a light blue. Luna looked up and grinned, then reached out with her open hand across the board.

"It's a draw?" she asked.

The alien withdrew its tentacles and changed its skin to a grey and white pattern, mimicking the playing board, equally distributing the purple and green colours of the game pieces across its body.

"Agreed."

◆ ◆ ◆

Luna sat at her desk, writing down her thoughts about her cultural exchange with Erial and how they had progressed in playing games together.

They had spent the remainder of their journey to Dol trying out more games, with Luna teaching the rules and winning the first rounds, then quickly losing against Erial. After Chinese checkers, they switched to checkers, then chess. She had to explain she had no idea why a game invented in Germany in nineteenth century was called after a country on the other side of the hemisphere. They looked it up and found it was a marketing scheme. While playing games they went on with their discussions, to continue the cultural exchange they were tasked to do. Erial had asked how she felt about marketing. They asked if the human tendency to advertise things that they once could buy or trade to an unbelievable extent was connected to an inherent pattern of wishing for something greater. They also asked if humans had the urge to be better than someone or something else and if this was connected to religion. The question caught her by surprise and she had to admit she had no answer, nurturing her doubts whether she was suitable for this exchange. When she tried to explain that she was out of her depth regarding the matter, she saw Erial's skin flush with surprise. She had to make clear that 'depth' here was meant as 'in deep water', sending them into a discussion of all sorts of fears humans and the Dolvar had.

Luna began explaining thalassophobia, the fear of deep bodies of water, which Erial compared to claustrophobia for the Dolvar. The Dolvar usually swam alone in the oceans of Dol and had never had the concept of rooms, ever. This also meant not all Dolvar were made up for flying into space in an enclosure, even if they could patch themselves into the ship and experience themselves as one with the ship, letting them experience space as one infinitely deep ocean. They both agreed that, in this case, the Dolvar were lucky not to experience thalassophobia. Luna remembered her tumbling and panic in the sim-sphere after the launch from Earth and couldn't see herself to be experiencing space in a way similar to Erial for a prolonged time.

Luna could mitigate her self-doubts about the exchange, when they both couldn't answer Erial's question that if given the previously stated, possibly inherent nature of striving for something greater, when given the opportunity to actually do so, if human fears would eventually take over and bring everything crashing back down to nothing.

The Dolvar's direct observation of an unpractical overload with fear in humans, as the Dolvar called it, was what had caused them to keep their distance from Earth for three more centuries, after their brief and painful first contact.

Luna finished writing down her notes and made her notebook and table disappear into the wall. The Dolvar were strict about things not floating around during launch, descent, breaking burn and orbiting with almost zero gravity.

She waved at Erial through the window, and watched them connect their tentacles with the respective counterparts extending out from the opposite end of their space into their room, to fully connect with the ship again and take over controls. At the same time, Luna stepped into the sim-sphere and sat down in the mould embedded in the curved wall, already adjusted to her body.

Over the course of the next fifteen minutes she felt gravity slowly decrease, until she was floating, just above the surface of her seat. The wall shrunk around her to keep her in place. She commanded the ship from inside the sphere, to turn on the outside view and she immediately floated outside in space, looking around from under the belly of the ship. She narrowed her field of view to decrease the level of immersion to a comfortable level. Planet *Dol* was a blue dot in space with marbled white clouds spinning on its hemispheres. Luna was wildly excited to be landing on another planet. Not just another planet, but an alien planet with alien life on it.

She had looked up the major differences between Dol and Earth. Their planet was spinning with an axial tilt of eleven degrees, giving it weaker seasons than Earth. The atmosphere was fifteen percent oxygen, eighty percent nitrogen and almost five percent carbon-dioxide making it unbreathable to humans, due to the latter concentration. With a diameter of nine thousand four-hundred and nineteen kilometres it was slightly smaller than earth, at just about three quarters the size in comparison.

Luna watched the ship flip around, split open to unfurl its tentacles, then ignite the engines across the surface, and decelerate their flight, dropping them out of a brief orbit. She spent minutes staring into the smoke of the rockets burning through the atmosphere, engulfing her inside, hiding the planet and the universe around her.

Her skin crawled with goosebumps, her body flushed with adrenaline. Impatiently she watched their approach with her mouth open. Eventually, the ship flipped over, placing her on top and they fell from the sky as if riding a gigantic cuttle fish, first through a thin layer of clouds, then through a thicker layer followed by rain. The wind rushed past, beating over the edges of the ship around her.

When the ship tilted upright, it fired its engines once more, this time with an audible, cracking boom, to decelerate them so they could hover above the surface of an endless ocean, gently plunging one tentacle after another into the dark waves.

Luna flinched and instinctively tried to stop herself from falling and submerging with the ship into the water, splashing through the surface without getting wet. When they resurfaced, she turned the sim-sphere to full immersion again and found herself floating on an endless ocean hid from the rain around her.

XIX (LUNA)

A thick rain fell sideways, seemingly through her, hammering down on *The Second Blue Marble,* hiding the horizon. The waves were bigger than what she had experienced in her month cruising on Earth, lifting her with the ship slowly up and down, through the moving valleys and hills of the ocean. She watched the wind foaming on top of the waves, pushing white ripples across the water.

"Home sweet home?" Luna asked.

"Yes!"

"Where are we exactly?"

"On Dol."

"But you know at least where we are, right?"

"Not exactly. Why?"

She spun around trying to get some orientation, but the only thing she could determine was that she was in the centre of the ship, surrounded by water, waves and a windy rain. She could hardly make out which was the pointy end and which one the tentacle end, almost a hundred meters to each side of her.

"But you will eventually find out, right?" She felt insecure, having to reassure herself that the alien knew what they were doing.

"No. Not directly."

"Ok. You mentioned the kelp blooms. If you don't know where we are, how do you know how to get there?" Luna tried to figure out what the plan was.

"We communicate. We know where we are relative to each other. The concept of continents, countries, states, cities, streets, houses, rooms, narrowing down where you can be and are allowed to be doesn't exist for us. We know where others are around us and we build a network. We only see a part of that network and exchange information about what we see. We often have conversations with each other over multiple hops, even if the Dolvar in between are asleep. More or less, at least. Do you understand."

"Why have you never mentioned this?"

"Why have you never asked? Why have you never looked it up? This seems to be new to you, but not to the relationship between the Dolvar and you, the Osvar. It would be easier if you turned your focus away from yourself from time to time."

Luna asked herself if she had been somehow too focused on telling all she knew about herself and humans and hadn't really asked enough questions. Maybe this exchange had been too one-sided until now. Thinking about it this way, her questions came flying at her, from all angles.

"Ok, but how do you meet with other Dolvar?"

"We usually don't."

"But if you do meet?"

"Well, if two Dolvar know where they are relative

to others, they can pick a place relative to each other. We are not confined to a plane to get around. If two humans are standing next to each other facing the same direction, left is left, and right is right. We don't care where up, down, left and right are. If the planet is below us, or above us. If we are swimming sideways or not, or in space. We could be facing the same direction but this still gives us an angle of three hundred and sixty degrees of freedom which way we are rotated. And in addition to this, depending on how deep you are, we don't even see each other. We might be able to glow, but not that far, so figuring out which way we are pointing is irrelevant."

Luna realised she had a lot of catching up to do. She remembered reading some of this, but never thought about what it actually meant, to place the facts into context.

"But why do you have this amazing skill of using your chromatophores?"

"In the first, lower conscious stage of our life we are not that much different from a fish, so adaptation is key for survival and hunting in shallow waters. And we still hunt. If we roam in the ocean, there is no hole in the wall which will give us food. We have to, and prefer to hunt our own. We will show you when we get to the kelp islands."

"So you know where you are and where they are?"
"Absolutely, no. Relatively, yes."
Luan felt relived.
"With how many Dolvar are you currently in con-

tact?"

"Directly, seven. Next hop, fifty-four."

"Doesn't it take a long time to relay a message to someone specific?"

"Yes, it does. But we live a lot longer than you, so then it doesn't matter. And if you remember, we don't actually meet, so who should this specific someone be?"

"Maybe your parents, for example?"

"We don't have your concept of parenthood either. Once a year on Dol we gather in the equatorial current and release our eggs and sperm, depending on what sex we have chosen until then. It's often mixed with millions of our variations of lower consciousness. This even is visible from space. But don't be afraid. Your kind of generational dependency is common among other alien species, so you don't have to feel alone in this regard. But we guess you have a lot of catching up to do. We assume that your general population will soon have access to the entire network of species."

Luna sat quietly in her transparent bubble, watching the rain change to a drizzle. She imagined a huge cum stain floating on the ocean, visible from space. She shook herself to get rid of the mental image, hoping that Erial wasn't watching. She wanted to change the topic.

"Ok, understood. You mentioned the seaweed earlier. Are we going there and will you stay on the ship or–"

She left the question open, hoping Erial would fill

in.

"We are already four kilometres to your right, six hundred metres deep, swimming in parallel. We will get there tomorrow."

She had to swallow.

"I'm alone on this ship?"

"Yes."

The answer stressed her and her mouth dried up. She commanded the sim-sphere to end. The immersion with the ocean waves and the rain around her immediately stopped, revealing the greyish wall of the space ship again. She got up from her seat and climbed out through the hole into the living room. Only then did she notice that Dol had only half the gravity of Earth. She felt even lighter, as if just putting down a heavy backpack after walking all day, as if her shoulders were pulling her up from the floor. In the living room, she stepped in front of the glass panel swaying with the movements of the ship, looking into the empty space filled with water in front of her.

She didn't sleep much that night. Luna had asked if there was a way to avoid the waves and the ship's voice confirmed this. The vessel then descended below the surface into the calm waters of the deep. She lay in her bed, with her arms above the bedcovers, staring at the ceiling, simulating a faint glow of stars to provide her with a comfortable amount of darkness.

Her head was moving too much information back

and forth, making it impossible to sleep. The planet – all water-, the tall waves, the dark clouds above, most of mankind was missing out on so many other species, from all over the universe.

And here she was, alone in the Dolvar ship, not knowing where she was, how deep she was, what else was swimming around her. She tried to imagine how far Erial was away from her, and when they would return. She felt helpless and entirely dependent on the alien. She felt alone.

After, three sleepless hours she eventually got up, grabbed her blanked, walked through the living room and crawled into the sim-sphere to create a new environment.

With the blanket in her hands she voiced her requests against the grey walls.

"I need a gras plane, at night, and a fireplace."

The sphere's top half turned into a night sky, displaying the stars as seen from Earth, the ground around her flattened and turned into a grassy surface. In front of her, out of reach, appeared a small, crackling wood fire, sending embers rising into the wafting air above. She could feel the radiating heat of the fire, then sat down on the grass and tucked her legs under the blanket. Around her the plane stretched out to the horizon in every direction.

"Now, add a dog for each Dolvar in the area, scale ten kilometres down to one metre, relative to me."

Next to her, a brown husky appeared, sleeping on its back, legs folded against its body and its black nose pointing towards the sky. She grinned at the wrangled shape of a sleeping dog, wanting to pet it.

All around her with a distance of ten to twenty metres, half a dozen other dogs appeared, some curled up and sleeping, others quietly sniffing at the grass, looking around, sometimes moving around in small steps. Further away, she saw more animals appearing, either asleep or minding their own business, like the others. She lay down, turned to her side, rested her head on her elbow and watched the dog representing Erial next to her. The animal looked cute in its unusual position. The simulated environment helped her forget that she was alone in an alien spaceship, diving somewhere in an ocean wrapping an entire planet, far away from her home. She finally fell asleep.

◆◆◆

Relieved, that the night was finally over, Luna had a quick breakfast, consisting of something resembling scrambled eggs with chives, and a long warm shower. She got dressed and immediately went back into the sim-sphere to meet with Erial.

Immersed in the outside world again, she found herself on top of the ship, floating next to a giant mass consisting of multiple layers of algae rising and falling with the ocean waves. The weather had cleared and the sun was shining climbing half way up to its zenith, surrounded by blue sky. The sun was twice as big as the star in the centre of the solar system, but it looked almost the same size from the surface of Dol, due to the higher orbit around it. She soaked up the blue sky trying to figure out if the blue was a darker blue than on Earth. The top of the algae surface was a brown, yellowish, grey curly mess of plants dried by the sun, floating like ramen in a bowl. Narrow cracks and channels opened up in places when lifted by waves, revealing the shimmering water underneath.

Across this shallow, moving aggregation of tiny islands animals were waddling around, taking off and landing. In the air she could make out the stretched arms of silvery hemmed transparent wings, grey scaly bodies and two feet that resembled fins more than feet. The heads she saw were round, with big dark eyes, long wide mouths across their faces and tiny beaks in the middle. Luna settled with describing them as a crossover of a potoo, a fish and a fruit bat, for her notes later that day.

On the conglomeration of islands the strange creatures hopped about, hissing and chasing each other or nibbling at the dried seaweed. Some were building nests, weaving intricate balls of the wet plant material, and others had seemingly nothing better to do than chase each other around and scream and flap their wings.

"Good morning Luna. Nice to see you." Erial greeted her.

She looked around trying to spot the alien. She knew this was meant literally.

"I'm lying on the edge of the algae."

Luna looked from side to side, along the edge of the shoreline, but couldn't see Erial's squid-shaped body anywhere.

"Good morning. Where are you? I can't see you." She checked all around her, assuming they weren't on the island after all.

"Look, I'll make it easier for you. See?"

Right in front of her the seaweed started to shift and wiggle. A chunk of weed briefly changed its texture, flattened its surface and colour to match the ocean with its two eyelids opening in the middle, revealing the four dark irises. Erial's shape quickly morphed back to resemble the crumpled seaweeds, but entirely escaping Luna's eyes this time.

"There you are! Impressive!"

She had seen the walls change in shape and texture within the sim-sphere, but seeing this on a living being was still mind-boggling to her. Erial had only played with colours and light in front of her so far, but not with textures. Now, she was curiously watching Erial, or the spot where they were.

"Is this any more difficult than changing colours?"

"No."

"Why haven't you done it before?"

"I didn't need to."

"What are you doing?"

"Hunting."

"What for?"

"Lunch."

She watched the scaly creatures in the distance. When they started into the air they flicked their tails, shot up and unfolded their wings, gently gliding away. Once in the air, they changed direction almost immediately, zigzagging like fleeing rabbits. At the edge of the seaweed they were feeding on fish, flying high up, then falling down, banging their heads onto the water, stunning tiny fish swimming directly below the surface, just to scoop them up and spit out the excess water through two slits under their throat. Another group of animals had just jumped up and were gliding towards Luna, headed for the open sea behind her. When they reached her, the seaweed below them moved. Luna flinched at the sudden movement of the textured, paddled tentacle shooting into the air, smacking one of the gliding animals with a loud, popping slap from below. The creature flew spiralling into the air, as the other gliders frantically flapped away into all directions like a firework, one so close to Luna, that she had to instinctively duck. Before the attacked animal hit the ground Erial reverted their camouflage and caught the animal with a fingered tentacle, wrapped around its prey like a snake, and sank back into the water between the ship and the floating island. Luna said nothing, stunned by her glimpse of Erial's physical power.

◆ ◆ ◆

Luna continued to study the *matsa*, as they were called by the Dolvar, until the afternoon. Virtual screens projected by the sim-sphere floated around her, providing her with access to the ship's data about life on Dol.

Each breeding matsa sat on a bundle of seaweed, holding it together with its fin-like feet. She learnt that they did build nests, as Luna witnessed, and laid their eggs inside, but instead of sitting on them to incubate them, they sat on them to dry and then glue the weeds into a ball with their excretions, to build a protective cover against predators like juvenile Dolvar swimming below. This kept these animals busy for a quarter of a year until the island reached the stormy regions, to be rolled around the surface of the sea like tumbleweed. The newly hatched *matsa* then spent their first months rolling around on the waves clinging to the seaweed and gobbling up whatever invaded their nests. Once they had survived the storms, their cycle repeated itself and they looked for islands of weeds clinging together.

◆ ◆ ◆

Eventually, she went back inside, fetched her lunch from the hole in the wall and sat down on the pile of cushions, holding a bowl filled with strips of chicken and rice in one hand and chopsticks in the other. She was ready to converse with Erial, who was slowly gliding over the half lowered edge of the living room window, gently making their way towards Luna. Luna was used to the alien's physical presence by now and she was trying to practice keeping someone company, which was still something unusual on a physical level for Erial.

"Have you ever thought about eating with your fingers?" said the alien, pointing at her bowl with a fingered tentacle, building up their towering body from just two metres away.

"No, usually it's too hot." Luna demonstratively blew across a piece of meat held between the two sticks in her hand to let it cool, while looking at the alien's irregular blinking interval. The creature was still adjusting to the dry air saying,

"When we eat something we hold it in our arms, so we can feel its entire texture. Even when ripping it apart we can feel the change in tension and structure. It's part of the experience for Dolvar." Erial collected the chess pieces on the board between them, neatly rearranging them in their home rows.

"I think there were times and regions on Earth were eating with your hands was the norm, but that was as least three to four hundred years ago. I think you might even find someone holding on to that as a tradition or heritage today."

She stuffed the piece of chicken into her mouth.

"And did they say it tasted better?"

"I can't remember to be honest, but I guess they'd say yes."

She said that with her mouth being full, smiled and continued chewing.

Erial shuffled their tentacles below their body, the long, paddled arms as thick as Luna's thighs pretzeled under it into a donut to support their towering body. She watched the smooth movements and recalled the moments from earlier, when she had witnessed how invisible Erial had been when hiding among the weeds. She remembered the speed with which they had smacked the animal into the sky, ending its life with a single blow. Luna's eyes were staring at the flat, paddled end of one of the tentacles, twice the size of her head, which quickly turned purple. She felt caught, impolite and intimidated at the same time and focused on her meal instead, fishing for another piece of chicken in her bowl.

"You don't have to be concerned. Intelligent beings are not part of our diet." Erial said with their neutral, nonchalant voice.

She looked up, feeling the alien had read her mind without requiring her to wave about with her arms or her skin blushing. All their paddled tentacles had turned purple, and they slowly shuffled them behind their body with their slippery gliding sounds.

"Luna, we have something else we would like to share. We have listened in on the interplanetary network this morning. We found a new habitable planet. We suggested you as the first contact and we would like to support you in this task."

Luna almost dropped her bowl.

"What? Really?" She was excited. "Who is 'we'? Have you suggested me?"

"No, we, the Dolvar have suggested you." Erial's body turned dark grey, with a bright orange disk in the middle, slowly dimming into purple.

"Wow!" Luna was looking for words. "What planet is it? What type of a planet is it?"

Erial moved a pawn on the chessboard, while answering her question.

"It looks similar to one of the planets from your solar system, like Mars."

XX (ELISA)

Reina's room was six by six metres, with a bunk bed, a cabinet and a desk on the left side and a yoga mat in the corner of the other. The rest was empty. There was a hole above the door with an arm of orange and grey cables reaching inside, running along the ceiling, forking away left and right to reach the bunk bed, desk and the other, empty walls, dangling down with plastic caps insulating the ends. The room had two vents, pushing in air above the door and out on the opposite side, above the desk. A bright, square LED panel in the centre illuminated the room in an even light. The yoga mat was lying in front of the empty wall that had been turned into a canvas showing a red Martian landscape blending into a terraformed green vision of what Mars could be some day in the distant future. In the centre was Earth, a small blue dot visible in the orange to blue gradient of the sky, going from left to right across the room.

"You can put your luggage in the corner." said Reina as she let them into her room.

Elisa entered and steered towards the mat at which Reina was pointing. Phil was right behind her.

A group of residents dressed in green or blue

onesies remained waiting outside. They had picked up an entourage while they were making their way to Reina's place inside dome H10. There were those who wanted to know more about Phil and Elisa, and those who wanted to keep everyone away from both of them.

Reina shouted at the group, standing in the doorway.

"Give us a minute, alright? We'll get back outside in a bit. We just need to get some fresh air and get organised. The past two days have been tough on them, okay? Thank you!"

Over Reina's shoulder Elisa watched how a small, round woman, shaped like a barrel, with thick, brown shoulder-long hair came shooing down the corridor, shouting at the crowd gathered outside.

"Alright, fuck off everyone! You got better stuff to do. Give the girls some time."

The strange woman closed the door behind them with a decisive bang, and the three were finally alone. From inside, Elisa heard the woman bossing around whoever was trying to stay outside the room and she wasn't taking no for an answer.

Reina's dorm was in the tenth habitat, one of fifty domes that housed the dormitories. After they had been in the empty halls of the cafeteria and the empty tunnels picking up Elisa's bags and Phil, the scene inside the dorm dome quickly changed. The structure was half under ground, the other half above the Martian surface, covered in a thick layer of concrete and regolith. Inside, the entrances to the dome were at the lowest level, five tunnels connecting them to the neighbourhood. The floors were arranged in rings, with a round double helix staircase in the middle, connecting eight levels. Corridors reached out from the centre column towards the outside to connect the rings of rooms, with the number of rooms decreasing the higher up the floor was under the curved dome.

Elisa felt like entering a prison every time she walked into a dome. People were sitting on the staircases, sitting on the balconies above looking down, with their legs dangling through the railing, playing on their terminals.

They had been recognised as soon as they had appeared under the double helix stair case, drawing increasing attention with every second. It didn't take long for a shouting match to ensue between Reina and the other residents, promising to provide crucial information once they had time to put the pieces together.

More parties joined the noise and opinions were being continuously added from all sides. But soon they were not the focus of anyone any more. More pressing matters were at stake: the darkness, and *The Mars Collective*.

There had been three major opinions being shouted at each other. First, there were those who believed that what they saw was the truth about the crash and that the recordings of the sky disappearing were fake. They wanted to fight against the coup. Others stated that they saw the glitches in the video stream and thought the opposite, that the crash was fake and the darkness real. These were trying to convince everyone to get rid of corporate management. Then there were others who thought that none of it mattered because of the ongoing alien invasion. They were trying to scream sense into everyone, to get them to prepare for an endless freezing darkness.

Elisa guessed the reality was somewhere in between these arguments, hoping that somehow things would go back to normal somehow, but doubted her situation had any chance of improving at all.

They had quickly made their way through the shouts and rants as they climbed their way up the staircase to reach the fourth floor. Elisa knew she had nothing left for this place. She wanted to go home, to Earth, and it seemed the world offered less and less options with every day that had passed since her flight got cancelled.

Elisa sat down on the yoga mat, catching Phil distractedly staring into the air again. She snapped her fingers, and waved at him to get his attention.

"Phil?" She looked at him, trying to hide her concern.

After having picked up their bags, she decided to push him to tell his part of the story and agree to decrypt the recordings they had stored on their terminals. Earth had disappeared and now the universe was gone as well and she didn't want to keep anything from anyone anymore. The thought that kept her afloat was payback.

Reina had copied their files onto her terminal, which was now connected to a screen bolted to the wall above the desk. Elisa typed in her half of the password and stepped aside to let Phil enter his second half. The two women had to painfully watch him type in the wrong password until he got it right at the fourth attempt. Elisa had typed hers into an editor to copy and paste it, but Phil insisted on typing it over and over again so he did not have to reveal it. She spent more than a painful minute, exchanging looks with Reina, crossing her fingers, hoping he hadn't forgotten his passphrase.

Once they had decrypted the video file, they watched it. The entire scene from Elisa losing her wits and bashing the sphere, the shouts and the sphere's response, the strobing lamps, the glowing, spinning animation until the sphere turned entirely dark. Reina joined the video with the file from the advertisement she had received via mail, and added a shot of Elisa talking to the camera, stating who she was and that the advertisement had been manipulated, urging everyone to join *The Mars Collective*.

When Elisa saw herself in the final video, she had to check in a hand mirror to see if she really looked that pale and exhausted. Taking in her reflection she noticed she looked even worse than in the last clip.

In the meantime, Reina opened the door to talk to the woman who seemed to be running the dome. They were waiting until the collective had bootstrapped a new local network to host the files for everyone in the dome. All communications had been cut from the station orbiting Mars. Even if she had sided with the takeover, out of spite, she was sceptic of what was to come from it.

As soon as the dome's local network was back up, they uploaded the video for everyone to access and distribute. At the same time Elisa was relieved to have the truth out, to show that even when she had attacked the sphere it had not responded, and that when it had responded it was in unison with the respective input and output.

Soon, the dome grew quiet, with many sitting outside in the staircase rewatching everything again and again, trying to shape their own view of the situation. Those who did not side with the majority in favour of *The Mars Collective* eventually left the dome in search for a place siding with their opinions.

There were still ongoing arguments further down in the hallways between those staying and leaving, but it all abated to people being too tired, in search for some rest. After another hour the dome was silent and none of the three had any energy left to begin or join any discussions in the neighbouring rooms and therefore remained inside Reina's.

It was late. Phil sat on the bottom bunk, Reina on the top bunk and Elisa cross-legged on the yoga mat, with her back against her duffle bags pushed against the wall.

Reina leaned down to pass back her joint to Phil.

"This is better than holing up down in the farm, right?" she said as he held the joint between his fingertips. The tip glowed as he pulled, he held his breath and eventually replied with smoke escaping from his lips.

"It depends." He took another hit.

"On what?"

Reina looked unhappy with his answer and leaned down to look at him, her head dangling upside down.

"Well, who's going to check on my plants tomorrow?" Phil coughed, blowing the smoke in her face.

"I will, and you will."

"But in all this chaos? I'm not sure that will be possible."

The woman on the top bunk lifted herself back up, grabbed her terminal from her pillow next to her and checked the screen.

"You're too pessimistic. Let's see what's happening."

She navigated the screen, refreshing and going back and forth. Reina described the situation.

"Some people are still up, and some have walked to the next domes. Apparently, more domes have started to pull up new networks, joining the collective. This taking over the city thing seems to be happening. See, this is moving into an entirely different direction than you are making up in your head."

Elisa pulled at her own joint, held her breath while she looked up at the other woman and shrugged. She let the smoke escape her lungs and adjusted her duffle bags to provide better comfort. Reina continued the conversation.

"So how have you two met?"

"Random job assignment. Auto-matching. I actually wanted to destroy one of those fucking balls. But well, seems like the fucking alien tech liked what I did to it." Elisa laughed, coughing out smoke and raised an eyebrow, staring at the glowing tip of her joint. She pulled again, watching the glowing ring travel down the paper, leaving behind burnt weed and ash. She inhaled deeper this time, holding her breath even longer, then slowly blew the smoke into the room watching it disperse and disappear into the vent under the ceiling. An additional set of filters had been screwed on top of it, to get rid of the smoke and it had four wires with a small PCB dangling out its side to temporarily spoof the sensor if the filter failed to do its job.

Phil stirred on the lower bunk.

"It is alien and it is alive. It has some sort of life at least. This is why I came here in the first place. Not to spend all the time looking after vegetables. That's why I signed up to analyse whatever these spheres are. Us two meeting was a coincidence."

He passed the joint back up to Reina, closed his eyes and smiled.

"Why do you dwell in that room of yours anyway? I've heard you're down there all the time by yourself? How do you do this? If we ever get out of this blackout or even if we don't, we will be stuck here for quite a while. Do you really want to stay down there all the time?"

"Yeah!"

"Why?"

Phil pointed at the drawing on the wall behind Elisa.

"Because this–" he waved his arm across the room. "–is bullshit."

Elisa focused on the glowing tip of her joint again, tuning out of their discussion. She watched the tip light up, realising why it looked so familiar and interrupted Phil mid-sentence.

"Phil, next time you pull at the joint keep an eye on the tip. I swear it looks exactly like the sphere. Those tiny fractals."

But instead of Phil's reaction, she watched how Reina's expression suddenly changed, how she quickly sat up, stretching her feet down the bunk bed, her face shocked, as if she had seen something she didn't want to see.

"Reina? What's up? Hungry?"

"No. Imagine being on Earth right now. What if this exact same thing is happening on Earth? Have you ever thought of this? What will actually happen if the sun goes out, goes out on earth? Here it's fucking freezing over in any case. But Earth?"

Phil scratched his head and rubbed his face. He looked as if he were to fall asleep any second, as he mumbled his response.

"I think it would get really cold pretty quick. It would get colder than Mars is right now, maybe within a couple of months? I don't know the exact numbers, or how to figure this out at the moment, but they would have a couple of days, maybe weeks to prepare, find shelter. The best would be to stay under ground. See?"

Reina looked mortified.

"Fuck. I need to know if Earth is really gone, or if they are bullshitting us on the station. I have to know."

"Why? You have anyone back there waiting for you? I've been here for twenty years, I'm sure most have forgotten I even exist."

Phil took the joint from Reina's hand without her noticing and finished it.

"Yes. My girlfriend, she flies one of the shuttles."

Reina's voice was quiet and she looked scared. She went on, staring at the blue dot on the wall above Elisa's head.

"What the hell is all this? Is this some sort of super gigantic curtain those fucking aliens have put around us to wipe us out, like pest control?"

Suddenly, Elisa felt a deep panic creep through her body. She had been so focused on how much she hated life on Mars, that she had pushed away thinking about the possible consequences of her actions.

If that's the case: I fucking caused it. Fuck. She thought, now staring at the floor, her breathing accelerating, hands gripping at the mat below her. Fear and guilt overran her. She rocked back and forth, not sure what to do or say. All she could focus on was the pain in her chest, her racing heartbeat, the sweat building up in the palms of her hands.

"Fuck. I messed with the sphere, and it turned dark. What if we were supposed to fucking leave it alone? Fuck, fuck, fuck!"

Reina jumped from the bed, sat down next to her and put one arm around her, trying to calm her down.

"No, no, no, no. Don't think that way! First of all, Earth disappeared first. Before you even arrived at the sphere, okay? So whatever happened to Earth is unrelated to what's happening here, okay?"

Phil leaned forward, fighting his tiredness.

"Maybe Reina's right and this still could be some pre-programmed shit after all, and we had nothing to do with it. Yes, maybe it reacted to you, but it doesn't have to mean anything. Overthinking is my part, ok? Even if you were a monkey that banged a cylinder onto it, would you go apeshit about a species which does not understand what the hell you are doing on their planet? Elisa, relax, this was not you."

Elisa sat hunched over her knees, listening to their words while Reina was carefully rubbing her back. She thought about what to do next. For the first time in a long while she was actually having a conversation with someone, even if it only revolved around her possibly fucking up the future of everyone around her. She looked up at Reina, and felt guilt overwhelm her. She hated the city, but it had never been her intention to destroy it, or their chances of survival. Tears ran down her cheeks as she stammered,

"With all that's happened, here... or whatever is going on, here... everything feels so out of reach, I have no idea what to do." She sobbed. "You cannot even imagine how badly I want to leave this place. But that seems too close to fucking impossible with every fucking day. Fuck these spheres. I wish I had destroyed it. Really!"

She buried her head under her arms, closed her eyes and mumbled onto her knees.

"What are we going to do? This sucks so hard for everyone right now. We don't even know what is happening, and we don't know what happened to Earth."

Elisa wiped her eyes and nose on the sleeve of her hoody and looked at Reina.

"These management motherfuckers will have to answer. They have to give us full access to whatever information they have up there. Let us try to at least take a look at where we really are, if there is really nothing out there or if we are just seeing nothing. And then we can see for ourselves if there is a way to contact Earth. They literally can't leave us hanging in the dark. There must be a way, you can't just let two planets disappear. That's impossible."

Elisa got up and excused herself, in search for some privacy. She intended to say she was going to get some fresh air, but knew that was practically impossible on Mars.

"I'm gonna go out for a bit." She said as she left the room and walked down the corridor until she reached the double helix staircase. Standing there for a while, she looked down the winding stairs. The bottom floor was four stories below. Occasionally, there were people walking around. To her surprise they just nodded at her and left her alone, confused. After the dome had almost exploded with people trying to nose around, those still up appeared to Elisa as if they were from a different world, calm and focused, going on their way.

In her mind, Elisa went over the last days over and over again. She felt as if she had gone through enough shit in the past fifty hours to fill a lifetime, hoping the next fifty hours would not be half as bad as the previous ones.

Eventually, weariness finally took over, and she walked back into the dorm room.

When she entered, the light was dimmed and Phil was curled up and asleep, snoring against the wall. Quietly, she closed the door and stepped through the dim light to her bags. She pulled out her pyjamas and blankets for the night. As she got up and turned around, she saw Reina was missing from her bunk and she seized the opportunity to change while no one was looking, double checking the room for any hidden cameras, grinding her teeth thinking of Iris' marketing video featuring her. She hastily slid under her blankets, waiting for Reina to return, fighting against her tiredness.

Within minutes Reina was back, stepped inside and placed her toothbrush back on its spot on a shelf between the bunk bed and the desk. She grabbed her pyjamas from the top bed, placed it on the desk in front of her and undressed. Without thinking, Elisa watched her from under her blanket, looking at her body in the dimmed light shining down on them from the ceiling. She saw the tattooed red lines go down Reina's cheeks, down her throat, then down her cleavage, bending outwards under her breasts, around her back, crossing over her spine to return to the front above her hips. The lines continued bending downwards and disappeared between her legs.

At least I know what the tattoo looks like. She thought as Reina turned her head towards her, and looked at Elisa, who was staring at her like a deer caught in the headlights.

She finished getting into her pyjamas and disappeared in the top bunk, effortlessly hopping up the ladder, aided by the lower gravity. Another constant reminder for Elisa that she was still on Mars.

XXI (ELISA)

The next day, Elisa observed how the city took on a life of its own. When she got up, Phil was already gone and she guessed he was already back to working on his experiments with Reina.

Sitting inside the shared bathrooms, she took the time to check up on the progress of the local network. The domes of the city were all re-connected, but all communication links to the station were cut. A decentralised platform had been rolled out to facilitate communication, a text based forum with files shared on a peer to peer network.

She scrolled through the posts ordered by popularity, and watched the videos of the recent days. Her compilation was ranking on top, with the glowing alien sphere as the preview image. There were thousands of comments. People were sympathising with her and others wishing she had cracked it open. But it was all already too much to read in one morning. She closed the post about her and her video, and distracted herself with the next, trying to push away the sensation of guilt inside her.

There was still no daylight outside. She skimmed through pictures of total darkness and the only visible light coming from the domes. The posts were tagged with 'the darkness'.

There had been messages from the station ordering everyone to comply, to re-establish the chain of command. They were ranked right below her own post, just to be taken apart in the comment section. Elisa was surprised to read so many voices speaking out against the previous status quo.

Files were piling up and comments were being added every second. Not even hours after the new network and platform was up it was impossible to catch up. Things had changed fast overnight.

She skimmed the latest media. There were recordings of fights with the newly appointed wards which had refused to give up listening to the chain of command. A boy not even in his twenties was excitedly reporting everything from his perspective, talking about how the wards had now been locked up in their own cells.

Elisa was surprised she had never even heard of the existence of holding cells on Mars and thought that she maybe wasn't that much different from Phil: both of them living in their own bubble at opposite ends of a comfortability scale.

She skipped through a number of speeches, suggesting it was time to hold elections, with a long trail of upvoted comments questioning what for.

The last video she watched was a report on herself. Someone had found the surveillance footage of the day she thought she was about to leave mars, with her middle finger raised high into the air when she left the cafeteria, then heading straight for the launchpad, a sign many interpreted in the comments as rejecting the corporation.

Looking at herself in the video, she felt ashamed of her actions. It looked childish. It had felt and looked so much better in her head versus watching her actions on a surveillance video from a third person's perspective. And she saw, what she couldn't see back then: noone even cared to look at her. Noone even looked insulted. Her lack of impact at that moment left her disappointed, not even being able to cause a stir in what she had assumed were her last days on Mars.

It confirmed her everlasting feeling she had had in the past years, that she never really mattered. That she was just a number in an equation from expanding a colony on Mars. To function and to work, and work more so others could join and work more.

◆◆◆

When she arrived at cafeteria C3, the dome wasn't even filled to a third. People were mostly staring at their terminals eating their breakfast between the green concrete walls and bushes. Many of the residents looked tired, but awake enough to eat something and keep scrolling, eyes glued to their screens. She guessed a large number of those present hadn't slept at all. Elisa lined up at the counter to queue for her breakfast, checking the popular posts, to see she had already bubbled down, ready to be forgotten. The top ranking post was titled 'The New Economy'.

She was disrupted when a man, roughly her age, in front of her turned around and recognised her.

"Hey, you're Elisa, right?"

Unsure if she wanted to talk or not, all she could do was agree.

"Yeah."

"I'm Arnab."

He held out his hand, fingernails bitten short. She accepted his handshake, his palms felt rough, and he continued talking.

"This last night, man, this was crazy. It's like, so many things happening at once. I haven't slept at all. But I swear it's as if this was bound to happen, man. There's this group for example, in sector C, they started this whole new currency thing. It was a pet project from one of the developers, which they worked on back on Earth. Decentralised currency. The stuff that was made illegal in the thirties. I don't know how it works, man, but look at it."

He fished his terminal out of his pocket and continued to explain, almost without pausing to taking a breath. Elisa tried to lean her head back trying to escape the constant stream of thought thrown at her, with way too many words for her head and the time of the day. She had no other choice but to listen.

"And it works! Look man, this is my wallet. It's not this credits crap they ran from the station."

She saw a number on his screen, trailed by the letter M. He went on.

"Right now I have nine-hundred and forty-six Martians. Have you checked yours? Have you already installed the wallet app?"

She shook her head and gestured with her hands to slow him down.

"Wait, please wait. I just got up and haven't had any coffee or something to eat. Slow down. Please. Can I look this up after breakfast?" She said hoping to escape the conversation.

She knew, algorithmically what crypto currencies on earth were about and how they had been only allowed to be operated by banks as the only entities yet again to be controlling the ledger, practically using the term 'decentralised finance' purely as a marketing scheme, and not actually providing any decentralisation, holding on to their monopoly on transferring assets.

She looked past his excited face towards the queue slowly moving forwards.

"No, you need to install it to buy breakfast. Let me show you!" He babbled on, sending her the application.

It was her turn before she had even managed to install and set up her wallet. She ordered a coffee and toast. Arnab excitedly walked her through everything, explaining every step she had to do to be able to get breakfast. She practically let him handle her order for her.

"They will show you the price now. See? Four Martians. Got to your favourites. Yes. Select the community wallet. Yes, that one, and confirm the transaction. Perfect!"

He tapped on her terminal and handed it back to

her. A progress bar stuck at the middle of the screen for a few seconds and then confirmed the payment process, returning the screen back to the overview panel. Her balance read 7230M.

"Oh la la, man you're rich already, look at that. Go check your transaction history. See where it came from! Everyone just started with a thousand."

She scrolled through her transaction history, cluttered with smileys, kisses, hearts or short messages attached. Wishing her a good morning or to enjoy her coffee. She looked around the cafeteria, most of the people around her were still glued to the screens or talking in small groups. Some looked up and lifted their cups or hands to briefly wave at her.

"This is so awesome, man. All this old school tech and shit. There is no way we are going back to credits. You get paid ten credits a day from the community wallet, and an extra ten if you work on something. It's simple, just post to get it verified, and then you will get your Martians."

Elisa was speechless, it all felt unreal, catching up with the new reality under the domes.

XXII (ELISA)

The darkness outside the domes remained unchanged and Mars was engulfed in a pitch black, endless night for the span of three days and nights. *The Gateway to Earth* had tried to negotiate with the city. The responses were typed out in comments on the local network and directly voted on by everyone who was interested. The strategy with the highest number of votes was pursued. The result was called "Let's keep them in the dark, lol" and the agreed upon details were, to let them say what they wanted to say and not respond at all. To keep them in the dark on an additional level.

Elisa had to laugh when she read about it. She enjoyed the changes on Mars as a form of entertainment, a form of payback. But over time she grew concerned if the most entertaining solution would always be the best or most humane. Any workers who wanted to return to the city from the station were allowed to come back. As far as Elisa was involved, she hadn't heard anything being mentioned about the orbital shuttles returning, which meant there was absolutely no way out.

Another highly voted-on strategy was that there was no need for any direct governance or representatives for Mars. The Mars Collective saw their works as done and left the remaining decisions up to the direct vote of the people. This didn't stop people from voting for a new representative each day, resulting in the daily routine of someone announcing themselves as the current representative of the city to the station, just to decline whatever management had requested or proposed. Given that there were more than twenty thousand inhabitants on Mars, it would take them more than fifty years on Earth to rotate through everyone to be the spokesperson of Mars for a single day.

Strategies were developed to handle strategies. A strategy was only to be implemented as long as there was a clear majority. Those strategies that failed to be passed by a vote, had to be exponentially delayed each time, to be reworked, and more information had to be collected for the given topic. Ideas that only involved a smaller circle could be voted on by lowering the number of required votes, for example for decisions only involving a single dome. So only those who actually lived there and were affected by the measure were selected.

Another popular strategy that was agreed upon was called *Fuck The Expansion*, an expletive headline followed by a long rant that it was practically insane to think that there would be a next wave. Seventy percent of the votes were in favour, which included Elisa's vote. She was happy about the result, believing that at least some sanity came from an unthinkable situation.

Her reasoning was that either somehow magically the universe around them appeared again and they could send a message back to Earth clarifying they wouldn't accept more than a couple of hundred settlers or noone was going to come in any case, because Earth was gone.

Still, a small group continued the expansion, working on finishing another dormitory dome, agreeing to disagree, and kept busy just for the sake of staying out of everyone's way and having something to do and still getting extra credits for each hour they worked on something. Higher priority tasks were voted on to pay out more Martians and were only assigned to those who were actually qualified to do the job or to those who were the last to earn something, in order to equally distribute the chance of work and redistribution of credits.

The Mars Collective had turned the city into a mode of self-organisation over night, growing on an unseen level of participation. Instead of working all day on expanding the colony, people were organising workshops or had the time to pick up hobbies for the first time on Mars. Small groups started painting the walls of the tunnels with graffiti and in the evenings, the domes were bustling with life, turning the cafeterias into one big festival during literally, the darkest times on Mars.

Elisa watched the rapid changes around her. She was impressed how fast things were voted on, how quickly decisions were made, and that things were decided collectively. It was something she yearned to see happening on Mars. At the same time she was troubled by the question how long it would take until this system backfired and decisions were made to the disadvantage of others. She arrived at a point where she realised, that it didn't matter what kind of system she was trying to integrate into, that there was always something she could find that could go wrong, voiding every possibility for her to truly enjoy the parts that actually did work.

During the days Elisa kept herself busy by helping out Reina and Phil in the Farms. She had offered five hundred Martians for someone to hold a public workshop, to explain how to reprogram the software of the utility robots. Within half a day she found herself sitting in a room with a handful of people listening to a youngster explaining the entire technology stack to her and the others. Without the constant workload of expanding Mars she had time to improve her own skills, without a superior breathing down her neck, telling her what to do and how. It was in these moments of listening and learning that she felt a level of calm that was for once not related to smoking weed.

At some point, Phil had dared to post his first message to the community, asking for volunteers to test his strawberries. He was looking for new customers, so to speak, testing out the waters of the new economy. He'd described the technology in detail, explaining where they were sent to in the past and the favours he had gotten, to get a clean slate and position himself. He gave the strawberries away for free in the end, but still ended up making over two hundred Martians in tips.

Comparing her own indecisiveness towards the current events, Elisa noticed how Reina had become quieter. She had watched her snap and defend herself in situations where neither was required. At first she wasn't sure if it was part of her personality or something else. In the end she remembered how Reina had looked after her and Phil on the day they had returned, defending them all the way into her room and helping them get out their message. So Elisa decided to step out of her usual observational role to ask if there was something she could help her with.

Elisa eventually found the right time and place, while they were sitting in the farm tunnels, between the vegetable panels, working on one of the harvest bots. Reina was sharpening the cutters of the thin bot that was looking like a praying mantis, while Elisa had connected her terminal to it to inspect the scripts that implemented the palette of actions that the AI could choose from. She put her terminal down and looked at Reina move the whetstone over the short blade at the end of the robotic arm.

"Hey Reina, I think if you need someone to talk to, I'd like to help, if I can."

Elisa watched her stop her rhythmic motion with the whetstone and looked at her.

"What makes you think that?"

"Actually, I don't know really, it's just a feeling about you, well, maybe because I've noticed that you are not your own self any more. Don't get me wrong, I wish I had half the character you have to say what you think and be who you are. But, I don't know. I have the feeling something has changed." She felt awkward to use so many words to break the ice.

Reina remained quiet, staring at the device between them. She grabbed one of the wheels and turned it. The device responded with a high pitched whine with each rotation of her wrist working against the motors.

"Reina, It's ok if you don't want to talk. But if there is one thing I've started to learn about myself, is that there is no point in piling up the stuff inside, and not talk about –"

"And how has that worked out for you?" Reina interrupted her. "You hated this place and the universe disappearing has now conveniently turned Mars into something you like. What's your point?"

Reina looked at the bot between them. Elisa felt being pushed away. The woman who convinced them to crawl out of the farms and had helped them get the truth out, was now arguing against her. At least she wanted her to know, that she wanted to help her if she wanted it..

"Hey Reina, you don't have to tell me anything, ok? I'd only like to help you, it's only fair. I don't want you to be alone."

"But that is exactly what I'm going to be. You and Phil you don't have anyone on Earth and noone here, so how is anything I've got to say going to make sense to you?"

XXII (ELISA)

Elisa remained silent and watched the other woman turn the wheel of the bot, rhythmically whirring the motor with each half turn, repeating the squealing noise.

"You see, while Mars is going full party mode with change and new-found purpose in every corner, time is ticking. It's slowly ticking away." Reine forced the wheel against the motor for another round of squealing rotations.

"Yes, but that's ok."

"Why is that ok? Tell me! Why is that ok?"

Elisa looked for words, she definitely had nothing to respond. Her words came out slowly.

"I don't –"

Reina cut her off again.

"Of course you don't know. Of course you don't fucking know. You both are social degenerates."

The woman with the red tattoos on her face was shouting at her. All Elisa felt she could do was look at her hand turning the wheels and let her continue to talk.

"If you don't have anyone you deeply care about, you cannot know. And with every fucking hour, it's another hour ticking on Earth. I can only think of two things that could have happened so far. The first is, Earth is gone for good and she's dead. Or, Earth is going through exactly the same shit we are going through, but without nice cosy tunnels and a heated environment built against the cold Martian surface. And don't tell me you are thinking otherwise. Lara's either already dead, or she is still sitting on a floating launch site in the middle of the ocean, waiting to freeze to death. Or she has made it to a harbour or a city, which wouldn't change the part about freezing to death, but it would possibly add even more people going crazy to the picture. We are just lucky the crazy part has turned into something positive here. This place is small enough to remain optimistic. Do you even know how lucky we are? Think about how this would play out if you had millions of people around you! On the surface. And not metres of rock and layers of air as isolation. Then you're done! Do you even realise how lucky we are? To be here on Mars right now? And with every hour passing, this feeling of uncertainty, fear and helplessness is growing inside me. I need to know what has happened to her!"

The two women sat between the rows of vegetables and fruit, with the bot between them, leaving just enough space to walk around it. No one said anything for a while and Elisa kept silent. Still, she was trying to think of a way that could help Reina. She really wanted to help her, even if talking about it wasn't her strong point. Elisa cleared her throat.

"Hey, what do you think of this: As soon as we get a chance, we will go up on that station and see for ourselves. We'll take a look at what is real and what they have heard from earth and figure out what we can do. If they haven't been telling the truth entirely, at least we will find out what the truth is. And you have every right to know. Should there be any way to get to Earth, I will personally go and look to see if she is OK."

Elisa thought about her last sentence, which had come out without thinking. It dawned on her, that deep inside her she still wanted to get away from Mars, no matter how much it had changed.

XXIII (IRIS)

Iris sat in the meeting room in the section neighbouring her flat, with her back towards the windows. For five days she had been enduring the darkness, trying to avoid it as best as she could, spending her time following the sparse trickle of news from the city.

She had to be the first in the meeting room before the other three could arrive. She had been twenty minutes early, continuously tapping her fingers against the screen, impatiently waiting. Iris repeatedly refreshed the screen, tapping and dragging her fingers across it. But every time she did so, it remained unchanged, displaying the same information and still no connection to the city.

They had been cut off. They were in the dark about the universe disappearing around them and in the dark about what was going on in the city. Only a different face showed up every day, declining their requests to access the network and let the stewards report to the station. She wiped the table with her hand where she had crushed the insect days ago, then looked up at the door, expecting any of the other managers to enter any time. She checked her shoes again and spotted traces of dirt on the insides of her soles. Grinding her shoes against the chair, she tried to rub them clean. Iris had spent the days walking up and down her terra-suite until the grass under her feet had been stamped into the ground leaving a brown skidmark across the green floor. She had been rewatching her husband's latest transmission many times, as well as the videos from the relay stations of the moment when Earth disappeared. The situation made her restless, she was in a position where she had no access to new information and she had no control over what was happening around her.

Mr. Ginn was the first to enter the meeting room. Her feeling of nervousness made way for a combination of hate and anger towards him and she didn't greet him when he entered, nor did he greet her. They had clashed in the previous days. It had been his idea to manipulate the video of the crash. To her annoyance he had responded in front of the others that it had been Iris' idea that the situation needed to be managed in the first place and that he had only acted on the recommendation of the simulations. She had screamed at him that he could shove his simulations up his arse and use his brain for a change.

With Mr. Ginn in the room time was passing even slower. It was tormenting her. Now with him present, she couldn't even continue to scrape off the remaining traces of dirt from her trainers and rub them into the carpet. She was locked in her own skin, trying to keep up her facade of staying calm.

Her glass of water was in the way of her accessing the controls of her screen and she pushed it to the edge of her screen, to avoid picking it up, revealing her shaking hands.

Iris quickly jabbed at the screen to refresh it, and hid her hands under the table again. The system indicated that there was still no contact from the surface. The only data that was updating, came from the ships connected to the station, crawling with grey little dots, confined to their respective ships.

It was Mr. Moreno's idea to keep the six hundred people on the ships and lock them out after he had been attacked by one of the passengers. Someone had hurtled a shrink wrapped kilogram of dried beans against his face leaving a grey, green, rectangular imprint under his left eye. A certain Mr. Hamza was the accused, who had been confined to his room on the spaceship as a result. Iris had said she had never heard the name or seen the man, who had complained about his missing credits.

Mr. Moreno and Mrs. Zhao were late. When Iris heard their voices outside, further down the corridor, she had to impatiently wait for them to come closer.

Her tension increased, when they didn't come closer, but stayed outside, whispering, inaudibly for Iris, adding to her rising anger, not knowing what they were discussing, effectively keeping her out of the loop. Iris didn't care about Mr. Ginn being kept out of the loop, but she had to know what they were talking about. Before she could get up and walk to the door to listen, they stopped talking and walked into the meeting room. They sat down and switched on their screens. Iris' eyes flitted between the two, trying to read their expression, to see if there was any information to be picked up from them.

I'm out of the loop!

Mr. Moreno began the meeting.

"We've got a small team working for us now. To shut down our sections, so we can conserve energy."

He shared his screen with a visualisation of *The Gateway To Earth*. Small pie charts popped up around the perimeter of each segment of the station: the green ones showed the battery capacities and the coloured pie charts showed the main power consumers. The bald man continued.

"The biggest consumers are the ships headed for Earth. Well, the ships that were scheduled to go to Earth, to be precise. With the current power consumption we are going to last two more days at the most."

Mrs. Zhao chimed in.

"We have decided to send the six hundred passengers back to Mars. Two of the flight crews have been instructed to report back on what is happening on Mars and to restore communication. It will take them two round trips with the four shuttles to get everyone down to the surface."

Iris narrowed her eyes. Her thoughts went in circles, tuning in and out from what was happening around her.

We have decided? Who is we? Why was I not in-

volved?

Iris inhaled sharply, to focus on the meeting again and without consideration, interrupted Mrs Zhao.

"*We* still have to vote on that!"

The woman opposite her went quiet and looked at the other two, looking for support. Mr. Ginn looked up from his screen and smiled.

"Yes, I told you. *We* need to vote on this." He agreed.

Iris' thoughts were juggling his words.

Is he mocking me? Or is he even taking me seriously?

Mr. Moreno raised his arm and Mrs. Zhao quickly joined and raised her arm as well. Mr. Ginn took his time to slowly hold up his hand, while smirking at Iris. Iris saw the three hands and faces look at her and she briefly raised her arm as well, putting it down again as quickly as she could to hide her trembling hands.

The meeting went on with Mrs. Zhao continuing her presentation. The animation on the screens continued, showing the four large space ships undock and land on the edge of the screen next to a pictogram of the city.

"This way, we will have more than enough energy for a month up here. Enough time for the ground crews to accomplish their tasks. Once they are done they will pick us up. Until then we have to move into a single section, to conserve energy."

Iris gauged his last sentences. She watched the animations, how temperatures were lowered in all sections but one. Her section stayed unchanged.

"Good choice!" Iris said delightedly and folded her hands under the table into her lap, briefly looking at the others and back onto the animation, nodding her head.

The others continued with the meeting. At some point Iris' attention was caught by a question from Mr. Ginn.

"What about food? What about water? How long will that last?"

Mr. Moreno bent slightly forward, looking at the other man who said nothing. He sat there waiting and staring. Iris watched the interaction, while picking at the skin at the edges of her fingernails.

The silence in the room eventually made the younger man uncomfortable and he defended himself.

"It was a serious question. What difference does it make if we can stay here for another month with the batteries up if we have nothing to eat?"

Nothing to eat?

Mrs. Zhao cleared her throat and answered the question.

"With a small maintenance crew we have enough food for half a year. We will make sure to take out enough supplies from the ships."

And while watching Iris, she added:

"We will have enough to eat."

Enough to eat. Good.

◆◆◆

Back in her terra-suite, Iris walked up and down

the room again, repeatedly looking at her reflection in the windows. The sprinklers had been running while she was away during the meeting and the brown track had turned into mud.

Oblivious, she walked up and down her track and the mud built up on her shoes. Over and over again she stopped in her tracks to look out the window. Staring at her reflection waiting for something to happen, for the sun to return, for Mars to reappear on either side of her luxurious space. But whenever she stopped she saw nothing but the reflection of the bushes and grass in the windows curving with the structure of the station. She alternated her routine of walking up and down the room with sitting on the chaise-longue with her eyes glued to the arcing screen on the shallow table in front of her. On it, she switched between refreshing the status windows showing the missing communication links to Earth and rewatching the latest transmission of her husband, up to the moment were the signal was lost, followed by the video feed of the Lagrange stations showing Earth disappearing into nothing. Iris repeated this process over and over again, but it did not reveal anything new to her.

At some point, she was briefed about the progress of reorganising the station to optimise the resource allocations. She watched the status animations of the other sections changing. The sections were being switched off one by one. Her section was the last one to remain running at full power. She thought it was the best section to be kept running.

Not because it had her apartment in it, but because it had something else, something she could not remember what it was, that made it different.

Irritatedly, she stood up again to walk up and down the long room. Every time she looked outside, all she could see was nothing but darkness. She had brought up the question of how they would know that Mars was still below them during the last meeting because they couldn't see a thing without any light when she looked out of the windows. Mr. Moreno had explained that the gyroscopes installed at the centre of the station would have detected if the station had changed its flight path and left orbit. As that was not the case, she could be reassured that they were still orbiting Mars. In addition, they showed her what each representative of the day had to say, that there still was someone in close communication range. Until then, it was the same message of rejecting their orders to reinstate full communications and control over the city again and again.

Iris stopped in the middle of her track, her shoes squishing on the muddy ground. She glanced at the screen on the table from where she stood.

Did the screen change? Was there any news from Earth?

From her location, she watched the animation of the station circling around Mars, her gaze switching between looking at the window where the planet was supposed to be and back at the animation. She understood the animation, it showed the station orbiting around Mars, but still when she looked outside she could see nothing.

How does this work? How does this even make sense? He said we are orbiting Mars. But are we really still orbiting Mars? We have enough to eat.

"We are orbiting Mars. We will have enough to eat." Even when she repeatedly spoke the words out loud to herself, alone in her terra-suite, she imagined how *The Gateway to Mars* was hurtling through empty space, all the stars extinguished at once, leaving the galaxy. She could feel darkness and emptiness engulf the station, waiting for her behind the window's reflections. The sun was gone. Without a sun, there would be no life ever on any planet again. Without the sun, their hours left on the station were slowly ticking away to either freeze or starve. Iris repeated the words again.

"We are orbiting Mars. We will have enough to eat."

She looked back at the windows stretching from the floor high up the curved ceiling. A bumble bee flew past her face and she aggressively smacked it away with her hand. The insect flew buzzing against the blue ceiling glowing around her and the windows, then spiralled down to land in the muddy track. She hurried over and stepped onto it. She looked at the walls.

Is this really the station? Is this a simulation about to end? Was my entire life a simulation, now coming to an end?

She looked around.

Was someone there?

"Hello?" She called out into the room and walked over to the deck in the middle and sat down again, refreshed the screen and rewatched all the videos. Her hands were trembling as she watched Earth disappear over and over again. When she refreshed the screen for updates she thought she heard something again as if someone had been next to her, just seconds ago. She called out into the room.

"Hello?"

Iris jumped up, out of the chair and walked around the furniture, looking around, her eyes frantically searching the room. She spun around and shouted at the ceiling.

"Hello? Who's there?"

Someone's here! I know it!

Then, out of nowhere, she heard the familiar sound of a strip of velcro being opened behind her head. She jumped and spun around.

"Hello? Who is this? Show yourself!"

Her hands were holding on to the back of one of the chairs, clawing into the fabric as tightly as she could with her trembling hands. Her knuckles turned red, then white, pushing against her skin.

Again she heard the velcro sound burst behind her head. She let go of the chair, jumped aside and turned around towards the opposite direction, stumbling backwards.

"Who is this?"

She was screaming now, eyes wide open.

"Who is this?"

She grabbed her hair, trying to feel if something

was at the back of her head.

The only response she got was another burst of velcro, like white noise, ripping into her head. She screamed, grabbed her head, pressed onto her ears as hard as she could with her flat hands and continued to scream, then started punching against her ears. She walked away and stumbled forwards until she fell onto the grass, her shoulder hitting the muddy trail.

And again, she heard the rough sound of velcro tearing, this time clearly audible, inside her head. She kicked out with her feet, struggling in the mud, screaming from the top of her lungs.

"Go away! Get out of my head!"

Suddenly, she felt something grab her at the shoulder. She instinctively twisted away, trying to escape it. She tried to look up. Through her tears, she saw several bodies standing above her, bending over, thin arms reaching out.

They are coming to get me!

She tried to defend herself. She screamed and lashed out at the arms and fingers trying to grab her. When she kicked out she could feel the bodies around her, until they got rougher, held her down, grabbed her arms and feet. Bodies knelt into her legs, pushed her into the mud. She screamed and cried, unable to move. A hand grabbed her head and pushed her face to the side and into the mud. Iris screamed and tried to defend herself, struggling under the arms and the weight of the bodies holding her down, as she felt the prick of a cold needle at the back of her neck.

XXIV (IRIS)

Iris woke up to the familiar voices of Mr. Moreno and Mrs. Zhao whispering at the end of her bed. She kept her eyes closed and tried not to move. The voices stopped and she heard the man whisper.

"Is she awake?"

She remained still, her eyes shut, trying to perceive as much as possible from the room, just using her ears. Mr. Moreno's steps came closer, walking over to her left side of the bed with slow and careful footsteps. At the foot of the bed she could hear Mrs. Zhao, stepping quietly from one leg to another, her fingers tapping against the frame of the bed. A shadow moved across her eyes, back and forth. Mr. Moreno's voice was much closer now.

"She's still asleep. We'll have to wait and see what condition she is in when she wakes up."

From the bottom of the bed she heard Mrs. Zhao.

"When she wakes up, we have noone here with experience to help her. Maybe one of the physicians down in the city have worked with a case like this in the past. We have to help her. We have to do something. We *have* to help her!"

Help me with what? There is nothing wrong with me. Is this a test? Are you testing me? Have you decided now that I'm the problem?

She lay still, breathing as calmly and steadily as possible, holding her breath for seconds while listening in on the conversation around her bed. Mr. Moreno moved away again.

"You are right. You are one hundred percent right. But what about the city? They are not telling us anything. We don't even know if it is safe to land! They could be at each other's throats, or at ours as soon as we arrive. We know absolutely nothing!"

Another test! Now you are trying to scare me! This is not going to work! You'll see, I'll know more than you soon. You are not going to get rid of me this way.

"But we can't keep her here on the station, there is no one here to–"

Yes, you keep talking. Trying to wake me up. You will see. This is a trap. You will not get rid of me on my last days before I retire. I know people like you. And what are you trying to hide all the time? Help me? Help me with what? I'm not the one hurtling through empty space. The station is. And next you are trying to convince me to leave in a shuttle so you have the station alone for yourself! Hah! I knew it! This is what you are trying to do! Get rid of people, grab everything for yourself! It's not my head which conjured up this infinite darkness. You have! I bet you have been part of this from the beginning!

Mr. Moreno was interrupted by the sound of doors sliding open behind him.

The door is to my left. Is this my bedroom? Who let them in? This is my room. Get out!

An unknown voice came through the door.

"The last shuttles have left the station, we are the only ones up here now."

"Thank you. We have to wait. Let's see what our teams report when they do."

Mr. Moreno sounded pleased and the door closed again.

Yes, it's all going according to your plan. You've got rid of almost everyone already, haven't you? We'll see! I've seen right through you, all the time.

Just as she finished her thought, Iris perceived a faint glow coming from her right.

What's that? Is that light from outside? Shit, I almost moved. What's happening?

Iris heard Mr. Moreno rush around the bed, towards the dim light.

"What happened? Where's that light coming from?"

Ah shit. Another test! Nice try! You think I'm awake and trying to get me to move! You'll see! You'll see! I'll make my move soon enough. I have more patience than you think!

Mrs. Zhao gasped.

"It's gone, the darkness is gone! Thank goodness! I can't believe it. Fuck, I'm gonna cry."

Trying to get me excited now, are you?

The two cheered and Iris heard their hands slapping against the glass.

Nice try!

"I don't believe it! Quick, let's check the other side. Mars is on the other side!"

Really trying to get me excited, right? Fucking liars!

Iris listened to how the two ran away from the windows, past her bed and out through the door.

Silence? The door is still shut.

She remained motionless in the bed.

I'll show you.

Iris opened her eyes enough to see if someone had silently remained in the room with her. Noone was in front of her. The room was empty. She opened her eyes and saw sunlight reflect from the ring, throwing shadows across her bed. When she looked up at the windows, she saw the metal of the station framing the glass, bright with sunlight. Further away she saw the white ring of the opposite side of the station, a bright band going across the windows.

This is real light! Quick! Get up!

She slid out of the bed and ran over to the control panel next to her door.

Yes, I remember now! This is the only section, this is my section! That was it! How could I forget this? Now, let's see, yes. Root. Yes! I can see you.

A cross-section of the segment appeared on the screen in front of her. Seven grey dots were in the meeting room motionless, in a bundle in front of the windows. One grey dot was her, in her room, a quarter section away from them. Two more were making their way to the group.

Wait and see, yes! I'll show you. You won't get rid of me so easy!

As soon as the last two dots had made their way into the room, the door that was depicted on the map closed. She tapped the icon and a menu opened.

Yes. Override. Lock. Revoke access. Gotcha!

Iris was getting excited.

You should see your faces! Do you see how easy it is when you know more than others?

Iris walked through the hallway into her garden and looked at the empty room. The grass was green besides the muddy path she had created over the last days. She walked over to the windows that faced Mars, an orange-brown canvas filling the windows, spinning under the station.

We are still orbiting Mars!

She turned around and ran over to the table.

Earth! Where is Earth?

She manually refreshed the status screen again, but there was still no communications link to Earth. The Lagrange points were also missing.

Wait! They moved everything to this section, this means I should have access to the radio systems.

In the overview panel she confirmed once more that the grey dots were still locked inside the meeting room. She closed the overview, navigated two levels up and two levels down into the radio and transmission controls.

Let's see. Where is the direct transmission channel to Earth? Here!

All channels were indicated as busy.

Zero encoded channels found? What do you mean? What do you mean, all busy? There is noone here who could be sending! I am the one who has to send a message to earth! Give me a transmission channel! They can't be all blocked, that's impossible!

She clenched her hands into fists and began to repeatedly slam them as hard as she could into the table, screaming at its surface.

I'm not going to give up so easy. You are not going to win this. I will show you.

Iris closed her eyes and took a deep breath. She navigated back into the overview of her section on the station, tapped on the room and turned on the camera. Inside, Mr. Moreno was hammering his fists against the door. Two other men were trying to pry open the door with their fingers. Mrs. Zhao was waving at the camera, trying to talk to Iris.

"Iris, we need to talk. Please!"

What do we need to talk about now? Talk about how you want to 'help' me?

"Iris, look outside. This is not our solar system!"

Not our solar system? Really? We spend six days in darkness, and suddenly we are somewhere else? Really? You are lying again!"

"Look outside! This is not the sun. Look at the other planets! There are other planets!"

Iris saw the others standing at the windows, looking outside, with their faces in awe. Mrs. Zhao was still talking to the camera in the corner of the room, repeatedly pointing with her arm towards the window.

"Iris, if you are watching this, you have to look outside. There are two big bright blue dots with moons! Look! Outside! Trust me. Look! Please! We want to help you! But you have to let us out of this room! Please! I'm begging you!"

XXV (GÉRÔME)

Esra turned her gaze away from Earth's surface shining bright in the sunlight four hundred kilometres below and looked at her husband.

"Gérôme, we both know this is over. There is nothing we can change. There is no infrastructure on Earth left to support this station. It's over."

He was still looking through the window, at the white clouds mixed with streaks of grey smoke covering Europe. For the past two weeks he had spent every day and night with his wife confined to their room watching Earth. Twice a day someone brought them food and water, at some point even a small bottle of wine.

She grabbed his shoulder and gave it a light squeeze to get his attention.

"Look honey. We are lucky the second shuttle came. Everyone can go back and no one is left behind. I know we have to find a way to live our lives entirely different from now on. It will be different from what we've imagined, but we *will* find a way. And noone on the station got hurt or will get hurt. You should give yourself credit for that."

Gérôme's eyes welled up and he could feel the painful lump of sadness at the back of his throat hindering him from speaking. The only sound he was able to produce was a squeak that turned into a whine. He felt his wife move closer hugging him tightly, while he rested his head on her shoulder. He exhaled and let go, crying, sobbing into his wive's arms. It hurt him to leave the hotel, something he had taken care of for more than a decade. But now it was all over.

He stayed in her arms for as long as he needed. She caressed his cheeks, brushing over the stubble that had been growing into a beard over the past week. When he felt he was ready to talk, he raised himself up and held onto her hands.

"Honey, I know. I know it's over. I knew I would eventually leave this place, but it shouldn't be the end of the station. For everyone to leave it. All the work and engineering that created all this. Now, it's for nothing..."

He wiped away the tears from his face and tried to brush away the wet streak he had left on Esra's blue pullover. He gestured at the room, looked at the ceiling, the walls, the windows and eventually down at Earth.

"It's just so painful to let go. It's so many things at once. All I ever worked for, the life we created up here, is gone."

He sat up, watching the bright surface slowly blend into the night over the Asian continent. Where once bright lights had traced the outlines of the border between land and water he could only see a few glowing speckles, as if organised civilisation had been reduced tenfold, hiding which country or continent was sleeping below. He looked at his slight reflection on the glass.

"And who knows what else is gone."

They packed their bags for the last time in space and were ready to leave when the door was unlocked from the outside. Without saying a word they complied to the instructions to follow the security detail through the station towards the dock where the shuttle awaited them to take them back to Earth. Their path took them around a third of the station towards their airlock. A trail of twenty people was following them, most of them staff. When they arrived at the dining hall Gérôme stopped and looked one more time through the biggest windows on the station, taking in the beautiful sight of their planet below. He turned around to face the opposite side, looking at the changed stars of an entirely different star system. He deeply inhaled and turned around to address his former staff.

"I'd like to thank you all. For everything you have done for me and for all the time of your lives that you have spent with everyone up here. Thank you, for the welcoming place you have made possible. From the bottom of my heart, thank you."

Gérôme looked back at the row of faces lined up behind them, each face adding to a tired trail of uncertainty, looking at him holding back his tears. His eyes stopped at the two security personal catching up with them in short, steady strides. His eyebrows tensed at their sight and he had no grateful words for them. They had taken away the station from him and his staff and separated everyone as soon as power was restored. The solar-cell coating of the station was fuelled by a new sun. All they had been told in the meantime was that they weren't in the solar system any more but in a new, unknown star system, with at least dozens of other planets nearby. Gérôme knew that everyone was as clueless as everyone else. All he knew was, that the things he saw were the new reality. The radio antennas had been picking up an unseen amount of noise, thousands of unknown signals every second which suggested they were not alone.

Gérôme took another deep breath and he continued his speech before the security detail could catch up.

"We will have to begin our new chapters of life back on Earth, and from there we will see how this new world will unfold. For sure, it will have an immense impact on each and every one of us. We will see what the future will bring us. We have to see this as something new." Gérôme pointed at the windows, away from Earth. "A new era."

He paused again, looking for words. He hadn't planned to say anything, but he wanted to remember his departure in a way he was proud of. It had been impossible to get in touch with his staff over the two weeks. He even tried shouting through the walls. He had been staring out the window for hours with his wife after they had spotted the other planets. They felt inhibited, not being able to share this moment with staff they had grown close to. But they had each other, to share their ideas or concerns about this new world suddenly unfolding around them. But in addition to the extreme change of their environment Gérôme was frustrated. He couldn't believe what he saw and he couldn't believe the situation they had been in. Locked away, controlled by a political opportunist.

They had spent a lot of time looking out the windows, and had given the planets their first names. The closest one looked like a bigger version of Earth, but with three tiny moons. It was now called *The Big Blue Three.* They had guessed its size assuming the moons were the same size as their own. There were more planets, further away to both sides of Earth, like a ring of coloured marbles best seen when the station passed exactly through Earth's shadow. They called the others *The Big Grey One*, followed by *The Two Smaller Blue Ones* and the *The Greyish One*. Earth's moon itself was still there, too. At no point had Gérôme and Esra been able to find out if, what they saw, was physically possible. But after five sunless nights anything was possible to him now.

"Keep moving!"

The shout came from the back of the group, from one of the security personnel. Gérôme turned around and continued walking through the dining hall. The group moved past the bar, past the empty shelves. Gérôme remembered once more the life and celebrations that had taken place in this hall, not even that long ago. He left the empty stage, framed by big windows and the thick red curtains raised, behind him. It was a stage he had never been on himself, and he now regretted he had never taken the opportunity to do so. When they arrived at the end of the dining hall he stopped once more and turned around, to have a last look at this magnificent place. He needed a second to mentally say goodbye and give it a place in his memories. He knew he would miss this incredible station built by humans, which orbited at more than seven and a half kilometres per second above the planet. Esra stopped with him, too. They stepped aside, to let the others pass. Gérôme felt sadness and the lump at the back of his throat return again. He took a deep breath, to finally move on and leave the hotel behind him when an arm reached out of the file of people that was catching up, pointing at something outside the windows. First the arm was slowly waving up and down, then it frantically pointed again followed by a scream.

"What is this thing?"

Everyone stopped in their tracks and turned towards the windows to look. Gérôme traced his steps back to look outside as well. The security detail at the end of the file started to radio back and forth, but Gérôme didn't understand their language. All he understood was that they were hectic, maybe even concerned. He looked out of the window. What he saw, made him tense, slowly forcing every breath in and out of his body. A thin oval shape was approaching the station, faster than any space ship he had ever watched. Esra moved closer and grabbed his arm, squeezing it tightly. The alien object spun around and split open at the tip, which now faced the station. Eight arms unfolded, opening op like an umbrella and in an instant lit up with bright blue flames shaped liked tear drops, stretching out towards them. They both jumped, not knowing what to expect, and held each other tight. The blue flames increased their burn, decelerating the unknown object. It increased in size with every second it came closer. It was impossible to tell how big it was without any point of reference for scale. Slowly, the dining hall spun away under it, eventually moving the object out of their view. One of the security detail ran towards the windows, radioing back and forth, trying to see, then turned around to the group and shouted a single word.

"Move!"

Gérôme couldn't allocate any thought to what he just felt. He didn't even know why he was running, following everyone, why everyone had to run. People were screaming. All he could puzzle together, was that they were definitely not alone in this world. He couldn't decide whether to be excited or scared.

"What was that?"

He asked the people around him but everyone was as clueless as him, as they were rushed through the station.

"Get to the shuttle, now!"

The security detail kept shouting, keeping up the pace of the group. One after the other they were rushed through the long, curved corridor, moving towards their shuttle, second by second, minute by minute. Doors were opening and closing the segments in front and behind them as they hurried through. He bumped into Esra when he heard another shout from the front.

"Get down!"

They scrambled to the side of the corridor, hunching down, onto their knees. A guard dressed in black ran past them with a gun drawn in his hand, pointing at something further down the corridor. Gérôme moved forward to get next to his wife, instinctively trying to cover her with his body, leaning on the wall with his elbow as she grabbed his sweaty hand. Two guards took position on each side of the corridor, trying to take cover inside doorways and a third knelt in front of the group. The fourth and last shouted into the radio behind them. Again, Gérôme couldn't understand a word. But he could read the room. There was panic. Further down the corridor the hole in the floor towards the airlock began to shimmer, throwing lights against the wall as on a ceiling of an indoor pool. He watched as the airlock filled with water from below, rising right up to the edge. A shadow moved below the surface of the water, in the glowing light. Gérôme inched closer towards his wife and gripped her hand tighter. Above the heads of the others he watched how a body shot up, out of the water, breaking through the surface, the size of a fridge. It had the shape of a squid. Tentacles quickly unfurled under its body, spreading out, reaching for the floor, slapping against the walls. Gérôme flinched and ducked closer towards Esra, watching the event unfold. Within an instant, the detail started shooting. A burst of pops and muzzle flashes unloaded into the unknown alien life form. It changed colour where it got hit, sending blue waves of glowing blotches across its skin, tentacles scrambling around, reaching out in front of itself, jerking away where the bullets ripped open its flesh and punched through its body. After seconds of gunshots and splashing it stopped moving. One of the two dark bean-shaped eyes had ripped open, leaking a transparent slime. The alien shuddered, tipped over to one side and fell on to the floor. The gunshots were still ringing in Gérôme's ears as he watched the tentacles slowly twitch from side to side, to the clicking sounds of the emptied magazines.

"Move!"

They were rushed up the stairs, to avoid passing the obliterated alien and on towards the shuttle. Once at the dock, they had to scramble down the ladder one by one into the ship, some of them slipping and almost falling. Their luggage was hastily thrown down the shaft. The two pilots with whom Gérôme had spent the first night were already inside, waiting. He wanted to talk to the pilot who had been looking for Mars, to tell her that he believed Mars would be among the other planets, but he could not find the right words. Instead he was rushed to his seat. There was no time to catch up. The group, which was collected from the other side of the station was already waiting, scared, curious faces looking at them, as they buckled into their seats. The last guard jumped down the shaft, hit the floor and limped to his seat. They undocked and left the station within minutes. Inside the shuttle, in the cabin, it was dead silent.

The seat around Gérôme adjusted to his body, as he watched the curved screen in front him. The outside camera showed the alien spaceship docked to the station, holding on to it with its arms grabbing onto the hull. He swallowed. He couldn't talk. He didn't know what to think. Even when his wife grabbed his arm and tried to gently shake him and asked what he had seen, he couldn't say a word. In shock, he floated limply against the straps pushing him back into his seat, as near zero gravity lifted him up. He felt empty inside.

◆◆◆

Esra grabbed his hand and he squeezed it back in response, holding on to her tightly. At the same time the seats spun around rotating them to face the ceiling. The spacecraft was shaking, rattling them through the re-entry burn. The screens showed the trail of smoke they dragged after them while braking their descent in the atmosphere. Eventually, the shuttle calmed, and the smoke subsided. The black sky above them slowly turned blue, the longer they fell towards earth, entering deeper into the atmosphere, in an eerie silence.

Without warning the view tilted towards the

ground showing snow-covered mountains in the distance and a burning city in between. At the same time the seats rotated forward again to level the passengers' backs with the ground. Gérôme felt as if he had just changed direction on a swing at the highest point, and was falling back down. The shuttle completed its bellyflop manoeuvre and tilted the spacecraft upright. The loud cracking rumble of the rocket engines igniting filled the cabin. Gérôme felt deceleration push his weight into the seat. The world stopped moving towards the camera on the screen and disappeared behind a plume of smoke kicked up by the landing burn. Deceleration then stopped completely and the engine rumble subsided. No one clapped. No one cheered for having experienced the trip of their lifetime of visiting space. Gérôme was unable to move, as he watched, in silence, like everyone else, the surveillance video of the alien creature bursting from the airlock and being shot to pieces.

XXVI (ELISA)

It was the morning the sunlight had come back to Mars. Elisa sat with Reina and Phil in a small nook inside the cafeteria dome, her nose hovering over her cup of coffee, while staring at the other two on the opposite side of the table. The square box of a service bot had just disappeared after leaving them with their three coffees. They were waiting for the throng of people queueing to get their breakfast to shrink away. Elisa had paid for the coffees with her pool of Martians, in an attempt to cheer up the mood. She had no clue why Phil was not talkative, but she had a good idea what occupied Reina's mind. Either way she had no intention to break an early morning of silence without having her first coffee and focused her eyes back on the hot, shiny surface in her hands. The queue slowly inched forwards. She was sceptical about whoever had the idea to change chefs in the kitchen just because someone suddenly felt that it had been their life-long calling to be a chef instead of a drill operator. At least the menu had surprisingly increased in length, apparently confirming the majority vote to be right.

As surprisingly as the light suddenly shone through the windows, the atmosphere inside changed with it. The first reaction was a natural duck or drop in whatever you were carrying, for those who had just got their trays filled up. Elisa had to rebalance the coffee sloshing in her mug from her own reaction. No matter if they were still in pyjamas, in a leisure suit or work clothes, they all immediately ran towards the windows, gathering around the brightness as if waiting for their favourite band to show up, pushing their noses against the glass to look outside, to see a world of regolith soaking up the sun. Elisa placed her cup on the table and stood up to get a better view. Eventually, she turned around and addressed the other two, who were still seated.

"Now that the queue is gone, we at least could get some breakfast." She was excited and pissed off at the same time.

They made their way through the middle of the dome, watching the crowd gathering around the windows. Some were moving closer with their trays to continue their breakfast closer to the natural light. Elisa decided for beans on toast out of habit and walked back to their table. Phil and Reina soon followed, both their trays filled with a new item from the menu: bread rolls filled with fried tomatoes and mushrooms. Elisa didn't care to ask if either of them wanted to swap, or at least let her try, but she regretted her routine for a moment.

Minutes later the screens on the ceiling turned on, showing a bright sky above their heads. It didn't take long until the first planets in their vicinity were spotted. A handheld camera zoomed in on a yellowish planet, slightly shaky across the screen, operating at the maximum possible optical magnification. Gasps went through the dome.

"What–" Reina couldn't finish her words and Phil remained quiet, biting at his fingernails, watching the screen above Elisa's head. She swallowed the last bite from her breakfast and leaned back to take in the screen on the opposite ceiling of the dome.

"Where the hell did this come from? This can't be our potato, right?" she asked.

She fetched her headphones from her pockets and let the almost transparent devices disappear into her ears. She tuned into the stream running on the screen above.

"– far we have spotted seven other planets around us, as if in the same orbit. The images you can see are live from one of the landing pads. The shuttles have returned during the night, bringing back the six hundred passengers originally destined for Earth, with two roundtrips each. We are being told that this had been a measure by the former management to increase their chances of survival on the station."

The view switched to a smaller planet half lit by the sun, then to another, both slightly greyish and blue.

"We kindly suggest that all physicists and astronomers in the city please check the local channels and share whatever insights they have on what we are seeing in the sky right now. The recordings are being uploaded as we speak for further analysis."

Elisa took out her headphones again and looked at Reina, who was still listening to the broadcast.

"What happened to our solar system? What the fuck has happened? Where do these planets come from? And how the fuck did that happen? You can't just displace a bunch of planets, not even a single planet within five fucking days! How?" Elisa was done with being quiet.

Reina looked at her, with a gaze that she read as her brain working full speed on what the new scenario entailed. Elisa continued to let her own thoughts come out, unfiltered.

"The last time I had an interest in possible future space technologies and theories is years ago. It has only left me with the impression that physics and gravity suck and it's impossible to obtain and maintain the energy to move even a single spaceship fast enough to get anywhere. If that had not been the case our future wouldn't have been digging holes on Mars right now. What has happened? What is this? I mean, what the fuck?"

Reina looked like she was listening to her own voice in her head instead of Elisa's thoughts. The tattooed woman began to talk, her words coming out carefully one after the other.

"Whatever this is. Earth disappeared before us, so there might be a chance that, no matter what this is, that Earth is out there, among those other planets. I don't care if it's technically possible or not. I need to know!"

Reina quickly fumbled out her terminal, placed it

on the table and started drumming away on a keyboard projected under her fingers. After her typing had stopped, she read out from her screen.

"Check for planets closer to the sun. Are there more planets, smaller and further away?"

She looked at Phil and Elisa and asked them to upvote her request. Soon, the question bubbled up the recent topics and was picked up by the stream. They turned their earpieces back on to follow the screens above them.

"– a good question! We are waiting for further views to be accessible from the cameras installed on the shuttles. They will be automated and less shaky. In the meantime, let's get back to the first responses we have from our astrophysicists. If we have understood them correctly, what we are seeing is technically not possible. We will wait and see if they can come up with further details and theories as soon as possible. But it looks like this is history in the making. To everyone else who has just tuned in: Yes, the sun is back! But as it seems, we are not sure if we are in a different star system or if we have new neighbouring planets in our own solar system. As soon as we have more details we will keep you up to date immediately. OK? Yes, let's switch the cameras to the shuttle cams. Let's get back to the question: Are there more planets, further away? The answer at the moment is: maybe. At the moment it's not clear yet if the spots we are seeing in this shot of the sun are sun spots or other planets. But indications are that the lower two are moving at a different speed, so at this point: yes, there could be more planets on lower orbits around this sun. Good morning everyone and to anyone who has just tuned in. The sun is back. And the solar system or this star system is not the same anymore. We will keep you updated as soon as we have more –"

Elisa removed her earpieces again and looked at Reina.

"Reina?"

She waited until she had her attention.

"Reina! Earth!"

◆◆◆

Half a day later they were sitting in Reina's room. After five days of darkness, Mars had cooled down more than ever and with the sudden energy radiating from the sun, the entire Planet was engulfed in a giant sandstorm. This time Phil sat on the empty yoga mat and Elisa in the lower bunk on top of her blankets. Reina spun in her swivel chair, bouncing from left to right. They were watching the screen above the desk and this time Phil was the one who was talking.

"This is strange and amazing at the same time. I have been working my ass off here for twenty years, hoping to get the chance to dig through Martian dirt and wait for an analysis to see if this planet has traces of life from millions of years ago. And now I'm staring at planets, stuck in the sky, and it's at least dozens of them! And if that isn't enough, there is all kind of noise going on in the radio frequencies of which a millionth would have been a jackpot for SETI a few decades ago!" He paused and looked around the room. "I mean this kind of pisses me off!" He looked displeased.

Elisa was thinking about Earth. Mars had been the only place to live on during the past five days in the visible or invisible universe they had been in. Now, with all the planets around them and the possibility of Earth being out there, it reminded her of her own views of Mars again, of what she had felt like every day in recent years. She turned her attention back to Phil who said,

"And regarding all this decentralised democracy shit going on; I'm pretty sure they will put a stop to that. And what's going to happen? There are investors and shareholders even living on Mars, it's only a matter of time until they want their control back of this place, just quietly waiting for something to happen, to point at the terms and conditions we signed with our contracts. We all signed fucking contracts. We depend on supplies from Earth, how is that going to change? Meds, chemicals, equipment. I mean, we are lucky the lights are back on, but the situation isn't significantly better for Mars. It's not that we have any leverage. So what's all of this going to be?"

Reina turned around from the screen and looked at Phil with a smirk.

"Dr. Scruffy, you sound exactly like Elisa, have you noticed?" She laughed and Phil looked hurt. At the same time Elisa felt she had been listening to herself through Phil and all she could do was to congratulate him:

"Welcome to the club!"

Reina turned towards them.

"I think it's not all as corpo doom and gloom as you two are making it out to be. Where is your effort to make it work? To be honest, if you call it a 'corporation' or a 'country', it doesn't make a damn difference. There will always be people who are in charge or believe they are in charge. Either way, you are never safe from those in a position of power to be actually qualified to do the job. Some just want the job for the title's sake, to put a symbolical medal on their chest. I like the situation that actually noone is in charge right now. Society should have no hierarchy. The new system makes us all equal. And the decisions impact on everyone equally. If Earth is out there, we will negotiate and there will be a middle ground."

Elisa wasn't convinced. She couldn't shake off the feeling that everything happening around her made her more vulnerable to so many things. She repositioned herself on her blankets, to talk to the other two at the same time and shared her view.

"What about all the different opinions? A majority outvoting a minority on something that doesn't affect them? How is this going to work for every topic? This would only work if everyone had an equal understanding of things, the same level of access to information and understanding, to derive conclusions, even for small groups. And even with that as a requirement, the human brain is still a nondeterministic neural network depending on too many things to account for. Feelings and needs and ideas all impact our decisions. In the past days we have been in a we-are-all-in-the-same-boat-situation, which I bet the management would have loved to use in a sentence. But this will dissolve over time and the common ground will fragment. My point and the way I see it is that over the past two hundred years, mankind has shown it doesn't scale. We don't scale in our consciousness. Our communities only work if they are small enough. I thought I would find a better system or whatever you want to call it here on Mars. But it's already too big. If Earth is out there, and I'm hoping this for you, Reina, as much as I do for myself, then my question is: What is going to stop them from sending another twenty thousand people our way? There will be not much of a choice but to continue exactly the same way as before, if it's a decentralised vote or a manager hiding on a station pretending to represent and work for what needs to be done? Who will stop our conscious and sub-conscious manipulation of others?"

The others said nothing. Reina didn't look too convinced, but Phil was quietly nodding, scratching his chin through his beard. Elisa felt as if she was looking at humanity as if it was a piece of code that was impossible to debug, but always full of flaws. Sometimes it worked and you didn't know why. But at other times you turned a cogwheel in one place and something broke somewhere else, not knowing

XXVI (ELISA)

if the two instances were related to each other or not. Deep inside herself she wanted to prove Reina wrong and at the same time she didn't know why she wanted to do that. Then, she had an idea.

"We can put this to a test. Do we have enough energy to create more fuel for the shuttles? Yes! Do we want to know if Earth is out there? Fuck, yes! Do we have enough equipment to radio back to Earth? No. So the only place we can at least take a look and ask the question, if they are still out there, is from the station. Put that into a question and see if there is a majority to give us a shuttle to go up and see for ourselves."

Reina raised an eyebrow, seemingly catching on to her idea. She spun around and unlocked her terminal.

It went fast from there. Reina typed in the topic "Let's reach out to Earth!" and added a description, arguing that there were no resource constraints stopping them from going up to the station. Within minutes it was voted down. And in addition the comments piled up: "Who needs Earth?", "We are Martians now!", "Let them suffer!" or "Go, Mars!"

The room was quiet with dissatisfaction. Elisa, on the one hand, was happy to see her opinion about how things went on Mars be validated so quickly, but on the other hand she had the confirmation of her dread of being stuck on Mars for much longer than she ever thought possible. And in addition to that she still wanted to go to the station and look for Earth, even if just for Reina's sake. Something needed to be done.

At this moment a sudden insight about herself hit her. Even if she found on Mars what she had tried to escape from on Earth, at least on Earth she had the space to get away from it all. Mars had turned out to be exactly the same, only condensed into an inescapable infrastructure, like a prison. This loss of freedom wasn't even an adequate sacrifice for science.

Phil looked pained and uneasy. He slowly got up from the yoga mat and waved at the two women to get their attention.

"You know what? Fuck this! We are going up there anyway!"

◆◆◆

It took them a week to come up with a plan. During the first days they had more company at lunch than in the days before. Those who shared their idea to contact Earth joined them, to ask if they had any plans on how to reach out to Earth and if there was a way to do this from Mars. At first they only listened. After three days they found a common ground with the pilots of one of the flight crews who had worked on the station until now. They, too, wanted to go back up and find out if Earth was still out there. They explained that they had the necessary permissions to manually set a course and launch a shuttle, and the only part they needed help with was to get to the launch pad. As the pilots had found out, the transfer pods between the city and the space shuttles had been shut down, with no way of activating them without the right digital signatures. Elisa guessed the effort required to re-flash them. To figure out how to reinitialise the operating systems or build a controller from scratch would take her at least half a month. In the worst case they would have this time, but they wanted to find a way to get to the station sooner.

To their surprise, Elisa found out that their access codes for the expedition vehicles had not been cleared. The plan was to manually drive to the launch pad through the current storm, only relying on inertial sensors and a limited visibility.

On the day of their planned departure, the dust storm engulfing Mars had begun to calm down, which worked to their favour. Unfortunately, they couldn't see the planets they had seen on the first morning anymore, which meant the screens in the cafeteria only showed a hazy, glowing sun. The images taken at night only revealed vague blotches in the sky. Enough to guess what was there, not enough to say for sure.

Elisa had packed her bags, yet again, and it had become a routine for her by now, living out of her duffle bags for weeks. She had announced on the network, that she was going to do maintenance on the vehicles for a few days, as she had been practically the last one to use them. The day before she had hooked them up to the power grid, to charge them up to storage charge capacity, the optimal value to keep them standing still for years, but still enough to get to the shuttles and back, multiple times, if needed.

She had announced to be unloading the cargo boxes and to clean the interior, but none of this was ever going to happen.

Now, she was impatiently sitting on the crates inside the vehicle, checking her space suit, checking the old but hardly outdated satellite images on her suit's terminal, waiting for the others to arrive. This time, there was no specific launch time, just the time they had agreed to meet up: two hours after lunch. She hadn't been hungry and almost choked on every bite, in contrast to Phil scoffing down as much as he could in half the time others needed to finish their own food. His method of coping with stress was apparently entirely opposite to Elisa's, and she wasn't even sure if that worked for him.

She walked around the vehicle, looking for something to do. Eventually she decided to sit in the front seats and run through the diagnostics on the vehicle's screens. She was impatient and hat to pass the time somehow. It was the day for her to finally leave Mars, at least make it to the station, even if it reduced the space she had around her even more, trading domes and tunnels with a single ring surrounded by vacuum. Before she had enough time to lose herself in the vehicle's config system, the two pilots walked through a small door entering the hangar. Two men, Felipe the flight captain, and his co-pilot Shantanu. Both wearing the same grey space suit as her, but with more signs stuck to their chests indicating their function and rank within the company. A small patch resembled a shuttle and another one resembled the station above Mars. One of them had a tiny star added to it, to indicate his superiority. Elisa smirked at the patches and thought of it as playing boy-scouts in space.

Nervously, she looked around to see if anyone else was joining them and greeted the pilots.

"Time to get away, right?"

"Yes, in a rush?"

"Long story." She was sure about that. But before she could elaborate, Reina already appeared with Phil in tow, their expressions entirely different: the tattooed woman radiated excitement, while Phil's face looked as if his farm had burnt down. They boarded the off-road vehicle and after a brief 'hello', Elisa sealed the airlock behind them, checked the life support system inside their cabin and proceeded to depressurise the hangar. Four minutes later the large doors to the ramp leading to the surface unhinged from the walls, released by the equal pressures from both sides and rolled up. The off-roader turned its wheels by ninety degrees and turned on the spot. Within a minute they had rolled up the dusty slope into the calming sand storm. Brown-grey dust hanging over the domes like a deadly mist.

Elisa compared the satellite images on one screen with the inertial measurement data, showing the count of wheel turns, direction, acceleration as well as the outside cameras of the vehicle. The screen showed the process of scanning the surface to remap and match their course. Throughout the thirty-four kilometre trip to the launch pads, Elisa had her eyes glued to the screen ignoring the hazy world around her. She was not going to let anything up for chance.

At the launch site, she got up and let the captain take over the controls, to check which of the four shuttles was the best candidate for their launch. She turned to Phil and Reina sitting on the unloaded cargo behind her.

"It's happening. I've been waiting for this, five and a half years on Mars are enough." She could feel her heart beat inside her chest. "I'm nervous to be honest."

"It'll be alright. " Said Reina.

Phil just nodded and looked away, tormented. Elisa turned to him.

"What's wrong, Phil?"

His eyes hastily went back and forth between Reina and Elisa, while the vehicle continued its slow roll towards one of the shuttles, a dark silhouette standing in the dusty curtains drifting around them. He scratched his beard.

"Okay, you two. Before we get to the shuttle I have to let you know: I've thought a lot about this. And this is going to piss you off, as I was the one who said let's do this. But I'm not going. I can't go."

His forehead was wet with perspiration.

"But, why?" Reina looked confused, even sad.

"I've thought about this a lot. Maybe too much. Elisa might understand me better than you Reina, but I tend to think too much. I have to work on this. When I'm in the farms I'm ok. But once outside, I've realised, again, it's getting worse. And I need more time. I just can't do this right now. I'm sorry, you'll have to go without me. I'm sure I won't be of great help up there in any case. I'm needed here."

He looked at both of them, but before Elisa could say anything he continued with his explanation.

"My head has been spinning in the last days. Maybe I will go up there, follow you eventually, but it's not going to be today. Even if life is out there, waiting for us, the question if life ever existed on Mars remains. I won't be bored. I still have something to look forward to, here on Mars. Please accept my decision, to stay here. I'm happy if I could help you get this far. And let me know if I can do anything for you from down here."

Elisa and Reina looked at each other and Reina was the first to act. She opened her arms and embraced Phil.

"Ok honey, we'll stay in touch, we're not going *that* far anyways. We'll send you a postcard. Don't think about it too much, just let us know you're doing okay, alright?"

Elisa, too, gave Phil a hug.

"Take care, and thank you!" She said as she held him tight.

She was sad to leave him on Mars, after all the plans to go back to Earth together. The feeling of having to leave someone behind who she actually cared about surprised her more than she wanted to admit. Her departure from Mars was suddenly connected to an emotion that had something positive in it. But she quickly reminded herself that she had to focus, had to see it through, to finally leave and pushed her feelings aside. Elisa glanced over to the pilots, steering the off-roader to park in front of the second launch pad. The jet bridge extended down through the sandy winds and connected to their vehicle, providing them with a pressurised set of stairs into the space shuttle. They said their good-byes to Phil, hugging him once more and the two women followed the pilots up the stairs.

Once inside, Elisa saw herself reversing her movements of the day she was meant to leave Mars, but this time it was only the four of them. The two pilots settled in the middle of the top deck, and they sat behind them, the seats automatically adjusting to their bodies.

Anxiously, Elisa watched the countdown. Her arms were tingling. She felt excited and scared at the same time. She watched the off-roader head back into the clouds of dust, navigating back to the city on a small window of the curved screen in front of her. The pad camera showed the silhouette of their spaceship, with brown, grey curtains rolling over the empty plane around them, hiding the other shuttles in the distance.

The countdown began, reading four minutes, and her heart jumped in her chest. This time she closed her eyes, and left them closed, hoping for the best. She waited in silence, for the audible countdown to

XXVI (ELISA)

begin. In her head she spoke out the numbers with the voice from the shuttle in her ears, her sweaty hands gripping hard onto the edge of her seat. "..., three, two, one. Liftoff."

The engines ignited on the last word of the countdown and the burning rumble shook the shuttle. She deactivated the noise cancelling of her headphones to take in as much as possible, to be engulfed in the noise, generated by force pushing them away from Mars. She felt the vessel vibrate. Her skin crawled with goosebumps as she was pushed into her seat, accelerating away from Mars.

Finally!

When she opened her eyes, tears were rolling down the side of her head into her hair.

XXVII (LUNA)

"Erial, if this were Mars how old would it be?"

Luna walked around the pillows in the centre of the living room. Erial was on the other side of the glass, strapped into the ship's controls, answering her questions through the walls.

"We don't exactly know. If this were Mars the possible range is somewhere between four point six billion and twenty billion years. Without going to its actual surface we will never be able to answer this exactly."

"Will we land on the new planet?"

"Maybe we don't have to. Let us arrive first. Then we will see. Please keep in mind that this is most likely not Mars. It's not impossible, but it's improbable."

Luna popped her head inside the sim-sphere to take another look at the images. They had been captured over the recent days and she repeatedly compared them with the handful of digital images that had made it through Earth's second middle age. The size estimation matched, but with the lack of features on its surface it was impossible to say if this was Mars. She had squinted her eyes to make them look identical, well knowing it was an unscientific attempt to make the look the same. No one had seen Mars since the blackout, a planet that had been considered missing for four centuries. But even the slightest chance of this discovery being Mars made her believe in the impossible. The correlation of the images was strong, but only if she ignored the timeframes in which Mars could have substantially changed, which was billions of years, which put the probability of this new planet actually being Mars close to zero. As curious as she was about the sheer possibility not being impossible, the more she appreciated to be chosen by the Dolvar to be the first contact. If this was not Mars, she still was going to be the first contact. A chance she would have never thought to be possible. She had been in the right time and place for either of these possibilities.

The result of all of this was that she had slept even worse in the days that followed the announcement of the planet. She was becoming increasingly restless with every hour, and it made it worse that they still had three more days ahead of them. Even a short interplanetary travel of just about a week seemed too long for her now, and she couldn't wait any longer.

"What if this really were Mars? How much time could have passed on Mars?" She couldn't stop exploring her idea of Mars from every angle.

"Luna, may we remind you that we have gone over this question numerous times. And the answer remains the same: The age of Mars could be anything, up to fifteen point four billions years. The possibility you are hoping for is incredibly small. If we were emotionally inclined to it we would say we regretted ever bringing this possibility up at all. We know you are a creative and overly optimistic species, but that makes you incredibly selfish and unrealistic."

Luna pulled her head out of the sim-sphere and returned to walking around the island in the living room. She stopped after a single rotation, top stand in front of the glass window. Inside, Erial was glowing with a soft yellow, resembling a mix of a lightbulb morphing into a Christmas tree.

"We do not mean to offend you, but it is like that. Would you like to play another round of chess? We will not use our arms to think, nor my mental capacity connected to texturing my skin for advanced and deeper planning. We would play fair according to your definition of fairness. Would you play because you want to win, or because you enjoy studying the game itself? Were you ever interested in your history to study the game or to find out if you had won?" The glow covering the alien turned from yellow to orange to green. "Do you see the difference between the Dolvar and yourself? Do you see the difference between the Dolvar and humans? This sense of being yourself: having an ego. You represent your species, but you let yourself get distracted by your personal motivations. What is the point of our interactions if your personal view and focus stand between our two species? We are not going to say that this was not entertaining, but it might turn out the same way as if you were watching and studying the matsa on Dol. You watched and learned. We watch and learn. But there never was any interaction between you and the animals living their lives on the islands. We are here to communicate. Please, remember, the goal of our exchange is to bring the consciousness of our two species closer together. Think of it this way: For an intelligent consciousness to prevail you need to be able to see yourself as a part of a bigger organism. Look at your body. Look at ours. We are all made up of cells. Each cell dies eventually, to be replaced by another. You should try to see yourself as a single cell inside a body, and everything that happens to you in relation to what's happening to the whole body. But if you keep thinking that you are a whole body on your own of course you will think that when you die the whole world ends. This is your selfishness. But this is not your role and it's not mine." Erial paused, their colours dimming. "We chose the last word explicitly to help you understand what we mean."

Luna watched the colours fade from the alien and she noticed her reflection in the glass. This was new to her. She felt the alien had put her in her place, compared her to a scaly, flying animal, butting its head against the water to hunt. She had been likened to an animal, intellectually and emotionally and she began to question whether she ever understood what this exchange was all about, or if any of the other humans had understood it. She stood there, questioning her own perspective. She remembered comparing their trip with herself looking after a pet, travelling in a van. Was she not that much different from a matsa to the Dolvar, just smart enough not to be eaten? Was the relationship between humans and Dolvar so imbalanced? Especially since the first encounter between humans and the Dolvar almost four hundred years before had ended so abruptly? Was this why the cultural distance between the two planets had been upheld for centuries with no one reaching out to Earth? Or had mankind been too busy with itself, undoing the centuries of technological advances within a few decades?

Over the centuries, historians had been in the dark about what really had happened the day humans had made first contact with the Dolvar. Only when the Dolvar had eventually reached out and provided them with their recordings did they obtain a first perspective of what had happened. As a result, many considered the Dolvar recordings to be a lie, and accused them of orchestrating the downfall of organised civilisation on Earth, to leave humans technologically behind to secure the Dolvar dominance in space. Luna believed that it didn't help that many of those who did believe the Dolvar, were of the opinion that the last humans onboard *The Gateway To Mars* were not to blame, because no one could have been prepared for the physical appearance of a Dolvar jumping out of an airlock.

In the end, humans learnt that the Dolvar were not the ugliest aliens out there by far and should consider themselves lucky with their match, especially considering the outcome.

Luna's thoughts returned to her reflections, to the uncertainties and about what she felt.

"Erial? I am scared." She tried to see the alien in the dark body of water in front of her. "I am scared of the possibilities. If this is Mars, I'm scared to learn the fate of our first and only colony on another planet. I'm scared to learn that this is not Mars, that its fate remains unknown after four hundred years. And I'm frightened to be a first contact." She turned away from the window and walked towards the cushions.

"It excites me to think about the best outcome of what I could find on Mars. To find a different kind of human society that has prevailed all that time. To listen to their stories, or to find their archives if there was no one left to tell it. It distracts me from all the other possibilities."

Mars was what kept her awake all these nights. An idea that developed a train of thought of its own, not having anyone to share it with. The probability to find a human culture that had changed over centuries, brought implications for Earth that made her realise that this exchange might eventually not be about herself at all. If this planet was indeed Mars and the colony had survived over hundreds of years, maybe even much, much longer, if the Dolvar were right, what would make these humans any less alien than the Dolvar? How could she make contact with this entirely different culture? How could she represent Earth in this case?

It made her rethink the way she had communicated with Erial, that if the Dolvar were as connected in space as within their ocean, she might have been talking to a collective after all. As much as she considered herself to be Luna, she was the result of growing up as a human being on Earth, shaped by her environment, the result of human culture rising and falling over millennia, now talking to the Dolvar. All she could really do was give it a personal touch.

She sat down on the cushions to set up their chessboard, carefully placing the pieces into their positions. She looked up and addressed the alien, who was now floating dimly behind the glass, watching her.

"Erial, we are ready to continue our conversation."

❖ ❖ ❖

"Good morning Luna! How did we sleep today?"

She heard Erial's voice as she walked out of her bedroom after yet another restless night. For seven days now, she had trouble falling asleep. She had been staring at the ceiling or at the insides of her eyelids for hours, wallowing around in her mind and literally in bed. Her thoughts were everywhere and nowhere, but always returning to human history and Mars. Asking herself the same questions over and over again. Did the same things happen on Earth as on Mars? How much time did Mars have

XXVII (LUNA)

before the blackout? Even if this wasn't Mars. What had happened to the colony? For how long did they survive?

The closer they got to their destination the more alternatives she could think of how history could have unfolded on the so called red planet. Was their society entirely different now? Was there anyone left on the planet at all? Three hundred and ninety-two years had passed on Earth since the blackout. Her own world had changed as drastically as noone could have ever imagined.

"Not so good, thank you." she replied, leaning against the wall, waiting for her breakfast to appear from the hole in the wall. As the wall opened, she grabbed the steaming bowl of matsa and seaweeds. To pass the time, she had agreed to prick her skin with a variety of needles to see if she had any allergic reactions to the foreign food, scribbling everything down in her book, describing the flavours of the things she could eat. Steamed matsa tasted like a mix of chicken and caramel and the seaweeds were closest in flavour to corn mixed with spinach. She settled down into the cushions, eating her breakfast with chopsticks. The sweet taste eventually gave her enough energy to look up at Erial floating behind the wall, slowly spinning around their axis. She felt like a child asking her parents in the front of the car, who were navigating the bumpy roads connecting the few remaining cities in Europe.

"Are we there yet?"

"We will arrive in half an hour. We have also spotted a station orbiting the planet at a height of eight hundred and thirteen kilometres. There are two tiny moons."

Luna stopped chewing and froze. The food dropped from her mouth into the bowl.

"What?"

"Yes?"

"What are the chances now?"

"It is Mars."

She looked at the shimmering alien spinning in the water, purple streaks and circles flashing across its skin and shook her head.

"No. Please. For real?"

"Very real."

She scoffed half her breakfast down as fast as she could and slammed the unfinished bowl back into the hole on her way into the bedroom. She rushed through showering and getting dressed, putting on a pair of purple pants, grey sandals and a white hoodie. She threw her pyjamas with the wet towel onto her bed and sprinted into the sim-sphere, plunging into the seat.

◆ ◆ ◆

They approached *The Gateway To Earth* as fast as Luna's body allowed. She watched the breaking manoeuvre from within the safety of her augmented sphere, hanging under the body of *The Second Blue Marble.* In front of her she saw the night crawl over the orange, brown planet. She zoomed in, to study the station in its orbit. There were no signals coming from it and there was no response when they tried to contact it. In some places she could see light coming from the windows. Luna had to focus on her breathing to stay calm, her excitement was building up with every detail she could perceive.

"There are lights in the windows! Someone could still be there! Erial, can you see anything on the surface? Is there anyone, can you see anything?"

"According to your history records, the city would be on the opposite side of Mars right now but even then, it could be hard to tell from the orbit."

Even if the planet and the station was in front of her, she felt the rapid deceleration pressing her down into her seat, embedded into the wall that was holding her in place. She had to close her eyes to avoid getting sick of her body getting confused of the mismatch of movements she felt and what she could see with her eyes. She had to force herself to breathe, pushing every hard breath in and out of her body past her lips. Erial was forcing her to her physical limits of travelling in space.

The manoeuvre stopped and she opened her eyes again, looking at stars of her own for a few seconds. She saw the dark tiles on the outside of the station move past her, almost close enough for her to touch. She watched the surface rotate beneath her, with sections of tiles entirely missing in some places. At the same time as they docked, the simsphere stopped and she found herself staring at the grey walls of the sphere, releasing her from its grip.

She climbed out and walked into the living room, noticing the lighter than usual gravity, even lighter than on Dol. Erial was already floating behind the window looking at her, their voice coming from the wall.

"We think from here onwards you should go on your own."

"What's the date today? For my notes, later."

"Seventeenth of September, 2478."

XXVIII (IRIS)

Iris stood in the empty, silent hallways of *The Gateway To Earth*. The only sounds she heard had been the doors opening and closing around her as she walked in circles, always ending up at the same place over and over again. Day in and day out. At times she thought she was walking through an endless corridor, never being able to reach her goal and her only option was to keep on walking. Even in her dreams she walked around the station. She could distinguish the corridors she walked through in her dreams from the corridor she walked in when she was awake.

When she was awake, the corridor never changed and always returned her back to her starting point. And as the days dragged on, it was her only way to distinguish dream from reality.

She kept on walking, hoping to end up in her own section, passing doors and staircases on both sides. Her eyes constantly looking ahead, staring at the floor reaching up into the next section. And then, she felt it happening again. With each of her steps, she felt the angle of the floor under her feet decrease, as if walking down a ramp. She moved towards the wall and reached out to the next doorframe, to hold on to the edge. Iris felt her feet slowly lifting from the floor, dangling almost sideways across the wall. She felt the increasing gravity pull at her. She screamed until she could not hold onto the thin edge of the door frame anymore. She fell, crashing into doorframes, tumbling down into an infinite corridor, her arms and legs flailing around her, breaking her bones when she hit the walls.

Iris woke up screaming, bathed in her own sweat, lying on the lawn of her terra suite. She wiped bits of gras from her face and looked around. A small, square service bot was next to her in the grass, upside down. Two wheels were bent and one missing. The thin aluminium surfaces were bashed in and split open at the seams, revealing the empty isolated insides consisting of thin pistons, wires and PCBs. Scenes of her smashing the artificial servant appeared in front of her inner eye. She knew those images hadn't been a dream. Iris remembered how she had crashed the bot into the animated surface of the table, braking it in the process. The transparent screen had dull white spots where she had repeatedly hit it with the service bot. The glass frame that surrounded it had broken into hundreds of pieces, lying in the grass. Small splinters glinted between the leaves, a mix of green and transparent blades.

I'm awake.

Iris looked around, most of her wardrobe was strewn across the floor, covered in mud stains. The furniture was covered with dead and smashed insects. She remembered swatting them with her clothes.

She picked up a wrinkled blouse and wrapped it around her hand. She picked up a long shard of glass, gripping it tightly through material, pressing it into the palm of her hand.

I need to get out!

The corridor stretched in front of her, bending slightly upwards with every new segment. She kept on walking, every section looking almost the same, in a repeating pattern, until she reached her apartment again.

I'm awake!

From there, she continued walking, the dirt on her feet travelling further each time, as if a brown brush had been dragged out of her flat, to travel around the station.

On her trips around the station, she passed by the meeting room. At times there were bangs or muffled screams that came from the room, which she ignored.

Earth will soon pick me up! They will make this right again. I will go to Earth. Soon. This will end! And I will tell them of your treachery.

She kept on walking, to finish yet another trip around the station. Only when she heard the double ding announcing the successful docking of a shuttle, she stopped.

Earth!

Iris walked towards to a wall terminal and looked

up where the shuttle had docked. She counted the sections between her and the icon of the interplanetary shuttle blinking on the screen.

Six sections. Time to go. I knew they would come for me! They will take me back to Earth!

Fifteen minutes later she arrived at the dock and looked at the ladder reaching down, her hand still clutching her makeshift dagger.

Where is everyone?

One by one she gripped the bars in front of her face with her bruised hands, biting through the fabric of her blouse into the shard of glass. She lowered herself down, step by step, until she reached the bottom and looked around.

This is not a shuttle! Am I really awake?

She found herself in an empty room connected to a long swimming-pool tapering towards the far side. The pool and the room were separated by a hip-high glass wall, with the surface of the water gently rippling against the edge of the glass. The only thing she recognised was a cylindrical, metallic filtration system or water heater in the corner of the pool, with its thick pipes leading into the wall. A small array of lights regularly blinked at the top, slowly dimming between blue and yellow.

"Hello? Is there anyone here?" Iris shouted against the naked walls, waiting in vain for a response. She watched the device at the side of the pool gently push a stream of water across the surface of the pool.

This has to be another dream! I have to wake up!

She shook her head and pulled at her hair. Even scratching her arms had no effect.

Why can't I wake up???

She walked towards the pool. As she bent over the edge to look at her reflection, the machine on the wall to her left stopped. She inspected herself on the steadying waves. Dark rings hung under her eyes. With her empty hand, she reached out to break the surface of the pool.

"Don't touch the water!" A voice rang from behind her, making her jump and spin around, slashing her dagger through the air, screaming.

"Not again! Where are you? You won't get me this time!" Iris attacked the air around her and screamed. She looked around the room, but there was noone.

She turned back to the pool and stepped in front of the water again, looking around, ready for gravity to change direction, ready for anything. She slapped herself in the face with her empty hand and looked at her reflection.

Why can't I wake up?

She quickly dipped her hand into the water, and splashed it onto her face. It smelled salty and tasted even saltier on her lips. With her eyes closed, she could feel it sting along her eyelids. She stumbled away, cursing, rubbing her face with her shirt, screaming in pain. Her eyes were burning.

What is this? Why can't I wake up?

She wiped off her hands, the water stinging in her hands. She screamed.

"Where are you?"

She spun around, holding the dagger in front of her, listening carefully. She screamed and pulled at her hair.

"LET ME WAKE UP!!!"

As she stumbled back towards the ladder, she looked back at the pool. The machine was back on, pushing out a steady stream of water across the surface, its lights blinking on top.

Before she could begin climbing up into the station, she heard another double ding of a successful docking.

XXIX (ELISA)

Elisa watched the curved display in front of her. Half of the screen showed them slowly approaching *The Gateway To Earth*. She felt elated watching the altimeter climb with every second, increasing the distance between her and Mars.

On another window she watched the view outside, the camera focused on the neighbouring planets, zooming in on them, one after the other.

The pilots sat one row ahead of her and Reina, idly watching their screens, were floating inches above their seats. Elisa doubted they actually knew how to fly a shuttle, all they had to do was to be in permission of the access keys to initiate the launch and configure a time and dock on the station before they left the ground. On a usual day on Mars this would have happened remotely, not requiring their presence. But today, they were part of the group of four sitting in the centre of the forty seats, empty rows stretching out in front and behind them, with another empty level of seats on the floor below them. All of them were watching the planets in awe.

Elisa turned over to Reina, sitting to her right. Her tattooed face was staring at her own screen. Elisa felt fortunate not be alone any more in wanting to get away from Mars, even if it was only her first step, only going as far as the station. In her head she kept repeating the same questions over and over again: Is Earth really out there? And if so, how to get there? Questions with answers she knew she wouldn't be able to find on her own.

Thinking about the possibility that Earth was gone, made her feel sorry for Reina. Elisa knew she didn't necessarily have to go to Earth, but rather had to get away from Mars. And if she couldn't get away, she knew she would have to compromise. Elisa could find a way to get along with whatever direction the city was going to develop, in contrast to Reina possibly losing the most important person in her life.

"We'll have to dock manually, we don't know why, but the automatic system on the station is offline." The captain's announcement brought Elisa back to reality. She exhaled loud enough to get Reina's attention.

"This place really is trying to put a spoke in our wheel."

"Yeah, I hadn't expected anything different. But what else could go wrong, right? Break a leg?"

They turned their attention back to their screens, just to be interrupted by the captain again.

"Uh, yeah, I don't know what that is about, but there is, errr.... a ship docked at the station. And it doesn't look like one of ours."

Elisa looked at the half of her screen showing station rotate like a clock. A long, round shape was

XXIX (ELISA)

connected to one of the airlocks, and it resembled nothing anyone of the group could recognise.

"Well, if it's docked to our station, it must be one of ours right? Who else would know how the docking mechanism works, right?" The captain sounded unsure.

They docked a quarter spin of the station away from the unknown spaceship, climbed up the ladder into the waiting area and looked around. The corridors to both sides were empty. Elisa assumed they would at least be greeted by someone of the remaining crew or management, but no one was there. In search for an answer she turned to the pilots.

"Since you guys usually work up here, what was your protocol on handling new guests again?"

"Uh, usually we have a few months to prepare, so this is a little bit, uh, …. different? Let me check where the others are." the captain replied as he walked over to the next terminal.

Elisa watched him tapping away on the screen. When he suddenly stopped, pointing at the screen, speechless, she knew something was wrong. She approached the terminal to get a better look. The pilot switched to a camera looking into a meeting room. People were either lying on the floor, sitting with their backs to the wall or around the meeting table in the centre. One corner was empty apart from a pile of jackets, surrounded by a wet stain seeping into the carpet.

"What... the... fuck?" The captain had finally

found his words again.

The others joined them to look at the screen. Her gaze met Reina's, pulling up her shoulders, also unsure of what was going on. The co-pilot turned to the captain.

"What's happening? What are we supposed to do?"

"Help them?" The captain replied, being unsure and concerned at the same time.

"But is that all of them?"

"I don't know! How many stayed behind?"

"What if this was, this… the unknown ship?"

"How should I know?"

Elisa couldn't believe they were bickering, and stepped away from them.

"One of them moved!"

"Of course they moved!"

"What do you mean, 'of course'?"

"Did you think they were dead?"

"Are they not?"

"That's why I said: of course they moved!"

Elisa waved her hand between the two pilots' faces, to interrupt them.

"Which way? Which way to the room?" She wanted to do something.

Both of the pilots stopped their argument to point into the same direction.

"Good! Thank you! We'll go ahead, you can either figure out from here how to help or keep arguing."

Apparently, Elisa wasn't the only one getting frustrated with the two. She saw how Reina had

XXIX (ELISA)

already walked off towards the direction they had pointed to.

"We will try to open it from here!" the captain called after her.

Elisa followed Reina down the corridor.

She had almost caught up with her, when the woman in front of her tossed away her helmet and turned her strides into a run. Elisa did the same.

When they arrived at the meeting room, they heard the pilots talk through the terminal next its door.

"It's here! It's locked, we can't open it."

Almost simultaneously the two women threw their bodies against the door, trying to dig their fingernails into the thin, vertical seam that separated the door into two sliding halves.

They shouted at the door, then listened for the people inside. Instead, the pilot's voice crackled out of the terminal again.

"Look, they are ok inside. They need food and water, but first we need to find a way to get the door open. You need to find a crowbar or something."

The women looked each other. Reina waved at the terminal and shouted back at the two men on the other side.

"Where?!"

But instead of a voice answering from the terminal again, a frightened scream echoed from the corridor, further ahead. Both of them spun around. A series of panicky screeches immediately followed.

"Those are screams for help." Reina whispered, then bolted down the corridor towards the noise. Elisa paused for a second, then ran after her. When they passed through the angle that connected to the next section, Reina stopped in her tracks, stretching out her arms to stop Elisa from running past her. At the same time a voice shouted at them from the middle of the section.

"STOP!"

Elisa looked down the corridor into the next waiting area. In front of the shaft that lead down to the airlock, a dishevelled, old woman knelt on top of a body. Her hair looked filthy, hanging in unkept strands in front of her face. Her eyes were bloodshot. One hand was raised, gesturing them to stop. The other hand was pushing something against the throat of the pale body below her. Elisa recognised the woman's voice quicker than her appearance had allowed it. It was Iris, screaming at them.

"STAY WHERE YOU ARE!"

Elisa watched as Iris put all her weight into pushing her knees into the body below her, grabbing her victim's hair with her free hand.

"WAKE ME UP! WAKE ME UP!"

Iris screeched, her hair shaking in front of her red eyes, repeatedly bashing the victim's head against the floor.

"WAKE ME UP!"

Elisa had no time to think.

"Iris! Stop!" she shouted in disbelief, her own stomach starting to cramp up.

XXIX (ELISA)

"Iris! Look at me! You're awake! Stop!"

She felt she was going to be sick and Elisa was forced to swallow, her own body fighting with what she was witnessing. The body under Iris twitched. Blood soaked through the victim's clothes, legs kicking out, arms failing to push the woman away.

"IF YOU MOVE I'LL KILL HER." Iris stopped shaking the body.

"Stop! Please! Stop! Iris, look!" They both shouted at the woman.

Iris first hesitated, then looked up.

"Yes! Good! Look at me! It's me! Elisa! Remember?"

A cold shiver went down her back as she looked into Iris' red eyes, lined with dark rings, the skin clinging to her skull. The woman she had met a few weeks before was almost unrecognisable.

Elisa raised her own hands in defence, slowly inching forwards.

"Iris, listen to me. Look at me. What happened?" She moved another step closer, keeping eye contact with Iris. "Iris, do you recognise me?"

She watched Iris' expression turn into anger and hate.

"STAY AWAY! You are not going to get me! This is a dream! A simulation! You are not real!"

Elisa froze as she watched Iris raise her arm, holding a stained shard of glass high above her head, blood running down her arm.

"I control this dream! I control it. I will prove it to you, it's a dream!"

Iris screeched. Elisa watched the body struggle,

trying to move away from under her. At the same time she saw the station move, as if a piece of the airlock itself moved out of the floor, right behind Iris. Then, two big eyelids blinked, vertically. Terrified, Elisa pointed at Iris, ready to scream. Iris reached back and plunged her hand down. As quickly as the two eyes had blinked, a snake-like arm shot out from underneath, slamming into Iris, before she could drive the shard of glass into the body below her. The force that hit her sent her flying into the wall of the waiting area with a cracking sound. Elisa heard how Iris' body landed on the floor with a dull thud.

Seconds later, she saw how a massive shape of a squid scrambled out of the airlock, tentacles branching out from under its body, slapping onto the floor to move the twisted towering shape of the alien towards the body on the floor. She felt her own stomach mimicking the twisting movements of the tentacles and had to bend over, to throw up between her boots. With tears in her eyes and vomit in her nose she tried to look back up, trying to see what was happening. The squid picked up the body, a woman, from the floor, and gently propped her up against a tentacle. At the same time a pair of tentacles stretched out towards the corner of the waiting area, where Iris had disappeared out of sight.

The woman looked younger than Elisa. She had multiple, thin cuts around her neck, with lines of blood trickling down her skin, her white hoodie drenched in blood. The woman coughed and looked at Reina and Elisa, who was trying to shake off

XXIX (ELISA)

her half-digested lunch from her boots, spitting out what had remained in her mouth.

Elisa was staring from the woman to the massive squid holding her up.

"What–" she began to say, but stopped as the alien changed its colours from matching the airlock to a grey-white triangular pattern with green and purple dots, allowing them a better view of its shape and size in contrast to the station.

"We are sorry. She is dead." Elisa heard the voice, but it didn't come from the woman, as the woman hadn't moved her lips. The alien blinked, with both eyes, two irises each.

"We are Luna from Earth and Erial from Dol. Welcome to the collectors' system."

Elisa moved her head forward as if to hear better, raising her eyebrows, swallowing down the rancid aftertaste of sick in her mouth.

"What?" Elisa was confused. "What did–"

Reina cut her off, "You just said Earth. Are you saying Earth is out there? With the other planets?" The injured woman cleared her throat.

"Yes, I'm Luna. I'm from Earth."

Elisa watched how Reina's eyes lit up as she pushed herself backwards against the wall and collapsed, then sat on the floor, arms resting on her knees, shaking her head. Elisa wasn't sure if Reina was crying or laughing or both, at the same time. Elisa was speechless.

"Are you the only ones left?"

"What do you mean by 'left'?" she didn't understand Luna's question.

"I walked through the station." Luna paused. "And there was noone here." The bloodied woman looked around the room, her voice breaking. "When I came back I heard this woman scream, she attacked me, screaming at me to wake her up." Luna hesitated, looking at Iris' body, hidden in the corner of the waiting area. She got up with the help of the alien and walked towards Elisa, with the massive squid following behind her, its tentacles bending and rolling across the floor.

"Are you the only ones left? Here? On Mars?" Luna asked again.

Elisa shook her head in confusion, and answered as best as she could.

"There is only a small crew plus the management up here. Everyone else is down in the city. We just came up to look for Earth."

Luna wiped tears from her face, keeping her eyes on Elisa.

"Who is everyone else?"

"Everyone here on Mars."

She watched how Luna carefully probed the skin around her throat.

Elisa was feeling suspicious about the questions, and asked back.

"Who are you? Why do you not know this?"

Elisa looked at Reina, fighting the urge to run away. The other two stopped inside the corridor, ten metres away from them. The alien changed its colour to a pale grey and shifted its body, to rest on its

XXIX (ELISA)

tentacles.

"May we try to clear a few things up?" Elisa heard the voice again, but couldn't find a mouth that made the sounds, while Luna looked at the alien and nodded.

"First, what year is it?"

Elisa's stomach was still rumbling. She looked at her terminal and read out the year.

"Twenty eighty-six. Why?"

"Twenty eighty-six?" Luna sounded surprised. "When was the blackout?"

Unsure what to make of the question, Elisa looked at Reina for help, but she just shook her head, staring at the alien.

"Blackout? The darkness you mean? Two, ..., two and a half to two weeks ago." Elisa stumbled over her own words and watched her confusion spread to Luna as well.

The alien turned dark. Small glowing spots appeared across its skin. Thin grey lines crisscrossed past the dots, then the whole image faded back to grey again. The alien blinked at Luna with one eye, while looking at Elisa with the other.

"We think there is an explanation to this. It seems that Earth and Mars started their journeys almost at the same time. But there was no guarantee for them to arrive at the same time. It's very likely that the route which the collectors chose for Mars was a different route than that for Earth." The alien turned both eyes at Reina and Elisa. "A route through the universe. The collectors work independently from each other, and come up with different solutions to moving a planet from its home system to the collectors'. A time span of fifteen point four billion years travelling through space versus a difference of three hundred and ninety-two years is still an error close to zero. The difference is a two and a half millionth of a percent. According to the collectors' calculations you practically arrived at the same time."

Elisa heard the alien speak. Every single word went through her head, but nothing connected inside her head. She tried to bring the words together to recreate the sentences, but nothing made sense. She just stood there nodding, listening to the alien.

"It's simple: For billions of years now, these entities have been roaming through the universe, to collect intelligent life. Whenever a species makes itself recognisable as such to the collectors, everything within the Hill sphere surrounding a planet is cut out of space and moved through what we know as the universe. This all happened when you experienced what you called the 'blackout on Earth', three hundred and ninety-two years ago. All collected life is brought to the same destination, this star system. This is what we call the collectors' system. We, the Dolvar, have been here for twenty-seven thousand, four-hundred and ten of your Earth years. We were the first to arrive and we have been watching the arrival of many species since then. The collectors, as we call them, are as far as we know, the oldest living being in the universe. It's the only species or entity capable of travelling at the speed of light, and it's the only species we know that can manipulate space and time on such a scale. The collectors are the reason why all the planets remain in orbit, tilting each planet to simulate its original orbit around its original sun. Hundreds of planets. We don't know why the collectors do this. We assume the motivation is to bring us together. Even if a species knows how to travel at the speed of light to search for another conscious and intelligent species, the distances even in your own home galaxy, the milky way for example, are still, in your own words: enormous. If you crossed your galaxy once and returned back to your home, almost a quarter millions years would have passed. The reality is that, with the chances of life forming on a planet, and intelligent life evolving from that life, this life will be unlikely to ever connect with another species. Distances are too big. The 'collectors' are an ancient technology with the only goal to collect intelligent consciousness in the universe and bring it together in the same place at the same time. Those spheres are non-biological life-forms, remnants of a long-dead species. They allow intelligent life-forms to meet at some point in the future, but never have the chance to participate themselves."

Elisa tried to visualise what the alien was trying to explain.

"Welcome to the collectors' system. Yes, Earth is here. But Earth has already been here for three hundred and ninety-two years."

The numbers tumbled through her head.

"Three-hundred and ninety-two years?" Elisa heard herself speak.

"Three-hundred and ninety-two years, yes. It's the year 2478 on Earth right now."

Elisa shook her head, quickly looked at Luna and back at the alien.

"How is this possible?" she asked, unable to hide her disbelief.

"During the blackout, you were disconnected from space around you, travelling at almost the speed of light through the universe, for fifteen point four billion years. Earth arrived first. Mars arrived second. Almost four hundred years later. All this happened during the blackout. As soon as each planet arrives, life goes on without time dilation."

Elisa slowly nodded, unsure if to trust what she heard. For a moment she just stood there, painfully aware of her own breathing, not knowing if she was the one who was dreaming. Her head was getting light.

"Why should I believe you?" Elisa had to sit down.

"I'm Luna. I was born twenty-five years ago, in the year 2453. I studied the technological history of Earth. Everything from the first contact with the Dolvar on Earth after the blackout, and the second middle ages that immediately followed. I can tell you everything that has happened in the last three centuries. Everything I know. The European Ice Age. That it took Earth three centuries to send a person to space again. How the population on Earth decreased from 8 billion to less than a hundred million. I've been travelling with Erial for two months now, as part of a cultural exchange between our two species, a first step to be accepted in this star system. The planet you call 'Earth', as you know it from only weeks ago, does not exist anymore. Earth has changed. Humanity has changed."

Elisa felt her pulse drum in her ears as Reina wailed and hid her head behind her arms, her body shaking. Then Elisa finally understood what all this implied. She had to force herself to talk with a painful lump in the back of her throat, tears in her eyes.

"Reina, I'm so sorry!"

XXX (ELISA)

Elisa watched Mars from her room on *The Gateway To Earth*. The days after their first contact were a blur. She had to accept a new reality: The aliens were real. The thousands of planets were real. Earth had moved on for hundreds of years while Mars was stuck in the past. Thousands of species, all scooped up from around the universe, had been brought into the same star system, called the 'Collectors' System', either willingly or unknowingly, as Elisa had triggered the collectors herself. The images of the sphere woke her up at night, when she gasped for air, after dreams of their encounter ending with a hostile species instead. She had messaged Phil, that they had been right with their thought experiment, searching for something that was looking for intelligent life.

She had been to the Dolvar ship, had sat on the cushions while Luna explained everything to Reina and her all over again, in her own words. Luna described what had happened to Earth and Mars, like two marbles lying on a pizza dough, stretched on a trampoline, bending down the soft sticky surface with their weight. She explained the collectors as entities who used tape to fix the dough in a circle around the marbles, to cut them out, move them to a bigger trampoline, and insert them into a pre-cut, taped hole again.

Elisa had watched and felt the sim-sphere with her own body, studying the recordings of other worlds.

For example the sea caves of *Adar*, caves tall enough to house skyscrapers, filled with huts and houses clinging onto the walls, connected with ropes and suspension bridges, high above the salty waters below. Cranes and elevators transferring goods and naked, winged lifeforms flying up and down, left and right. A constant stream of boats leaving and returning from the sea covering the floor of the cave.

The depths of *Dol*, swimming with the sim-sphere, accompanying a new generation of hatchlings, watching the process of cocooning and the first time a juvenile, five brained Dolvar resurfaced. She saw Dolvar hunting for fish and matsa, riding the waves of giant storms.

She dropped her chin, as she flew past the European woodland cities on Earth, sky scrapers like thin, mirrored blades of grass reaching into the sky, surrounded by endless, thick forests. Elevators racing on the glass walls of the skyscrapers, in every direction and sometimes disappearing into the walls. She passed the crumbling dome cities of Asia, a legacy of a fight for survival against the forces of nature and humanity itself. Broken and slowly disappearing monuments, left as a reminder of the past.

The jungles of *Proa*. A species Elisa had initially thought were fruit bats if it weren't for the long beaks, and scaly bodies, living in huts woven into the tree tops. A species capable of spaceflight, building space ships mostly out of wood, while maintaining a long lasting tradition of courting and nest building.

At some point Elisa had to take a break, to give her time to adjust to the new reality, to stop herself from drowning in a flood of information which was catching up with her at night.

She often thought of Phil and how he was handling the situation. She had mentioned the Dolvar as well as the scale of this new star system to him and tried to explain the abundance of intelligent life around them. He'd said he'd need his time before he could delve deeper into this world.

With the help of Erial they connected to the interplanetary communications network and exchanged first messages with Earth, to send the first signs of life from Mars back to their home world after three-hundred and ninety-two years or, three weeks, depending on the perspective.

Mrs. Moreno, Mrs. Zhao and Mr. Ginn, had to face their new reality that they were working for nobody anymore, and that they owned nothing. They were offered to live on the station, or in the city, but as equals with everyone, starting with their initial balance of a thousand Martians. They had no more authority than anyone else. After burying Iris on Mars, next to the graves of those with whom she had no relation, they opted for helping out with reconfiguring the Martian interplanetary shuttles to be adjusted to allow for a longer travel back to earth.

As the news and understanding about the system spread, only a third of the population wanted to stay on Mars, which included Phil. He felt at home where he was, under the Martian surface, building up a team to finally, truly analyse the planet's history.

The original passenger list destined for Earth was reinstated, giving Elisa her ticket back. The suites had been redesigned to allow for additional capacity, such that Reina managed to join her. She had to see Earth with her own eyes to be able to absolutely believe and understand the new circumstances.

After a month of restructuring the four interplanetary shuttles, they were on their journey back to Earth, escorted by eight Dolvar ships, one clinging onto each shuttle, and another four as support. Luna was on one of them. Reina and Elisa shared a room on one of the now ancient ships making up the squad, connected together, spinning around each other for artificial gravity.

After twenty-five days of travelling through space, a fifth of the journey, Elisa sat in the community kitchen, which had been very much improved by the Dolvar. She held a fresh cup of coffee in one hand, the other scrolling through data projected on the table in front of her. She had been surprised to learn how restrictive the society on Earth was in regard to technology, giving her the uneasy feeling of not knowing if she'd feel at home on Earth. Since they had launched from *The Gateway To Earth*, she spent most of her time learning, almost non-stop every day. She had set herself the goal to understand as much as possible about the available technologies, to catch up, at least with the three-hundred and ninety-two years of Earth, but likely more than that. The projection in front of her showed a compatibility matrix of alien species, a simple dataset presenting which species were able to co-exist within the conditions of their respective home atmospheres, and vice versa. Another layer displayed information beyond atmospheric compatibility, whether a species was allergic to the hair, scales, fumes, powders or other secretions of another. In addition to biological differences, Elisa was surprised that a large part of the planets refused to communicate or participate in any way, even defended their home orbits aggressively, prohibiting anyone to pass through their hill sphere. Even Earth had been part of the excluded planets for three centuries. The complexity of interplanetary life was higher than Elisa had ever thought possible.

After finishing her coffee, she headed back into their cabin, to make space for other passengers in the small yet effective kitchen. Elisa found Reina sitting in front of a desk, with teary eyes and a video paused on the screen.

Elisa quickly stepped inside and closed the door behind her.

"Reina, what's up?"

The tattooed woman connected Elisa's earpieces

to the audio stream and restarted the video without taking a look back at Elisa.

A frail old woman, maybe in her eighties, sat on a roof top, between laundry hanging on a line on one side and a small roof top garden with vegetables growing on the other. Above her was a dome, mixed with glass and solar panels, some of them broken, or missing. Behind her, the rooftops continued, stretching out like a chessboard under the dome. The old woman cleared her throat and quietly introduced herself.

"Hello Reina, my dear. It's likely you don't recognise me at this age." The woman on the screen rolled up her sleeves, and held her forearms into the camera. Dull red stripes started from her wrists, up her forearms, disappearing under her crinkled blouse. She cleared her throat again. "I remember when we both got our tattoos. Mine are a lot paler now than what they used to be. Look how the edges have blurred over time."

Elisa compared the tattoos in video with Reina's, which looked new in comparison. She listened to the quiet, wheezy voice continue.

"I'm eighty-three now. As you can see I'm now what we used to call 'an old fart'." The old woman chuckled and smiled at the camera. "In the past twenty years I have lived on one of the first dome ships slowly travelling around the planet. I survived the blackout on *The Gateway To Mars* and I was there when we made first contact with aliens. I saw it happen from our last shuttle to fly in space. Live on my screen, while we waited for the last passengers to leave the station. We didn't know what to make of it back then, and unfortunately we weren't in the best company to make first contact with an alien species. I still remember the eerie silence onboard the shuttle when we landed, not understanding what it meant. Only a few years ago I learnt it was a Dolvar. They, and everyone else, are staying away from us for good. When we got back to Earth, we found ourselves in a world that had fallen apart over night. A long night. The years that followed are the years I'm the least proud of. It was a fight for survival. To survive, I did things that you will never forgive me. Things, after which you will be happy never to see me again. And I will say it without leaving any room for interpretation: I have killed to survive, out of fear and out of hate. I'm haunted by these times to the present day. Day and night. I became the person I've had to become, to survive."

Elisa watched the old woman cough and wheeze.

"I've been waiting for you for a long, long time, looking at the planets and stars at night, knowing these stars could not be the same stars you might be looking at. For a long time I thought you were out there, out of reach, on the other side of this new sun, or in a different star system. Maybe even thinking the same, just like me. For a few years, I now know, you were not. The Elari responded to our signal, only to let us know where we are and how we got here. That it took us over fifteen billion years to get here, and that there was no planet like yours in this system. Many think I'm a crazy, old lady for believing you might still be on your way, arriving years, centuries or millennia later. It's been my wish, my entire life, to at least leave you a message, to let you know I'm still alive, or was alive. That I survived. Even if it was not good. I know I'm not going to be here for much longer, and I hope that this last message will receive you well. I truly hope you will get to see this wonderful star system, filled with more life than I had ever imagined, and more than I will ever have the chance to see. I truly believe you are still out there, on your way."

Elisa watched the woman in the video cough and pause to catch her breath.

"And if you receive this, you might be still a bit younger than me. If that's the case, try to be better than I have been. Live your life. See what this melting pot of consciousness has to give, and give something back. I know you love me and I have always loved you. For billions of years."

She kissed her fingertips on her right hand and waved them shakily at the camera.

"I love you Reina. This is goodbye."

ABOUT THE AUTHOR

Hi, I'm Paul. In my spare time I build open source things. During the lockdown of 2021 I began to write about my ideas that go beyond the things I build in real life. I hope you enjoyed this book as much as I did writing it.

More on my book projects:

    instagram.com/therealpaulanthonysmith

More on my maker projects:

    p3dt.net
    instagram.com/pauls_3d_things

Cover art by Vitaliy Ostaschenko, see https://artstation.com/ kruger7215 for more.

Printed in Great Britain
by Amazon